IN ANOTHER REALM

David Berardelli

IN ANOTHER REALM

GRAVESTONE PRESS

PART ONE

IN THE REALM

CHAPTER ONE

I found myself standing in a thick carpet of soft green grass in the middle of a lush meadow.

A forest of towering pine trees loomed majestically at the top of the grassy slope, about a hundred yards straight ahead. Flowers grew wild all around me, their sweet scent filling the air. The sky was clearer than I'd ever seen it.

I heard no traffic sounds--no car horns, police sirens, or the distant wail of a train. There was no sign of a building or even a power line. No jet streams overhead. Not even the barking of a dog. Nothing but peace and tranquility, and a sense of calm I'd never experienced before.

This vision was breathtaking. I knew right then that something was very, very wrong.

I didn't recognize this place at all. I couldn't even remember when or how I'd gotten here. All I knew was that this wasn't my condo or my office, and I shouldn't be here. Right now I should be sitting at my desk, sipping coffee while going over my itinerary for the workday. But this obviously wasn't the case. I'd somehow bypassed the trip to the office and come here instead-- wherever "here" was.

This sense of serenity was alien to me. I'd been living in cities most of my life. I lived less than half a mile from Semoran Boulevard, one of the busiest highways in Central Florida. I worked in Orlando and took frequent business trips to Tampa, Miami, and Atlanta. I lived by myself but wasn't alone very much at all.

My new surroundings seemed to be telling me that I'd somehow wrenched myself loose from my existence. Yet I felt no fear, no panic. No stress, no tension. Even so, I found myself growing uneasy.

The last thing I remembered was that I was getting ready for work. Work meant getting out of bed, showering, shaving, dressing, fixing a quick breakfast of coffee and buttered toast, and driving to my office. In the evening I'd come home and unwind with a glass of bourbon and an old movie. Sometimes I put Journey or Foreigner on the stereo or CD player; other times, when I felt particularly done in, Moody Blues. I even had a small collection of Coltrane, Louis Armstrong, and Miles Davis CDs for particularly tough unwindings. And, of course, old recordings of Led Zeppelin, CCR, Three Dog Night, and a dozen other classic bands my parents had left me, which I played when I felt the need to zone out completely.

Until six months ago, my wife Claire had served as my sounding board while having drinks before dinner. Now that she'd left, something else was needed to quell the flames of my daily business pressures. For the past few months,

6

relaxing on the sofa after work with my bourbon, listening to "*A Whiter Shade of Pale*," by Procol Harum, "*Nights in White Satin*," by Moody Blues, or "*Stairway to Heaven*," by Led Zeppelin, before fixing supper, seemed to do the trick.

This morning, however, something strange had happened to upset the works. I had no idea what it was, but I was determined to find out. It hadn't been long since I'd left the condo--an hour, maybe, based on my best guess. This meant two hours had passed since I'd gotten out of bed.

My routine hadn't varied much over the years. It was the same regimen I'd followed since I'd graduated from college seventeen years earlier and started the Personnel Counseling job at Drayson Industries in Orlando just three months after that. I'd been at Drayson ever since and was highly thought of at the company. I did my job well. I knew how to deal with people and was largely responsible for achieving the "family feeling" atmosphere Drayson had been known for since I'd started with them.

What was different this morning? What happened after I'd left the condo? And why was I here in this beautiful open field instead of in my office, logging on to the computer while listening to my voicemail?

How did I get here? Had I blinked my eyes at some random moment and somehow accidentally reset time itself, like in some strange sci-fi novel? Or had the gods of the universe decided to relieve boredom by displacing me somewhere else on this one particular day?

The morning had been no different from the hundreds of others preceding it. I couldn't remember doing anything differently. I hadn't gotten out of the bed from the wrong side or hit my head stepping into the shower.

Still, nothing explained what I was doing here or how I'd gotten here. Nothing gave me any clue of what happened from the time I'd left my Winter Park condo to the moment I opened my eyes and found myself in this beautiful field.

I had to find out what happened. I couldn't lie down in the grass and mentally transport myself back to where I was before all this happened. For one thing, I had no idea how to transport myself. For another, I didn't even believe in this concept. Otherwise, I'd simply close my eyes and click my heels. Not a particularly constructive thought, I realized right off. This place--as far as I could tell--wasn't Oz. And I sure as hell wasn't Dorothy Gale. Besides, I'd grown out of that phase when I was a kid. It was a difficult time for me. It had taken the deaths of my grandparents, my pet dog, and a childhood friend, to make me realize magic was merely illusion, and dreams seldom came true. Fantasy was something you saw in movies or read about in books. Reality was what everyone had to contend with on a daily basis.

This felt like fantasy, but the cynic in me told me otherwise. I wanted to believe this was some sort of hallucination. If so, what had caused it? Booze? I'd only had two shots before supper the night before. Drugs? I'd experimented a little in college, but other than booze, I hadn't put anything stronger than an occasional aspirin in my system during the last twenty years.

But even weighing these odds, this still felt like some sort of surrealistic trip. In my world, logic was everything, and if something made no sense, I considered it illogical, and would ignore it. Even so, my brain worked feverishly, struggling to convince me that this was somehow real. And even if I discovered that it wasn't real or logical, I still had to solve it.

The one fact that hit me the hardest was the most obvious: I hadn't come here under ordinary means. The second fact, just as obvious, made even more sense: I didn't belong here.

I'd been working with computers since grade school, but once I matured and began looking at things more objectively, I realized computers were much more limited than what most people thought. Modern technology never provided simple answers, only complicated solutions understood primarily by well-educated, computer-savvy techs. I preferred working with people. The problems associated with people were often just as complicated as any computer glitch or system Abend, but much easier to solve. With a person, a handshake worked wonders. Or a kind word, a simple suggestion, or compromise. With a computer glitch, a tech needed to be called in. Someone else was then required to listen to the tech's recommendations and translate them into everyday language to the workers. With an Abend, calls were made, the job was repaired and rerun, a trouble report written and submitted, and no further action was necessary.

I tried to use my command of logic to evaluate this present problem, but nothing would come. It was almost as if my brain refused to work. Perhaps this was because I couldn't give it any information to work with. I had no memory of coming here, no idea how I'd gotten here, why, or even when. As far as I knew, it happened moments ago. The only thing that registered was the nagging sensation that this beautiful meadow was some sort of destination--or drop-off point-- that began with my workday.

Everything I'd done that morning, as far as I could remember, had been routine. Nothing gave me any indication or clue suggesting that once I left the condo and got in my car, the pattern of my everyday life would unravel and propel me into this strange, beautiful world--

Semoran. My brain had blipped when the image of the rush hour traffic flared in my mind.

Was I involved in an accident?

What else could cause something like this? What else could explain my memory lapse, or why I wasn't in the office right now?

I tried very hard to ignore the sense of ultimate tranquility I was feeling. For that, I had to stop gawking at the meadow, the flowers and the trees, and force myself to focus. There were more important issues here that needed to be resolved. This place was beautiful; I felt better than I'd ever felt before. But I couldn't let this cloud the main issue.

Just as I began to focus, another thought came to me. Unlike the others, this one made my blood turn cold.

I must be dead.

What other explanation was there? Right after I'd left the condo, got in my car, pulled onto Semoran, merged into the morning rush hour traffic, and headed south, my existence had just *stopped.*

Stopped. There was no other term I could think of that could describe any of this. Everything I knew, that had been a part of me, had ceased. My life had simply run its course, and my existence ended.

This latest revelation made me think I might be right about this strange world being my destination. Perhaps I *had* died and entered this beautiful meadow. For me, eternity could have just started. In this case, there was no need to coax my memory to bring back images of my past.

Even so, that part of me obsessed with facts, with cause and effect, still longed to connect the dots. But no matter how hard I tried to remember, I came up empty. A solid void of nothingness had swallowed up all thoughts, images, feelings, and emotions. As soon as I tried grabbing at anything squirming into my consciousness, it faded and fell into the dark void that had become the center of my mind. At first I thought I remembered hearing the loud, angry roar of an engine--a truck, perhaps, or train--but as soon as the image began to form, it disintegrated, making me wonder if I'd just imagined it.

Dead or not, I had to force myself to forget my fears and do what was necessary. I couldn't just stand here and wait for something to happen.

My heart racing, I closed my eyes and took in some of the sweet air. Ten seconds later, I opened my eyes and looked down. I was wearing the same dark-blue jacket, matching slacks, white silk shirt and light-blue cotton tie I'd put on before leaving the condo. The shiny pointed toes of my tan imported casuals glistened in the sunlight. I hiked up my pant legs and was relieved to see the same black silk socks I'd pulled on that morning.

I was on a roll and saw no reason to stop at this point. I pushed up my shirt sleeve. The wristwatch Claire had bought me nine years ago, on my thirtieth birthday, winked at me. It said 9:07, but the second hand had stopped. I stared at it for a few moments--it didn't move. I brought it to my ear. I heard nothing.

9:07. It had stopped at 9:07. As I stared at it, I immediately began calculating. I always left for work at 8:45 and usually pulled into the parking garage in Orlando at around 9:30--sometimes at 9:45, if the traffic was particularly heavy. 9:07 normally put me a mile or two north of Colonial Drive.

So now I knew something had happened at 9:07 to bring me here. Whatever it was, it had stopped my watch.

Or had time stopped itself?

Enough. All this thinking was making my mind glaze over. I'd already figured out a few things, and except for the dead watch, I should be somewhat relieved. I was standing in a strange meadow in my suit. I could see myself and still had feeling in my limbs. This, of course, meant my nervous system was still working.

Maybe I wasn't dead after all.

To make sure this wasn't just the result of my imagination, I touched my neck...and then my jaw...and finally my nose. I even mussed my hair.

Nothing felt different or weird.

More importantly, everything felt *the same*.

For good measure, I brought my hands together and clapped, producing a sharp echo that made me flinch as the vibrations hopped up the grassy slope.

I took another deep breath. I discovered that I felt much better than just a minute ago. I was alive. I could feel myself. I still had substance.

So where was I? And what happened?

I needed to investigate. If I could get my brain working again, something might pop out of the darkness and tell me something. I might even find some way of getting out of here and going back to my former life.

I turned back to the slope leading to the pine trees on the other side of the crest and waited for some spark of familiarity. Nothing leaped out, yet I couldn't help wondering if I'd been here before. Was it because the trees themselves looked familiar? The slope? The grass? What was it about this setting that made me feel like I'd been here before?

Bits of my memory trickled back. I remembered growing up in a subdivision on the outskirts of Weirton, West Virginia, in a three-bedroom brick ranch home. The front yard consisted of a narrow strip of lawn my older brother Ned mowed each week. There was a front walk, a mailbox, and a few bushes growing in a reasonably straight row beneath the living room window, and a sidewalk running from the main street at one end of the block to the other end, where another subdivision ran perpendicular to our street. Our back yard went down a grassy slope leading to several hundred acres of woods separating the neighborhood from a large dairy farm. My fondest childhood memories were of Ned, the other neighborhood kids and I playing in the woods and exploring the winding country roads on our bikes.

That was a long time ago, and too many other things had happened to dull the memories. I hadn't gone back home since college but had heard that the neighborhood, like most built in the last half of the century, had gone to seed. I hadn't thought of my childhood home more than half a dozen times since graduating college. I hadn't even thought much about Ned, who stayed in the neighborhood and ran a successful body shop until he'd died of a heart ailment two years ago. We went our separate ways years earlier and saw one another only occasionally, usually during the holidays. Five years ago, Dad died of emphysema at 61. Mom now lived in an assisted facility outside Wheeling. I saw her once a year, on her birthday.

I wondered why my childhood had suddenly flashed by. The last time that happened was when Dad died. A barrage of memories had slammed into my consciousness during the plane flight from Orlando and on the drive to the funeral home.

Had this sudden trip down Memory Lane come back to me because I was frightened? Because, in spite of my recent evaluation, I couldn't stop wondering if I was dead? Or was it because the woods had brought me back to my childhood?

Although most forests looked alike, the underdeveloped areas in Florida had their own signature--palmettos, palms, scrubs, snakes, mosquitoes and flies. Florida pines had their own unique look--tall, slender and anemic, oftentimes standing stooped, their branches wilted and lowered in surrender.

This place looked nothing like Florida, West Virginia, or even Western Pennsylvania. The trees were too massive, too healthy-looking, the brush and the grass thick and robust, the flowers bright and happy.

Once again, I concluded that the answer to this mystery lay elsewhere. The only way to find out what had happened was to start walking.

My mind made up, I left my comfortable spot in the lush grass and began climbing the hill.

My steps felt strange. It was almost as if I was gliding rather than walking. This of course made me wonder once again if I was dreaming. I advised myself not to rush to any conclusions, but to reserve judgment until I'd ascended the hill and looked around. If something clicked, then I could work from there. But until then, my best option was to take it one step at a time.

I reached the top of the hill.

Then I saw her. She was standing a few feet in front of the tree line, watching me.

CHAPTER TWO

Although we were more than a hundred feet from one another, I could see her quite clearly.

She was tall and slender, with long black hair and dark eyes. She wore a maroon V-necked short-sleeve shirt, jeans, and white open-toed pumps. Stray strands of her windblown hair clung to her cheek.

She was looking up at the sky as I ascended the hill. She seemed confused, possibly as confused as I was--and was trying to get her bearings. When she first noticed me, she turned briefly toward the trees on her right. I feared she might dart into the woods. Instead, she turned back and faced me. She didn't even push the hair away from her face. She seemed to be studying me.

I stopped about ten feet away and continued staring. She was certainly a vision, especially in these strange circumstances. I didn't want to frighten her with any sudden movement. I was frightened as well but knew better than show it. As a man, I was expected to be strong--to keep my fears in check. I was the hunter, the stalker; running away from a beautiful woman was something no sane man should ever do.

I considered the positive aspects of this new wrinkle. Up until just a few moments ago, I faced this strange new world alone. But now there were two of us, and the other person was a beautiful woman. This in itself should cause me instant relief, but instead of rejoicing, I stood stock-still, unable to move or speak.

What was wrong with me?

I had to stay focused. Only moments ago, my brain had suggested that I explore my surroundings. This was why I climbed the hill in the first place. But the sudden appearance of this beautiful creature had changed everything. Now I found that I had no idea what to do next.

I was a grown man, for God's sake. I was a respected businessman and dealt with all sorts of people every day of my life. I'd known a lot of women and had affairs with some of them. I'd even been married and divorced. In other words, I should have learned all about the facts of life long before now. What was my problem now?

It was trust, of course. I wasn't sure if I believed my own eyes. I feared that if I moved even one step closer, this woman would vanish, and I'd be alone again.

She continued staring. I tried reading her expression, but in my present state, I didn't think anything I could come up with would be accurate. Was it suspicion I saw in her eyes? Or relief? Did she want me to approach her? Or was she waiting for me to turn around and leave her in peace?

Once again, I expected her to vanish.

What if she was just as real as I was? What if she was waiting for me to start talking?

I began wondering if she lived around here. She might be taking a leisurely morning stroll. For all I knew, she might own all this beautiful land. If so, I was trespassing, and she wouldn't appreciate my being out here. This could be why she was staring at me. She could be waiting for me to turn around and get off her property. I expected her to reach into the pocket of her jeans and pull out a cell phone.

That could be a blessing in disguise. If she called the cops, they'd show up in just a few minutes and arrest me. And once they took me to their station, I'd know where I was and maybe even discover what happened.

She continued watching me. Then she reached up and pulled some hair away from her face. "Hello."

Her voice startled me, and my thoughts disintegrated as if they'd just been swallowed up by the same dark emptiness that had taken over my mind earlier. The vision had actually spoken.

"Hi."

"Is this...*your* place?"

I felt some relief when I suddenly realized that a portion of the puzzle had just been cleared up. She'd just asked me where we were. If she lived here, she wouldn't have asked that question.

Apparently she was just as lost as I was.

I realized right then that this was probably not a good thing.

"No."

She continued staring, the confusion clear in her large dark eyes. "This is gonna sound really odd, but I have no idea where I am or how I got here. Do you happen to know what's going on?"

"I wish I did." I was surprised that my own voice worked. I took a few slow, cautious steps in her direction. I expected her to back up, but she didn't.

"Any idea where we are?"

"None."

She turned back to the woods. She still didn't reach into her pocket. This made me wonder if she even had a cell phone. I noticed that she wasn't carrying a handbag. This was very, very odd. I couldn't remember ever seeing a woman walking around without her handbag. I'd never been with a woman before who didn't have one with her at all times. Not out of the bedroom, anyway.

But this was an extreme situation. She was also wearing high-heeled, open-toed pumps--not the sort of footwear suitable for walking around in the woods.

When she turned back to me, she appeared frightened. She reached up and pushed more hair away from her cheek. Her hand shook a little. "Do you happen to know...*how* we got here?"

Lying to her wouldn't accomplish anything. It might make her feel better temporarily, but then I'd have to keep the lies going, and I'd never been a good liar.

"I wish I did, but I don't have a clue." I stopped about ten feet from her and took her in without being obvious about it. I'd learned years ago that women liked being admired--as long as the man was sensible about it. But since she was obviously on edge, things would go downhill in a heartbeat if she suspected she had to worry about me as well.

Still, I couldn't help noticing every delicious detail about her. She was about five-ten in her two-inch heels, making her just an inch or so shorter than me. Her eyes were very large and dark brown, with thick lashes. Her lips were full, her cheekbones high and sharply chiseled. I guessed her to be in her early or mid-thirties. She was small-breasted, with a tiny waist and long legs. Her hands were large, her fingers long, her nails long, manicured, and painted red. I wondered if she'd once been a model.

"This is really strange." She took a few steps to my left in the tall grass, careful to pick up her feet so she wouldn't trip. Her butt was shapely and the perfect size for her figure. "I'm sure I've never been here before. How about you?"

"I don't recognize this place, either."

"But we're both *here*." She began trembling.

"Yes."

"And neither of us knows how we got here."

"Right again."

"And this obviously happened quickly, before either of us knew

what was happening."

I perked up. "What makes you say that?"

She gestured. "You're wearing a suit."

I'd been so preoccupied in trying to determine if I was alive or dead and hadn't considered that minor detail. She'd just made me feel like an idiot.

She had another look around. Some of her hair had fallen in front of her face again. She pushed it away, this time more impatiently. Then she took a deep breath. When she turned to me, she looked angry. "Aren't you curious about all this?"

"Of course."

"You're holding it in pretty well."

I shrugged. "I'm struggling with it, too--believe me."

"Maybe if we start from the beginning, we might get an idea of what's going on."

"What do you mean?"

"If we start talking to each other, maybe we can figure out why we're here...or how we got here."

"That sounds like a plan. You go first."

"All right. Where'd you come from?"

"Originally?"

"What's the first thing you remember?"

"I was standing in that meadow, about a hundred yards from here."

"Nothing before that?"

"Not a thing."

She thought that over. "All right, you were in the meadow. Then what happened?"

"I decided to climb the hill back there so I could see what's on the

other side of these woods. I wanted to look around and check out this place. I'm hoping I'll eventually find out something once I start looking. What happened with you?"

"I opened my eyes, and I was right here. I was about to walk down that hill to do some

22

exploring myself, but when I saw you, I...well, I thought maybe you lived here or something."

"I thought the same thing about you."

She shivered. "Damn, this is scary..."

"And you were right here when you woke up?" I asked.

"Actually, it didn't feel like I woke up."

"How did it feel?"

"Ever watch a movie where they change the scene so abruptly, you feel like they took out something?"

I nodded. "You're on the right track, but to me, this feels a little different."

"How?"

"You're sitting through an endless batch of commercials. You zone out, and when the show you were watching finally comes back on, you suffer a brain blip and can't remember right off what you'd been watching."

"That sums it up, too. In this case, it feels like a huge portion of our lives was just snatched away in an instant." She rubbed her temples. "I should be freaking out by now. I don't know why I'm not."

"It won't solve anything. At least there are two of us now. That's something, isn't it?"

She blinked. "How does that help?"

"Two minds now, rather than one."

"I guess that's one way of looking at it..."

"It's the only thing we've got. So I guess our only option right now is to keep our heads and figure this out a step at a time."

She frowned. "And just how do we do that?"

"By doing what we were doing a minute ago. Let's get back to the moment you found yourself here. You said you were right here, in this spot."

She nodded. "I was so shocked and confused when I saw all these trees, I was afraid to move. And you were in that meadow?"

"Yes."

She looked past me, squinting. "It seems to go on forever. Did you see anything else?"

"All I saw was the meadow."

"I can understand why you wanted to check out the woods."

"I think that's still a good idea."

She didn't reply. She began trembling again.

"It beats standing here and wondering, doesn't it?"

"But those woods...they look like they go on forever, too."

"We've got to find out, don't we?"

She nodded.

"Who knows? There might be a subdivision on the other side of the tree line, for all we know."

She smiled. "With wild kids running around, screaming? And stray dogs lying in the middle of the street?"

"That's it. Aim high."

She laughed.

"If we're *really* lucky, we might even find a Walmart at the end of that trail."

She laughed again. "You're starting to sound delirious."

"You've got a point there." I moved toward the path leading through the woods.

She stayed where she was. Even after our faint attempt at humor, she was too frightened to leave her spot. She probably felt more secure there. But I didn't want to leave her here. Even though I now knew she was real, I didn't want her to vanish if I turned my back. "Well, why don't we both start walking and see what happens?"

She just stared at me. She probably didn't want to tempt fate in those heels.

"Think you can walk in this thick brush?"

"Why wouldn't I?"

"Your shoes. They're not exactly hiking footgear."

She looked down as if she'd forgotten what she had on her feet.

"I'll be all right." She raised her head slowly. Her brows pushed together. She'd obviously remembered something.

"Something wrong?"

"I think...I think I've walked through the woods in heels before."

"These woods?"

"No..."

"Somewhere else, then?"

"Yes--*no*." She shook her head. "I don't *know*. Maybe I'm just...I

don't know. I thought I remembered something, but..." She shrugged. "I *just don't know*."

"We'll be okay." I figured she needed reassurance.

"You're just saying that."

"No. I really think we'll be okay as long as we keep our heads and don't switch off."

"Easier said than done."

"We've got no choice."

"Tell me how I'm supposed to do that."

"Do what? Keep our heads? Or don't switch off?"

"Yes." After a few moments, she smiled.

"Keep smiling," I said.

"Why?"

"Just do it. It's helping, believe me."

"Are you gonna smile, too?"

"I really don't smile much."

"Why not?"

"I don't think I have a very good smile."

"Why not?"

"I've always been the serious type. When I was in high school, some girls told me I had a stupid smile."

"You're not in high school anymore."

"I know."

"You're older."

"Thank you."

"You're welcome. Now do it."

"Do what?"

"Smile."

I did what she said.

She studied it and scowled. "Nothing's wrong with your smile."

"Really?"

"Really."

"You're not just saying that?"

"No. You have a nice smile."

26

"Thanks. Let's go."

She took a deep breath and nodded. Then she reached out for my hand. I took it. It was cold, but I held it firmly. She bit her lip and nodded again.

"We'll do this slowly." I felt more confident since she'd taken my hand. I didn't know if that had been her intent, but that's how it made me feel. "I'll be right beside you."

She closed her eyes and nodded. She still grasped my hand, and I felt the pressure increasing slightly. This was my cue to stay calm. I had no idea what I could do if we suddenly faced danger, but at least now she realized she wasn't alone anymore. Sharing something horrendous with someone frightened could turn awful quickly. I was scared too, but I couldn't show weakness. If I did, she'd come apart.

"You're making me feel...a little better."

"Like I said, I think we'll be all right."

She continued squeezing my hand. "Okay..."

"It beats standing here, waiting for someone to rescue us, doesn't it?"

Her eyes grew. "You think that might happen?"

"Have you seen a plane out here? Have you heard any traffic?"

"You're right. We're on our own, aren't we?"

"For now, anyway."

She nodded. After a few moments, she let go of my hand.

Together, we began moving cautiously through the thick brush.

CHAPTER THREE

"I'm Alison."

"That's a pretty name."

"Thanks."

I sensed some resentment in her voice. Normally, I didn't like getting personal, especially with someone I just met, but since this was an unusual situation, I didn't see any harm in getting to know her better.

"I take it there's a story behind this."

"Story?" She glanced at me. "Who said there was a story?"

"You did."

"Really?" Her features tightened. "When did I say *that*?"

"Just a second ago, with your tone of voice. Now you're doing it with your eyes."

"You're pretty good."

"I deal with people for a living."

"You're a psychiatrist?"

"I'm a Personnel Director. So what's the story with your name?"

She shrugged. "My father wanted a boy. His name's Alan."

"It's still a beautiful name."

"Thanks."

We trudged through the wild brush. I could feel her eyes on me.

"What's *your* name, silly?"

"No, it's Jack. And yes, sometimes I am pretty silly."

She reddened. "I really didn't mean that. Sometimes I get a little impatient."

"I don't know any woman who isn't a *little* impatient. Except Claire, my ex-wife." Strange, how quickly that came back. "That woman's *extremely* impatient."

She didn't say anything.

"Forget I said that. It just slipped out."

"It's all right."

A little while later she said, "Maybe we should talk more about ourselves. It might help us relax."

"You mean it might make us more comfortable with one another?"

"Like I said before, it might give us clues about why we're together. Don't you agree?"

"Does this involve my talking more about my ex-wife?"

"Not if you don't *want* to talk about her..."

"Then it sounds like a really splendid idea."

She laughed, and I had a feeling she might already be growing more comfortable with me. I couldn't judge her by how she'd been acting since we'd met. The circumstances had brought out our fears and inhibitions too much.

"Where do you live?" she asked.

"Orlando."

She frowned.

"What's wrong?"

"My ex-husband...moved to Orlando about a year ago."

I could tell by the hurt in her eyes that the divorce had not been amiable. I decided to move on. "Where do you live?"

"Flagstaff."

"Really?"

"Why?"

"I guess our common denominator has nothing to do with where we live, obviously."

"You think this might tell us something else?"

"I honestly don't know. Nothing's made sense since I found myself standing in that meadow."

"You're right about that. And by the way, that's a good idea." Mindful of her heels, she stepped carefully over a deadfall. "Your common denominator idea thingy."

"Can you remember exactly what you were doing right before you found yourself here?"

No reply.

I wasn't sure if she'd heard me, so I went on. "My memory's still kind of fuzzy. Some things have been trickling back--"

"I'm trying to, but…" She'd stopped next to a scrub oak and stood totally still. She began staring at the broken limbs lying in the tall grass at her feet. "I'm coming up with a total blank. I can't remember anything before I woke up. Nothing. How about you?"

"I'd just left the condo. I was going to work."

She blinked. "How can you remember what you were doing, and I can't? And why can you remember other things, like your ex-wife? Your

30

job? Stuff like that? All I can remember is that I'm divorced, and that my ex lives in Orlando."

"How was your memory before?"

"It's always been pretty good. Yours?"

"In my line of work, my memory has to be excellent. It makes my job much easier, especially when I'm studying someone's file and have to make an evaluation based on the facts in the file and what I remember about this person's job performance and, more importantly, my assessment of their personality."

"Maybe that's the answer. Your memory is obviously much better than mine."

"Not necessarily. Your memory might be just as good as mine--maybe even better. We're not considering all the variables here because we don't know what they are."

"There's obviously a lot more to all this than just memory."

"I might have remembered a little more than you did, but it sure didn't come out easily. For a while I thought my brain had just packed up and left."

"That's how mine feels right now."

"Maybe we need to keep the discussion going. Something might actually help one of us remember something else that's not even related to anything."

"Sounds like a plan," she said. "Where do you work?"

"I live in Winter Park and work in downtown Orlando. I've been the Personnel Director at

Drayson Industries for the last seventeen years. I was on my way to work, and…"

"Wait a minute." She stopped walking.

"Remember something?"

"Orlando. I was there, too."

"When?"

"I can't remember exactly. Something's coming, but it's in bits and pieces."

"Nothing jumping out?"

"No, but I've got this feeling it wasn't very long ago."

"What were you doing there?"

"I'm not sure--wait a minute…" She turned away and stood with her back to me. She seemed to be staring at moss hanging from the pine tree a few feet from her.

"What is it?"

She didn't move for the longest time. Then she turned around. Her eyes were enormous. "I think I just went there…on business."

"A convention, maybe? Orlando always has conventions. If you went there for one of those, it might prod your memory and help you figure out why you were there specifically, and then you might remember your profession…"

"The rest is a blank."

"You can't remember anything else about your trip?"

She shook her head.

"Don't try to force it. You'll start imagining things, and then you won't be able to determine what's real and what's not…" I stopped talking.

She was no longer looking at me. She was staring at something behind me and to my right. I turned.

Something lay beneath an oak tree about a hundred feet beyond us, down the grassy path. I couldn't distinguish what it was, but I could see bright colors. Whatever it was didn't blend in with the woods.

"What *is* that?" she asked in a whisper.

"I don't know..." My pulse had quickened, but I knew I had to walk over there and investigate. We'd entered the woods to find out what was going on; now was not the time to be timid. Besides, it was my idea to explore the woods, and I intended to do just that.

Swallowing a lump in my throat, I quickly found that my legs weighed a ton. Here I was again, letting my fears overwhelm me.

This was ridiculous. I couldn't let my fear of the unknown stop me in my tracks. If I choked on this, I might as well head back to the meadow, lie down in the grass and stay there.

I've got to do this, dammit.

We couldn't just walk on by without getting closer. It was practically in our path. We could veer off to the side and head down the hill through another grove of trees. That would be a cowardly thing to do. Besides, my curiosity had gotten the better of me. I wouldn't be able to think of anything else and would end up coming back anyway.

"A-Are you going over there or what?" she asked, her voice unsteady.

"Eventually." I couldn't take my eyes away from the shape beneath the tree.

"Then why aren't you moving?"

"My legs forget what they're supposed to do."

"Just put one foot in front of the other."

"I'm working on it, believe me."

"You're scared, aren't you?"

"You could say that."

"Don't feel bad. So am I."

I managed to get my legs moving, coaxing them one by one, through the heavy brush. Behind me, I could hear the crunching of dead twigs as Alison followed.

As we drew nearer, the object became much more distinct. My gut tightened with each step, and I soon realized why I'd been so frightened.

A body lay beneath the tree.

***

"Wait." I held out my arm so she wouldn't pass.

I didn't want her to see the body. I knew she'd followed down the hill and would discover it shortly, but I still wanted to protect her.

"What's wrong?" she whispered.

I turned around and moved closer to her, hoping I could block her view. If I could get her to stay right here until I investigated this further, I might be able to keep her from freaking out. "I think we should--"

"Oh my God!" She'd sidestepped and gawked at the sight, her eyes filling the sockets,

34

her hands covering her mouth. A raspy squeal squeezed out of her throat. "L-*Larry*?"

My heart raced. *My God.* She knew who this was. Everything had gone from bad to horrible in an instant.

She rushed past me through the thick brush, nearly stumbling in her pumps. She stopped a few feet from the figure lying at the base of the tree and stood there, shaking, her hands covering her cheeks. I could hear her sobbing quietly as she dropped to her knees, bent, and began stroking the man's cheek.

My mind spun with wild images as I knelt on the other side of the body, facing her. This was making less and less sense. Now there were three of us in this strange place, and one of us was dead. Nothing that had happened from the moment I found myself in the meadow contained a single modicum of logic.

In a soft voice, I asked, "Who…is he?"

"Larry and I were married…for nine years," she replied in a whisper.

"I'm *so* sorry, Alison…"

She didn't hear me. "Larry is--was--a computer designer. He specialized in animation. He was very good, actually. He was offered a job at Disney several months after we divorced. That was about a year and a half ago. I'm…in the tourist industry--" Then she stopped and looked at me. "I'm remembering… My God. My brain is actually working again!"

"The shock of all this obviously caused the jolt necessary to bring it all back."

She turned back to Larry. "I was sent to Orlando. My company picked me as their rep. I think you were right when you mentioned a convention. Now that some things are coming back, I do remember talk of one."

"But what does Larry have to do with all this? Can you remember anything else?"

She sat silently for about half a minute. "I think Larry might have heard about it."

"How?"

She went silent again. I waited for her to say more, but she remained silent. She was struggling to put everything together.

"Like I said before, don't force it. At least some of it seems to be coming back…"

"Larry has a sister. Eileen. She and I always got along. Eileen lives in Phoenix, and Larry's mom lives in Tampa. Their mom moved there a while ago, but the three of them were always close."

"You think this is how he heard about the Orlando convention?"

"I can't think of any other way. Our divorce-- well, it was pretty awful, but Eileen and I stayed in touch. Our breakup was hard for her, too."

"Divorce hits everyone hard."

"Larry, well, he--" She shook her head. "The details are kind of hazy, but I do remember that he hurt me really badly."

I totally understood. "It's all right. It'll come to you later."

"Eileen might have gotten in touch with their mom. She probably called him right after that. They tell one another everything."

"It makes sense, but why would he want to see you? Was the divorce final?"

"Yes. No. I...can't remember."

"You don't remember if you're actually divorced?"

"I was the one who filed, but I can't remember if it was finalized. I seem to remember that we'd been separated for quite a while before that. Larry jumped at the chance when the job in Orlando came up."

"Maybe you didn't get the final papers in the mail."

"Maybe not."

"You're sure he signed them?"

"I was pretty insistent."

"But the Orlando thing is still a blur?"

"I imagine Larry heard about my trip from his mother then called me. He might have called before I left to tell me he wanted to see me. Maybe he wanted to meet at the airport."

"Are you sure you don't remember if you two are getting back together?"

"No, he wouldn't try...I would never go back..." She shivered. "We had too many problems. He was always very possessive and very controlling, but he also had a roving eye. He could never control himself with women. He also had a drinking problem."

She'd just told me everything. If Larry was the type she'd just described, he'd want to see her again. There was probably a lot more that went wrong with their relationship, but since he was obsessed with maintaining control, he'd still want Alison back in his life. Or maybe he just wanted one last fling for old time's sake.

My marriage to Claire fell apart for other reasons, but there were still parallels between our relationship and Alison's. When the person you love and depend on betrays you, you never get over the hurt. You can never trust them again. You know the day will come when the anger will be manageable, but you'll never actually forgive them.

But that was something I didn't want to think about right now. I couldn't understand how her ex-husband had gotten here or why he was lying in these woods. I still wasn't certain he was dead. I couldn't see a wound, blood, or any other sign of injury. His eyes were shut and if he was breathing, it was extremely shallow. He was either dead or unconscious.

Alison must have been thinking the same thing. She felt his neck for a few moments and shook her head. Her eyes were still wet, but she seemed to be holding herself together. She was a strong lady.

"How do you think he got here?" she asked in a whisper.

"The same way we did, I guess."

She sat there, watching him. I kept waiting to see some sign of life, and I was sure she felt the same. She finally bent forward and slid her hand under his neck. "I can't feel any blood or bruises."

She moved closer and examined his head carefully, rubbing and touching his skull. "No knots or wounds."

"No lumps? Anything wet or cold?"

"He's awfully warm, but I don't see or feel anything weird."

I felt his forehead. It was warm, but that could be the result of many things. It could also mean he wasn't really dead.

"If he's dead, shouldn't he be cold?" I asked. "He's...warm."

"I was thinking the same thing."

I grabbed his arm and pulled until he lay on his left side. Alison held him while I examined his spine. I was no doctor, but nothing felt out of the ordinary. No bulges, cuts, or blood--no stains on his clothes.

"Anything?"

I shook my head and we returned him to his former position. This was baffling.

"Larry?" She tapped his arm.

I felt his wrist for a pulse. There was none.

"I didn't feel one either," she said, "but something's not right." She watched him for a few moments. Then, with a deep sigh, she raised her head and looked around. Her eyes were still wet. "What *is* this place, Jack? Where the hell *are* we?"

"I wish I knew."

"Why is Larry here? And what happened to him? He seems to be dead, but we're not sure. If he is, what killed him? And if he's alive, why isn't he waking up?"

She'd raised some important issues, and I certainly wanted to know the answers just as much as she did. The only thing that made sense to me was to ask more questions. Whenever I'd faced problems I couldn't solve, I started asking questions and hoped one of them would shed enough light on the issue to give me a clue.

"You honestly can't remember how you ended up in Orlando?"

"Not really."

"You don't remember Larry meeting you somewhere? The airport? Riding with him to the hotel? Having breakfast?"

"I vaguely remember talking to him on the phone in Flagstaff, but as far as the conversation? The trip to the airport? It's all a blank--from the phone call to finding myself here. A big, fucking blank!"

I could tell she was ready to lose it. I recognized the signs--the anger, the trembling, the abrupt movements, the flushed skin. Most of all, the anger.

"Don't give up," I said. "Stop thinking about it for a little while, and maybe something will--"

"I picked you up," Larry suddenly said, his head rolling in the grass.

Alison gasped. I did, too.

His eyes opened and he struggled to sit up.

CHAPTER FOUR

"Larry? Are you…d-did you…say something?"

"I just said I picked you up. Can't you remember?" He took a few deep breaths and rubbed his eyes. Then raised his head and squinted. "Where the hell…where the hell *are* we? What's going on?"

I reached out to help Alison pull him into a sitting position. He noticed me and flinched. "Who're *you*?"

"Just a guy in the same boat as you and Alison."

As soon as we pulled him upright, he bent his legs at the knee, turned on his side and tried to stand. He was obviously too weak and dropped back down with a grunt.

"Sit there a minute," she said. "Rest."

He took a few deep breaths and sat there, looking around. Anyone could tell he was confused. "This sure doesn't look like Disney Village."

"No, Larry…"

He put his hand in the grass and, bracing his arm, tried getting up again.

"Larry…"

"I've got to get back on my feet, dammit."

"Let me help." I took his right arm, pulled it over my shoulders and grasped his wrist. Then I put my left arm around his waist and straightened. With Alison's help, we got him to stand. He was a

41

couple of inches taller than me and solid. He probably went two-twenty or so. It took us quite an effort to get him to stand.

He swayed a little. We held on until he could stand on his own. Then he reached out with his left hand and leaned against the base of the tree. He seemed to be all right but was slightly out of breath. "I think I'm okay," he whispered. I let go, but Alison kept her arm around his waist. A little while later, he said, "It's all right, babe, I can stand on my own."

"You're sure?"

"I think so."

She backed away a foot or so.

He began looking around again. "This is weird. It's pretty out here and all, but…where in holy hell *are* we?"

"We don't know," Alison said. "Jack and I just met--"

"Jack?"

"I'm Jack." I held out my hand. "Jack Clarkson."

"Larry Grant." He had a large hand and a tight grip. "Thanks for the help."

"No problem. Wish I could tell you where we are, but Alison and I just got here ourselves, and we can't make sense out of any of this. How about you? Remember anything other than picking her up?"

He rubbed the back of his thick neck. "Last I recall, I was picking up Ali from the airport. She and I were gonna go on over to the Vista."

"Where?" she asked.

"The Vista Resort. It's one of the best hotels in Disney Village. You have a room booked there. They've got this killer breakfast buffet, and I figured we could spend a little time together before--"

"You said you picked me up at the airport?" Alison asked.

He squinted at her. "You honestly don't remember?"

"I remember flying to Orlando, but not much else."

"How about my phone call?"

"I remember you calling me when I was back home in Flagstaff, but nothing we talked about rings a bell."

"Mom told me you were flying to Orlando, so I called you the day before you drove to the airport and we made a date to meet at Orlando International. That was yesterday. You got on the plane early this morning. At least, I thought it was this morning. Either of you happen to notice a calendar nailed to on one of these trees, by any chance?"

"We made a date?" Alison struggled to remember.

"Yeah. A date." He blinked. "You know. Two people get together and go somewhere? Usually at the same time? Like we used to do? That sort of thing."

Her eyes narrowed, and I could feel the tension growing. "Funny, Larry. Very funny. It's a shame you're wasting it, though. I'm really not in the mood right now."

43

"Babe, you don't know where we are. Neither does he, and *I* sure as hell don't, either. Don't get on my case for trying a little levity to cope with this."

"It isn't helping."

"Sorry about that, but from where I'm standing, the only thing that *will* help is if one of us figures out where in holy hell we are. And how we can get the hell out of here and find our way back to Orlando."

"That's what we were trying to do when we found you."

"But it obviously hasn't worked yet, has it?"

"We were heading toward the other end of the woods when we saw you," I said.

"And I was lying right here?"

"Right underneath this tree."

He took a few slow, awkward steps away from the tree and stared at the indented spot in the grass. Then he looked around. "Can't see anything from here, but I can tell we're definitely in the middle of nowhere."

"Thanks," Alison said. "We were able to figure that one out already."

He ignored her comment. "It looks like there could be good fishing out here." He took a deep breath. "Air smells clean enough. Sure is quiet. I started fishing a couple of months after I moved to Orlando, but this place doesn't look familiar. Doesn't have the same feel, either. And it's *too* quiet. There's not one damned place in the state of Florida where you can't hear the gulls. If we don't hear gulls, this can't be Florida."

"Where do you fish?" I asked.

"Lake Monroe. Know it?"

"I'm not familiar with the area. I live in Winter Park, and I'm always too busy working and never seem to have the time to take off and do any fun things."

"Where do you work?"

"Drayson Industries in Orlando."

"I've heard of it. Interior designing? Stuff like that?"

"They have dozens of subsidiaries."

"I work at Disney."

"Alison told me."

"Really?" He turned and stared at her. "What else did she tell you?"

"Not much." I suddenly realized I'd just entered hostile territory. "We were just trying to figure out why the two of us ended up in the same place." I hoped the explanation would suffice. I had no intention of opening up any old wounds.

Larry remained silent as he watched her. Once again, I could feel the growing tension in the air.

"I was scared, Larry," she said. "In fact, I was terrified. I don't know what I would've done if Jack hadn't--"

"So you decided to talk to a stranger about us?"

She shot him a glare. "I didn't tell him anything *personal*--if *that's* what you're worried about."

He continued staring.

45

"I was trying to figure out why I'd gone to Orlando. My memory had gone blank and refused to work, so I tried looking for a way to jump-start it. Since you were a part of what few memories were floating around in my head, I thought I should mention it. I hoped it would clear things up."

"It apparently didn't tell you anything, did it?"

"What do *you* think?"

"I think we're all lost, and none of us knows why."

"Thank you. I'm glad one of us finally figured it out."

I began walking down the path as quietly as possible. It seemed more comfortable than staying there, being in the middle of their problems. Claire and I had gone through the same rocky period for several months after our divorce. Luckily, we'd managed to get over it and were able to maintain a more or less civil, even friendly, relationship ever since. Claire's daughter Lexi was largely responsible for that. Lexi and I grew very close during the eleven-year marriage. Lexi considered me her father as well as her best friend, and our relationship was based on mutual trust and respect. I loved Lexi very much and hoped I'd have the chance to see her again.

A clearing loomed about a hundred yards straight ahead. The pines and brush huddled too close together and were too thick to make out anything beyond them. I decided to head down the path for a better look. I might even discover

46

something interesting by the time Alison and Larry decided to stop their bickering.

"Sorry about that." Alison, slightly out of breath, caught up with me. Her cheeks were red, and a thick vertical black line stood out boldly between her slim dark brows. "I've tried several times to maintain a cordial relationship with Larry since our divorce, but each time I'm with him again even for a minute or two, he makes it very clear right off why that'll never happen."

"It's really none of my business."

"It's so frustrating. He's bitter, and always on the defensive. I'm hoping he'll mellow one of these days, especially for our daughter's sake. I don't know why he even wanted to meet me at the airport."

"I'd rather concentrate on looking for a way of getting out of here."

"I just thought you should know why--"

"Alison, you don't owe me any explanations."

"I honestly feel that I do."

"Why?"

"We're going through something really bizarre together. I feel like we've bonded in many ways, and this makes our situation much more tolerable than it was. Because of you, I'm not nearly as afraid as I was before."

"Why's that?"

She smiled. "You're nice to be around. Comfortable."

"Like an old sofa?"

"You're not *that* old..."

"You ought to do standup comedy."

She laughed. "I really mean it. And I meant what I said before. If I hadn't met up with you, I probably would have just gone off the deep end."

"Don't sell yourself short." I noticed just then that Larry wasn't with us. "Did you leave him back there?"

She stopped walking and turned around. "Larry? Why are you still back there? Is something wrong?"

He was still standing in front of the tree, watching us. He was clutching his gut with both hands.

"Larry?"

"Something's wrong. He doesn't look too good."

We both hurried back up the hill.

Larry, still clutching his gut, watched us with glazed eyes. His face had turned pale, and a look of terror had taken over his features. He opened his mouth, but nothing came out.

"Larry?"

Just then, he began fading. His lips moved, but nothing came out of his throat. His eyes bulged, his jaw dropped. He looked like he was about to scream.

But we still heard nothing.

He raised his right arm as if he was about to wave. Then he vanished before our eyes.

***

Alison and I both stopped cold and stared at the tree.

There was no sign of Larry.

"What *happened*?" Alison stood close beside me, her hands clutched tightly together in front of her, as if in prayer.

"He's gone..." I couldn't think of anything else to say that would make any sense.

"He disappeared..." Apparently Alison couldn't process this, either. "He was right there..." She turned to me. Her wet eyes were enormous, and she was shaking. I could see the terror taking over. "Where did he go, Jack?" Her voice was a harsh whisper. "Where in heaven's name did Larry go?"

"I wish I could tell you, but--"

Without warning, Alison dashed up the hill. She stopped in the same spot where Larry had been thirty seconds earlier. "Larry?" She craned her neck and stared up at the tree. Then she circled the tree. She looked down and studied the ground. Then, finally, she turned to gawk at me. Her wet eyes filled the sockets. There was one moment when I thought she'd say something. She took a deep breath, spun around, and dashed into the woods, screaming hysterically. *"Larry Grant! Where the hell did you go?"*

I found her about a hundred feet farther in the woods. She was doubled over in front of a deadfall, sobbing and shaking, her arms crossed in front of her. She cried out in surprise when I knelt next to her and placed my hand gently on her arm. "It's me, Alison. Jack. Jack Clarkson."

She pushed the hair away from her face and squinted at me through her tears. When she realized who I was, she lowered her head and began sobbing again. Her hair dangled, forming a black shroud hiding her face.

"Listen. We're going to get through this. If it's the last thing I ever do, I'm gonna make sure--"

"Jack, what in heaven's name is happening to us?"

Before I could reply, she'd scrambled to her feet and ran back down the path. She stopped a few feet from the tree and scanned the area again. Then she looked up at the treetops and held out her arms. "Larry! Eileen! Mom! Dad! Kendra! Where *is* everyone? Where *are* we? What *is* this place?"

I stayed where I was and tried to remain focused. Watching Alison coming apart was tough. It also made the situation unbearable. I couldn't give in to the panic. One of us had to maintain an air of calm during all this.

But it made no sense. No matter what I saw or what I thought I saw, what just happened defied all logic. People just couldn't disappear like that. There had to be some rational explanation for it.

However, nothing I could come up with made any sense. Alison and I had both seen it with our own eyes. Larry had been lying beneath that tree. Although we both thought he was dead, he was alive, but just a few minutes later, after talking to us, he faded into the atmosphere.

Bizarre, to say the least. Impossible, to be sure. No one could fade...or disappear...or just vanish. It simply made no sense. Still, I struggled for an explanation. There *had* to be one. And I was determined to find out what was going on.

A few minutes later, Alison, clearly exhausted, lay on her back in the grass, staring up at the clear blue sky that showed beyond the highest tips of the towering pines. I went over to see if I could talk to her. I knew she needed rest, but we had to get a move on. Staying here like this would only feed her depression. We needed something to keep our minds active. We needed a purpose--a combined goal that might prevent us from feeling the total insanity of this situation.

I had a very strong feeling we should proceed down the next hill. I couldn't explain it, nor did I want to share my thoughts with Alison. In her vulnerable state, I didn't want to say anything that might give her the impression that I knew more about this than she did. This feeling had come to me only moments before, while I was watching her come apart. I didn't know if my gut was trying to communicate with me or if this was my subconscious suggesting we should move on because we wouldn't accomplish anything by staying here.

But whatever was feeding this urge, I strongly felt I should listen to it.

"You okay?" I sat down beside her.

She continued staring at the sky. "I just saw my ex-husband vanish before my very eyes."

"I know."

"So did you."

"Yes…"

"How can I be okay after that, Jack? How can you? How can anyone?"

"Alison, I think--"

"Jack, he was *right here*."

"I know."

"No. You don't get it." She pushed herself up and clutched my forearm. Her hand felt cold with fear. "Larry was *right here*."

"I saw him, too."

"He *disappeared*."

"Yes."

"He vanished. Like a puff of smoke. He was here, and then he wasn't." She tilted her head. "Do you understand what I'm saying?"

"Yes."

"What am I saying?"

"I guess you're wondering if we're both insane."

"What would *you* call it?"

"I'd rather consider it more like a shared hallucination."

"Why?"

"I just don't want to think the two of us might be insane."

"How could this be shared, Jack? You didn't know Larry, did you?"

"No…"

"Then how--"

"I don't know." I got to my feet. "All I know is, we need to get out of here."

"Why?"

"I just don't think we should stay here."

She watched me closely. I could tell she was trying to read my expression. "You think there might be answers somewhere else?"

"Maybe."

She grabbed my hand and I pulled her up. She faced me, standing less than a foot away, and looked deeply into my eyes. This time I felt her trying to penetrate my thoughts to determine if I actually knew something. She *wanted* me to know something. I couldn't blame her. But I didn't want to get her hopes up.

"You honestly think we should move on? I mean right now?"

"Well, there isn't anything very enlightening where we are right now. Just some really weird and unpleasant memories both of us would like to forget as quickly as possible."

She thought about that for a moment and smiled. "Thanks, Jack."

"For what?"

"For not lying to me."

"How can I lie? I haven't been here before, either. How would I know what's beyond that hill?"

"You could've said something to make me feel better--or just to shut me up. Any other guy would have done it--especially after watching my meltdown. Guys tend to get scared and intimidated when they see a woman having a meltdown. They don't know how to handle it."

"What meltdown?"

She smiled and kept her eyes on me. They were penetrating, making me feel uncomfortable. "I meant what I said before."

"When?"

"When I told you I feel much better with you around."

"I'll bet you say that to all the guys you're stranded in the woods with."

She laughed. "Just the ones who keep me from freaking."

"I must be slacking in my duties, then."

"It could've been much worse, believe me."

"I believe you."

"Good. Now let's concentrate on what we're supposed to be doing and try to find a way out of here."

"Sounds like a plan. Which direction?"

She groaned. "You really think it makes a difference?"

"No, but I'd feel much better if you pick."

"Why?"

"If it turns out wrong, you can't blame me."

"That's *so* typically male."

"I'm a typical male."

"Hardly." Alison slapped my shoulder. "C'mon. Let's go find something."

I followed her down the hill. As soon as we rounded the pine tree and reached the clearing, I heard a soft voice inside my head, saying, *You're gonna be okay, Dad. I love you, and you're gonna be okay.*

It sounded like Lexi's voice.

CHAPTER FIVE

"Jack? What's wrong?"

"I just...heard a voice." I hadn't wanted to frighten Alison. I was also afraid of saying it aloud because it might mean I'd lost my sanity. But then it occurred to me that I might have actually heard it. And if I had, I should tell her. Despite that strange feeling I'd experienced only minutes earlier, I didn't think it wise for either of us to keep things from one another.

Alison watched me closely. I imagined how perplexed I must have looked, but I couldn't help it. I'd just heard Lexi's voice. I knew that it was probably in my head--which meant that I might have imagined it. But something was off because Lexi's voice was just as clear as Alison's. Yet Alison was the only one here.

"What sort of voice? I mean, did you recognize it?"

"It sounded like Lexi, my stepdaughter."

"And you're sure you just heard her voice?"

"Sounds weird, doesn't it?"

Alison blinked. "After all that's happened, you can actually stand here and ask me if something sounds *weird?*"

"Sorry. That *was* stupid."

"Where exactly did you hear it?"

"Right here."

"And you're sure it was Lexi's voice you heard?"

"Definitely."

"What did she say?"

"She said I was gonna be okay."

"That was all?"

"She also said she loved me."

"That *is* weird. And you're sure you actually *heard* it? I hate to sound cynical, but maybe you were thinking about her at that same moment and imagined hearing her voice."

"Maybe."

"But you don't think so, do you?"

"She's not here, is she? I don't see her." I gave the woods a quick scan. Thankfully, I didn't see her. I loved Lexi and desperately wanted to see her again. But I knew I would have literally jumped out of my skin if I saw her right now.

"No, Jack. No one's here. No one but us. That's our problem."

I knew what the problem was, but since I was pretty certain I'd just heard Lexi's voice, I realized I was facing a much bigger issue. Despite what I felt, what I hoped, I had to face the fact that I might actually be going crazy. There was no other way of describing any of this. It made me wonder if I'd been imagining everything all along--the pasture, the woods, Alison, Larry.

But I had to be sure.

"Alison, tell me what happened over there." I pointed to the tree where Larry had once been standing.

"Whaddya mean?"

"I have to decide if I'm crazy. If I've been imagining all this. I need to work this out in my head."

"If you're crazy, I must be, too."

"I'm not even sure if you're real, or just a part of my hallucination."

"Touch me."

I hesitated.

She reached out and pressed her palm against my cheek. It was warm and made my body tingle. Even so, it didn't convince me she was totally real.

"I wish I *was* a part of your hallucination." She lowered her hand. "That would mean the real me was somewhere else--hopefully in my hotel room at Disney--or back in Arizona, getting ready for my trip here. But if I'd had any idea something like this would happen to me, even if it was just some stupid bad dream, I'd cancel my trip in a heartbeat."

"Humor me, okay? I need to figure this out. What happened over there?"

"We found Larry."

"Then what?"

"He woke up. We helped him up and he looked around for a minute or so. Then he said some things that irritated me, as he's always done, and I got angry and walked away. You and I began walking down the hill. We talked a little and then noticed he wasn't with us. He was still standing in front of that tree. When we went back to see what was wrong, he stared at us, grabbed his stomach and disappeared."

So far, so good. But it didn't explain Lexi's voice.

"Satisfied?"

"It'll have to do."

"Good. Now let's get out of here."

"But I've got to find out--"

"Later."

"But--"

"I said later. We can talk about your voice thing on the way."

She was right. I couldn't solve anything standing here, agonizing over what I'd just heard, or thought I'd heard.

Without another word, we went down the grassy path. I was tempted to turn around to see if Lexi was following us or standing in the path behind us. I even expected her to pop out from behind a tree, smiling at me with her big blue eyes.

But I knew better and tried to convince myself that her voice had been a figment of my imagination. I'd been grasping blindly at things, desperate for something familiar to latch onto. Since Lexi and I had always been close, she was never very far from my mind. I could only surmise that my imagination--as well as my fears--had caused her voice to materialize amongst my confusion.

"How old is Lexi?" Alison kept a watchful eye on me as we plodded through the thick brush.

"She turned seventeen last September."

"She's still in high school, then?"

"She'll be graduating in June. She skipped a year."

"She must be very bright."

"Extremely." The images of Lexi huddled over her laptop, her long blond hair spilling over her shoulders, made me smile. "She makes me feel like an idiot most of the time."

Alison laughed. "I've got a brainy daughter, too. Her name's Kendra. She's eight and lives with my parents. She's reading books I couldn't get into until I was in high school."

"Sounds like your memory's finally coming back," I said.

"I think it has something to do with my meltdown back there."

"Makes sense. A shock like that would stimulate your entire system and flip all the breakers on again."

Alison sighed. "Now everything's coming back--both good and bad."

"That's the thing about memory. Unless you've got some sort of mental block, the mind doesn't discriminate. But your memories of Kendra are good ones. That's great that she reads. Reading's rare these days--especially with young people." Most people I knew spent their time chatting, texting, or engrossed in video games. Even Lexi spent a lot of time chatting, but hardly texted, and wasn't addicted to her cell phone like most of her friends.

"Kendra saw *Wizard of Oz* a year or so ago and has been hooked on this kind of stuff ever since," Alison said. "She asked me to find the Baum books for her. I remember ordering one from eBay. She wanted the rest, so I ordered half a dozen more, and she read everything very quickly. She's been reading ever since. She even found an old copy of *Black Beauty* my mother gave me when I was little, and read that in just a few days. Likes Harry Potter, too."

"Lexi loves to read sci-fi, thrillers, and horror once in a while, but doesn't like gore, just stuff that plays havoc with the mind. She once told me sci-fi stuff helps her with her math. She can read a book in a day--which always amazed me."

"Does she take after her mother? Or her dad?"

"I never met her dad, and she never talks about him. He wasn't in her life much when he and Claire were married."

"Did he travel?"

"He had a substance abuse problem and spent much of his time in Rehab."

"I guess you're Lexi's *adopted* father, then. No wonder you two are close. I'm wondering if this is why you heard her voice."

"It could be something like that."

"Your subconscious might have been thinking about her at the time, for all you know."

"You're probably right." Still, I couldn't help thinking that there was something more tangible about Lexi's voice than just some fabrication forming in my mind.

"On the other hand, she could be thinking of you, too. If you two are as close as you say, there's a definite bond there. And they say strong bonds never break."

"According to Lexi, I'm her *real* father. Even after Claire and I divorced, Lexi never stopped coming over to spend time with me. She comes over at least twice a week, sometimes just for fifteen or twenty minutes. She even spends her Sundays at my place when she wants to chill and just hang out."

"Claire doesn't mind?"

"Claire has never stood in Lexi's way." I laughed. "She knows what would happen. Lexi would probably want to move in with me. That girl's got a mind of her own. She's more stubborn than her mother."

"Does she get along with her mother?"

"Generally. I really have to give Claire credit for treating Lexi like a person--not just her daughter, or a little girl. Lexi is much more mature than most girls her own age."

"Most daughters are closer to their father than their mother."

"How about Kendra?"

"Kenny was close to both of us growing up, but when Larry started spending more and more time away because of his drinking and whoring, Kenny and I grew closer to one another. I guess I became her anchor. I feel horrible about the divorce. It devastated Kenny. She turned inward and wouldn't talk much at all to anyone for the longest time."

"Did she have any idea why the two of you were splitting up?"

"She knew Larry drank. He did most of his drinking after office hours and was usually careful about what he did when he was home, but you can't hide something like that from everyone. He was good at it, but as I told you, Kenny's pretty bright. She told me she could smell it on him."

"At least she didn't blame you for the divorce."

"She blamed both of us. Since Larry and I had been separated for more than two years before our actual divorce, Kenny didn't see too much of him, but she knew he was close. He'd come and see her every weekend, but like I said, she'd already turned inward. She talked to him but didn't trust him. Kids are much more perceptive than we think."

"Was there a custody battle?"

"Before we even got that far, he was offered his new job with Disney shortly after the divorce was finalized. When he moved to Orlando, Kenny's whole world was shattered once again. She didn't want to move to Florida because all her friends are in Flagstaff. She wanted to stay there because it was her home, and unless Larry came back to see her, she'd have to fly to Orlando whenever she wanted to see him. Fortunately, Larry agreed to return to Flagstaff and stay with his sister one weekend a month. She seems okay with it so far." Alison went silent for a moment. "Now, after what just happened back there, I don't know *what* that poor child's gonna think…"

"Neither do we," I said, "especially since we don't know exactly what happened."

"I'm sure we both have a pretty good idea."

"But we can't be certain."

Alison shook her head.

"So…Kendra lives with you?"

"We both moved in with my parents. They live just a few blocks from my old apartment and not far from her friends and school. She loves being with them." Alison smiled. "My mother has a boarding stable, and Kenny has always loved horses. She's very good with them. She'd like to be a trainer one day."

"I take it she still doesn't know the details of the divorce?"

"I tried my best to keep everything from her. An eight-year-old doesn't need to know about stuff like that. But even though I tried so hard to keep Larry's secret to myself, she saw Larry with another woman one time. Kenny and I were at the Mall one Saturday afternoon and saw them. Kenny asked me about it and I told her the woman worked with her dad. I don't know if she believed me."

"If she's as smart as you say, she'll figure it out one day and realize you weren't really the bad guy."

"Even so, it'll always leave a scar--especially since she was so young, but old enough to know something awful was going on."

"Divorce isn't easy for anyone."

"It's horrible. My parents separated for nearly a year when I was little. That was the worst year of my life."

"But they obviously got back together."

"Yes, but I'll never forget how scared I was when Dad left and stayed away. I know exactly what Kenny's going through. I just couldn't do anything to help her cope with it."

"You had more than enough on your plate at the time."

"I still felt guilty for putting her through it."

"My parents managed to stay together, but once my brother and I reached our teen years, we both could tell that whatever love they'd once had was dead. Kids can tell when their parents just tolerate one another. At least Kendra's mature enough, even at her young age, to understand that this wasn't her fault."

"It still doesn't make it any easier, especially when she sees that her dad is no longer--"

She stopped talking when we reached the clearing.

I turned away from her and froze. I couldn't believe what I was looking at. It was at that moment, as I gazed numbly at the wondrous sight, that I suddenly realized this place couldn't be real.

"What's wrong?" she asked in a whisper.

Alison was staring at *me*, rather than at the glorious sight directly ahead. That fact alone sent shivers through me. "You don't...see that?"

"See what?"

"You're kidding, aren't you?"

She still hadn't taken her eyes off me. Her expression was grim. "Jack, what would I be kidding about?"

This told me the chilling truth: Alison couldn't see what I was looking at. "Alison, I need you to look straight ahead and tell me what you see."

She turned and stared. Then she shrugged. "Trees, of course."

My pulse fluttered. "That's all?"

"It looks like...well, a couple of them are missing."

"Nothing else? Just trees and a place where a couple are missing?"

She turned back to me. "What do *you* see, Jack?"

At the end of the clearing, standing boldly between two pine trees, a sparkling doorway blocked our path. It was a little larger than a normal door, and rectangular in shape.

"It's some sort of doorway with gold colors in its center."

Alison turned toward the front and gazed straight ahead. "A *doorway*? With gold *colors*?" Her eyes filled the sockets.

"I also see orange and white glittering inside."

Alison sighed brokenly. "You're serious, aren't you?"

I swallowed and felt my limbs turn cold. "As heart failure."

Without looking away from it, she said, "Jack...why aren't we seeing the same thing?"

"I wish I knew."

She slowly turned back to me. Her face had gone pale; she was trembling. "What's happening to us?" Her voice was unsteady.

Before I could reply, I heard Lexi's voice again. It said, *"I'm right here, Dad. I love you, and I'm waiting for you to come back."*

It sounded like it was coming from inside the doorway.

CHAPTER SIX

"Jack?" Alison was shaking my arm. "Are you all right?"

I forced myself to snap out of it. I pulled away from her and looked around. Part of me wanted to believe I'd just blacked out for a moment. But I knew I hadn't. Worse, I knew I hadn't budged from where I'd been only a moment ago, just before I'd heard Lexi's voice.

Trees. As before, we were surrounded by trees. There was a clearing straight ahead, but something was blocking it. It was some sort of portal with glittering colors inside. And Lexi's voice had come from inside it.

"Jack? Talk to me, please?"

Alison stood very close to me. It was her voice I'd just heard--not Lexi's. Alison--*not* Lexi--was standing beside me. She was worried, too, watching me as if I had a bomb strapped to my chest.

Or as if I'd just lost my mind.

Yes. That possibility still hung in the air, like a dark cloud. Had I gone insane? Is that what this was all about? Would it explain the meadow? The woods? Alison's presence? Larry? His disappearance? Would it explain Lexi's voice? This glittering doorway?

"Jack? *Talk* to me..." Alison was trembling.

"I'm okay."

"You're sure?"

"What happened? What did I do?"

"You cringed and just stood there, frozen. I thought maybe you had a coronary."

"I heard her voice again. It was just as clear as your voice."

"Jack, I know this is getting to you. It's getting to me, too. I mean, a doorway glittering with *bright lights*? In the middle of a *pine forest*? I'm having a big problem with this, so I need all the help I can get. But since you're the only one with me, you're the one I'm asking for the help. But you've got to force yourself to keep your head clear. I know you love Lexi and all, but she's not here. Did you hear me, Jack? Lexi's not here, but I am."

Yes. Alison was here. But that didn't mean I wasn't going crazy, did it? Alison was right here beside me, yet she hadn't seen the glittering doorway. Instead, she saw only a place where some trees were missing.

And why hadn't she heard Lexi's voice?

I tried a gamble. "Did you hear Lexi?"

She sighed. "No, Jack. I didn't."

Slivers of ice trickled down my spine. This was bad. If Alison couldn't hear Lexi's voice…what did this mean?

Was Alison real?

I'd asked myself this before, but was I certain she wasn't just some strange manifestation of my imagination? I'd *touched* her, for God's sakes. And she'd touched me. Under normal circumstances, this would be all I needed to convince myself. But somehow I needed more reassurance.

I reached out and touched her face. It was warm…and smooth…and soft…and most of all, *real*.

She didn't pull away, but her brows bumped together. "What are you doing?"

"You're real. You have to be. I'm *not* going crazy. I *can't* be going crazy. If you weren't real, I couldn't feel you, could I? My hand would have gone right through you. But it didn't. It touched you. Your skin…it felt real…"

"I *am* real, Jack." She moved closer and put her hands on my shoulders. "You touched me before. I was real before, and I'm still real. Can't you understand that?"

"Yes. Of course I understand."

Her right hand came up and gently touched my cheek.

It felt good, but this wasn't the time for distractions. I had to stay focused. In spite of Alison's beautiful face being so close and her hand touching my cheek, I had to keep my head clear.

"If I wasn't real, you couldn't touch me and I couldn't touch you, right?"

"You're real. You have to be real." I placed my hands on hers. They felt warm. Warm meant real. Warm meant alive. Alison was real; she was alive. At least that part of the puzzle had been solved.

"I *am* real, Jack. For God's sake, believe it. I'm real, and I'm right here, with you."

"Then why can't you see the doorway? Why can't you hear Lexi's voice?"

"I don't know. I wish I did--I really do. All I can say is, just because I can't see or hear what you've seen and heard doesn't mean I'm not real. Can you understand that?"

"I wish I could…"

"Can't you honestly believe I'm real, Jack?"

"Yes…"

"You're not sure."

"I'm not sure of anything."

She reached up and placed her hands at the back of my neck. "Be sure of this, Jack." Then she kissed me, hard and passionately.

I knew right then that she was real.

She ended the kiss--much too abruptly, for my taste--and pulled back. "Convinced now?"

I sighed and felt the familiar tingling heating up the appropriate areas. "Yeah. That sure was real, all right."

"*Thank* you…" She sounded disgusted, and I couldn't blame her.

I forced myself to get back on track. It was difficult, so I reluctantly turned away from her and focused on the glittering doorway again.

"Where exactly did you hear her?"

"It sounded like it came from the other side of that doorway."

"You mean where those trees are missing?"

"Yes."

"What did she say?"

"Her voice…it sounded so *clear*. She said, "I'm right here, Dad.""

"Is that all?"

"She said she loved me. She said she was waiting for me."

"And you're sure you heard her--"

"*Dad...*"

I held up my hand. "I just heard her again. She called my name."

"Are you sure this isn't just your subconscious turning this into--"

"No!" I turned to face her. She stepped back, and I realized I was glaring. I closed my eyes, took a breath, and told myself to focus. "I'm sorry. I just don't want to think this is all just my…" I turned back to the door. "My God!"

The doorway had disappeared. Only darkness remained.

***

"Wh-What's wrong, Jack? What are you looking at?" Alison stared straight ahead.

I gawked at her. "You don't see that?"

"See what?"

"The doorway. It's gone."

Alison gazed into my eyes. "Jack…what's going on?"

"I just told you. The doorway…"

"What do you mean, gone?" She turned back to where the doorway had once been. "What do you see now?"

"It's gone. The doorway's gone."

"Tell me what you see, Jack…"

"Darkness."

"You mean, where you once saw the doorway?"

"Between those two pines trees. The lights inside...it's all gone. Now it looks like...like some sort of dark entrance." I couldn't believe I was the only one who could see it. "Don't tell me you still don't see anything."

"I see that same space between the same two pine trees, Jack. There's some grass growing there, a mound of pine needles, and a few broken twigs. Nothing else."

My temples began pounding and I trembled. The fear was trying to take over again. "My God. I *am* going crazy."

"*Dad, please come home...*"

I froze. "Lexi's voice again."

Alison stared at me, then at the two trees, but said nothing. I could tell she truly wanted to hear the voice.

"You still don't hear it, do you?"

"Where did you hear it this time?"

I turned back and cringed. The darkness had become a tunnel. "There's a tunnel there now."

Alison turned sharply. "You mean...you see a *tunnel* now?"

I swallowed. "And you still don't see anything?"

She shook her head.

Something wasn't right. Up until the time I'd seen the doorway, Alison had seen everything I'd seen. But now the situation had changed. I was seeing and hearing some strange things that defied all logic. I found myself once again doubting my sanity. This time, my doubts--as well as my fears--had grown much stronger.

"Jack, what's going on?"

"I wish I knew."

"*Dad, I'm right here, and I'm not leaving until you come back...*"

"Lexi?"

"You heard her *again*?"

I nodded.

"Did it sound like it was coming from the same place?"

"I think so…"

"What do we do, Jack? Something very strange is happening to both of us right now. I know it feels like it's happening only to you, but since you're seeing and hearing all these unusual things that I can't see or hear, this concerns me just as much as it concerns you."

"I know."

"I'm no scientist, but I kind of think we should be seeing and hearing the same things. We're both here in the same place, looking at the same trees, the same meadow, and the same sky. That means I should've seen the doorway, the darkness, and the tunnel. I should've also heard the voice. But that just isn't happening, is it?"

"No."

"I mean, we both saw Larry at the same time. We both examined him, heard him when he came to, talked to him and even helped him stand up. We both saw him disappear at the same time. That should mean something."

"I know."

"But something's different, Jack. For some reason, everything's changed. You saw a doorway

72

with bright lights while I saw an empty space between two trees. Now you're seeing a tunnel. You still see it, right?"

"Right. And you still don't see anything between those trees?"

"Nothing but grass, pine needles and twigs."

"Damn. This makes no sense."

"So...what do we do about it?"

"I don't *know*..."

"*Dad*?"

Lexi's voice had grown louder and clearer and sounded much closer.

"Lexi?"

"*Dad*?"

My heart raced. "Can you hear me, Lexi?"

"*Dad, I'm right here...*"

"Jack, *please* tell me what's going on." Alison sounded frightened.

"She can hear me, Alison. I don't know what the hell's happening, but Lexi can hear me!"

"How do you know?"

"She just answered me!"

"Are you sure? I mean, really *sure*? You don't think...you don't think you're just imagining that she's hearing you, do you? It's possible, isn't it?"

"Maybe..."

"You don't sound convinced."

"Alison, I've got to go in there and find out what's going on. I have a feeling Lexi's in that tunnel."

73

Alison said nothing. She stared straight ahead, possibly forcing herself to visualize the tunnel.

"There *is* a tunnel there, believe me."

"I believe you, Jack. I may not see it, but I truly believe you see a tunnel."

"Thank you. And since I don't know what's in there, I think I'd better go in there alone."

"No. We're going *together*." She grabbed my arm with both hands. Her grip was warm, almost hot, and really hurt. She was obviously very frightened and desperate. I could feel the panic pulsating through her.

I knew I had to find some way of calming her. "How about if I go over there first? You can stay right behind me, and I'll let you know when it's safe to--"

"No! We're going in there *together*, understand?" Alison's face had become a tense mask. Her eyes glistened. "I don't know what's happening, Jack, but I won't let you leave me--get it? I *won't let us split up!*"

"It'll only be for a second, I promise."

"I don't *care!*" She moved closer. Her face was only inches away. "I've got this horrible feeling that if we split up, we'll never be able to be together again!"

"Where's *that* coming from?"

"I don't know, and I don't care. I don't like it one bit that you're suddenly seeing and hearing things I can't see or hear. That's scaring me, telling me something terrible is about to happen. *Please* don't leave me, Jack! *Please!*"

"All right." I saw no reason to argue. The white terror on Alison's face frightened me. I didn't know what she was feeling, but I could tell she was deadly serious. I clearly understood. I even agreed with her. I really didn't want to go in there by myself. I'd wanted to go in alone because I wanted her to stay at a safe distance in case something bad happened. But it made better sense that she should be right there with me if I needed help. "Let's go."

Holding hands, we cautiously approached the tunnel.

"Whatever happens," Alison whispered, "I'm right here with you."

"I'm right here with you, too."

"Don't let go of my hand."

"I won't."

"Promise?"

"Of course."

The pressure on my hand suddenly increased so much that I winced. "Can you ease up…just a little?"

She sighed. "Sorry." But she relaxed her grip only slightly.

"Thank you."

"Promise me with all your heart and soul that you won't under any circumstances let go of my hand."

"Whatever this feeling is, it sure has you terrified."

"Promise me, Jack."

"I promise. Feel better?"

She nodded.

75

We crept closer to the darkness. I could feel cool air coming from within the tunnel.

"You feel that?"

"Feel what?"

"Cold air."

"Cold *air*?"

She obviously had no idea what I was talking about. This made me feel even more suspicious, and I wondered once again if I was actually going crazy. Crazy or not, I had to follow Lexi's voice and find out once and for all why I was hearing it.

We took two more steps, then three, as we moved unsteadily over the tall grass. The tunnel awaited us just ten feet away. The cool air grew cold and much stronger, and a faint smell of minty antiseptic assaulted my nostrils. "I take it you don't smell anything, either," I said, glancing at her.

She sniffed and shook her head. "Are you trying to say you smell something coming out of there?"

"I'm trying to say--"

"*Dad*?" Lexi's voice, louder than before, came from within the tunnel.

"I'm coming, Lexi!"

"You heard her again, didn't you?"

"It was louder than ever. It sounded like she's just ten feet away." Three more steps and we were just a few feet short of the threshold. The cool air enveloped me, as did the antiseptic smell.

Alison began pulling me in the opposite direction. I turned and tugged at her. "I thought you wanted to go in with me."

"That isn't me, Jack!" She was trembling. "I'm trying to stay close to you!"

"What the hell are you talking about?"

"I mean, I'm not *doing* this!" She pulled harder, gritting her teeth. Her eyes filled the sockets as she gawked at the hand that gripped mine. She was staring at our hands as if she had no idea what they were. "What's happening? Why am I pulling *away* from you?"

"*Dad, I'm right here...*"

"Lexi?"

"*Dad?*"

"Jack, *please* don't let go of me!"

"I'm holding onto you as hard as I can!"

"Hold on *harder*!"

One more step and I was inside the tunnel, enveloped by cold and that sweet antiseptic smell. Alison's grip tightened, but I could no longer see her. The darkness had thickened, enveloping us, and she'd quickly faded.

"Jack? Where are you?"

"I'm right here!"

"Don't let go of me*!*"

"Alison? Where the hell are you?" I held on tightly, but I still couldn't see her in the darkness. "Come closer so I can see you!"

"*Dad?*"

"*Jack!*" Alison's voice sounded much farther away.

Her grip grew even tighter. A moment later, she suddenly stopped pulling away. The darkness thickened and I could no longer see anything--not even the hands locked around my own.

"Dad, please come back..." Lexi's voice was loud and clear, filling the tunnel. *"Dad, I'm right here..."*

Lexi's voice sounded like it was coming from my right, where Alison had been only moments earlier.

"Alison?"

No reply.

"Alison? Where are you?"

Still no reply.

The darkness gradually lifted, and I could finally see her face.

It wasn't Alison's face, but the face of a pretty young girl. She sat beside me, holding my hand, and her big blue eyes glistened with tears.

CHAPTER SEVEN

As the thick cloud in my head lifted, I realized I was lying in a bed in a small white room.

My hands were wrapped in bandages and my head was similarly wrapped. I ached all over, and my legs were numb. I wanted to sit up but discovered that I had no idea how to begin to do so.

As soon as I stirred, I heard a gasp somewhere on my right. A pretty young girl, her honey-blond hair tied in a thick ponytail, suddenly appeared, stopping abruptly against the metal rail of my bed and jarring the mattress a little. She'd obviously been sitting in a chair close to the bed. She bent over me and I caught a faint whiff of vanilla as her ponytail slid down over her shoulder and dangled just a few inches from my chest. It was really nice to look at, but she quickly grabbed it and tossed it behind her back, where I could no longer see it. She wore a turquoise tank top and jeans. Her big blue eyes glistened with tears. I immediately felt her hand covering mine. It was cold, and trembled. "Dad?" Her voice was a soft, unsteady whisper.

Dad. She was looking right at me, and she'd just called me "Dad." I couldn't remember being someone's dad. It didn't tell me anything, but that was no surprise; at the moment, I couldn't remember much at all. I had a vague notion that my name was Jack something. That name seemed to drift lazily out of the darkness, but not much of anything else. The rest of my existence was nothing more than a distant blur.

"Dad, it's me. Lexi."

Lexi? Still nothing. I closed my eyes and hoped the darkness filling my mind would reveal more of this mystery.

Lexi. Her name was Lexi. And she'd just called me "Dad."

She was watching me closely, probably hoping I'd smile, or say something that would make her feel less awkward. I didn't know what to say. I didn't even know if I could speak at all right now. Even if I could, I certainly didn't want to tell her I didn't know who she was. She probably wouldn't be able to deal with something like that. But by the same token, I wasn't sure who I was, either.

After what seemed an eternity of awkwardness, she finally said, "I'm your daughter, Dad. I'm Lexi. Don't you remember me?"

Lexi. My daughter. *No, Lexi, I don't remember you. But don't take it personal because I don't remember much of anything. Hell, I don't even remember my last name.*

I tried to smile, but my facial muscles wouldn't cooperate. They were as numb as my legs. I mumbled something I thought was "who am I?" but the only thing I heard coming out of my throat was a soft groan. My entire mouth and throat felt numb. I shook my head--or thought I did.

80

This didn't seem to matter to her. She just smiled and squeezed my hand. Then she placed her other hand over it. "Don't try to talk, Dad."

Dad. The way she said it made me feel better even though I couldn't remember anything. But it didn't make sense. If I was her father, I should remember, shouldn't I? But I didn't. I couldn't even remember if I'd seen this lovely young girl before.

Shadows moved along the chalky white wall on my right. They continued moving along the wall facing the bed, and out of the corner of my eye, I saw three of them. As they drew closer, I saw that they were all dressed in white. One of them was a woman around forty years old, with red hair and small, crinkly blue eyes. She wore a funny white cap. I'd seen caps like that before. She was a nurse, and immediately began fiddling with the bandages covering my skull. One of the men, a tall, skinny guy with thick gray hair, stepped next to Lexi and practically shoved her aside as he bent over me. I didn't like him doing that. I wanted to grab him by the throat and choke him. I couldn't even feel my arms, let alone raise them. If I could have been able to speak, I would have told him he was an asshole and ordered him to let Lexi stand where she was standing a moment earlier. All I could do was groan. I imagined choking him, but he didn't notice. If he had, he wasn't letting on. I was obviously much too weak to concentrate properly on anything.

"Mr. Clarkson," he said in a soft voice, "can you hear me?"

Clarkson. He'd called me Mr. Clarkson. Apparently my name was Jack Clarkson--that is, if I was right about my first name being Jack. My memory still didn't seem to be switched on yet. It wouldn't tell me if he'd gotten my last name right. I still couldn't recall anything familiar about this beautiful young girl with golden hair who told me her name was Lexi and that she was my daughter. But I decided that if Clarkson wasn't really my name, Lexi would have corrected him.

That wasn't the issue. I didn't like the way he'd bullied his way in between Lexi and me. I wanted to see Lexi, not him. She was much nicer to look at. Besides, his grim expression told me he had things to say that I wouldn't like hearing.

But I figured all this nonsense was necessary. He was the doctor, and one of his duties was to tell me what happened and why I was lying in this bed.

"Mr. Clarkson, you've been in a coma for five days..."

I didn't hear the rest. Once his message had sunk in, his voice quickly trailed away as another heavy cloud of darkness drifted my way.

A coma. He'd said coma. It sure as hell had sounded like coma. I'd been in a coma for five days. That would explain the hospital room. The bandages. My injuries. Most of all, my total lack of recall.

Five days of my life were gone, and I'd never get them back.

I'd been lying here for five days. I'd actually been dead for five days. Now I lay here, fully awake, my brain filled with darkness and a heavy sense of nothingness...

A bright flash flew across my vision and quickly vanished. It happened so fast, I was unable to get a good look. I closed my eyes and saw a lush green meadow and some pine trees.

Then darkness.

Another image, this one darker and more ominous, overshadowed the darkness for an instant. A tunnel. I'd gone through a dark tunnel, but I hadn't been alone. There was someone else with me, following me, staying close behind me...

A woman.

I'd gone into the tunnel with a woman.

That didn't make any sense. What was I doing in a tunnel? Where was this tunnel? Who was the woman with me? And what did that the lush green meadow and pine trees have to do with this?

A dream, most likely. It had to have been a dream. Nothing else made any sense.

"Jack, please don't..."

The troubled voice thundered through my head with the force of a freight train and then vanished. Had I done something to offend this woman? Why did she sound so frightened?

Who was she?

What were we doing in the tunnel?

Since I couldn't see her face, there was no way I could tell. And if it was indeed a dream, it didn't matter, did it? Dreams were merely disposable material; they meant nothing.

How did I know that? Had I read it somewhere?

The doctor was still going on about my injuries and what to expect. I barely listened. I knew my name, that I'd been severely hurt, and that I wasn't in the mood right now to listen to him. I had a beautiful young daughter named Lexi but couldn't remember anything about her. And I'd just had a strange dream about a meadow, pine trees, a tunnel, and a mysterious, faceless woman.

As the doctor droned on, I began growing more and more tired. I relaxed on the pillow and closed my eyes. The blackness instantly enveloped me. I sighed deeply and let it take me into the quiet, relaxing state of blissful sleep.

***

I opened my eyes sometime later.

The pretty young thing calling herself Lexi sat beside my bed, punching keys on one of those computer things in her lap. It looked like some sort of --

Laptop.

An image registered in my brain. Laptops were portable computers, easy to carry around so you could work with them anywhere, and everyone seemed to have them. I vaguely recalled that they'd been around for a while and that I might even have one.

The image of a desk instantly flashed in my head. It was kind of large and looked vaguely familiar. There was some sort of wooden plaque sitting on the surface of the desk, facing the wrong way. I wondered what it said, if my name was on it. A laptop covered the center of a green blotter. On the right, next to the phone, a framed photo of a pretty young girl with long blond hair and bright blue eyes sat facing me...

It was a picture of Lexi.

I struggled to remember other things about her. Her mother, for instance. She was, after all, my wife, wasn't she? I should remember her, shouldn't I?

The only thing that jumped out was the fact that she wasn't in the hospital room with Lexi when I opened my eyes. I knew this should tell me something, but I wasn't quite sure what it was.

I sent my mind back to recall more details about that desk. I discovered that a few things that should have been there weren't.

There was no other photo on my desk. If I was married, there should be a picture of my wife right there beside Lexi. But there wasn't. There was no picture of Lexi and me or of Lexi, another woman and me.

During my mental chaos, the shadow of a brown-haired woman walking away from me flared in my memory and instantly dimmed. She wore a business suit and carried a briefcase. She didn't look back, so I couldn't see her face.

The image vanished.

Another image instantly appeared amidst the rubble in my brain. This woman was tall and slender, with long black hair and dark eyes. She wore a maroon V-necked short-sleeve shirt, jeans and white open-toed pumps. Her hair was windblown; long black strands clung to her cheek.

She stood amongst a group of pine trees, gazing up at the sky. She looked at me, and her eyes were wet. She began walking toward me.

"Jack? Where did you go?"

The hazy bubble dimmed, as did her image. An instant later, the sky and the pine trees vanished as well.

The heavy blackness that had been hovering so close above me dropped over me once again.

CHAPTER EIGHT

Lexi was working on her laptop when I awoke.

One glance at her told me I'd been asleep for quite a while.

Her hair was totally different. Before I'd surrendered to the heavy curtain of sleep, she wore it in a thick ponytail. Now it swept down her back, stopping just a few inches above her waist. She'd also changed into a tan tank top and faded jeans. I couldn't raise my head much from the pillow, so I couldn't see what she had on her feet.

The books on the small white table beside her hadn't been there before. She'd obviously been gone long enough to grab a few new books as well as change her clothes. This made me wonder how long I'd been asleep.

I felt a little better, but the back of my head throbbed, and the inside of my mouth was as dry as kindling. My legs and back ached. I'd hoped my memory had improved, but it still felt fuzzy and dark in the very places I needed light and clarity.

Noticing I was awake, Lexi jumped up from her chair, set her laptop on the padded seat and approached the bed. She covered my right hand with hers. It felt warm--probably from her keyboard.

"Feeling any better?"

I tried asking for water, but my tongue wouldn't cooperate. I couldn't even lick my lips without making a mess of it. My arms weighed a ton, but I managed to raise my left hand about six inches. I was able to turn my hand and use my index finger to point to my face.

"Thirsty?"

I managed a slight nod. I wanted to kiss her for being so perceptive.

She went back to the table and picked up the small white plastic pitcher sitting beside a stack of brown paper cups. "They don't want you drinking anything yet, but they said I could give you some ice. Is that all right?"

I gave another nod. Lexi poured some into a cup and brought it over. She took out half a dozen small slivers of ice with a red plastic spoon and carefully dropped them between my lips. The sensation was like a frosty blast that immediately stimulated my mouth and made my flesh stand out. I groaned and closed my eyes.

"Would you like more?"

The ice quickly melted. I swallowed the tiny drops. A moment later I could feel it tingling in my gut. It felt nice and quenched my thirst, but I wasn't quite ready for another blast. I shook my head.

She leaned against the safety rail and took my hand again. "Mom was here."

Mom. The woman I was married to, obviously. The woman who'd brought this lovely young girl into the world.

I tried hard to remember, but my brain refused to cooperate.

I frowned as the heavy waves of frustration shimmered through me. The darkness that had taken over my mind was just as impenetrable now as it was before my nap.

Lexi smiled and patted my hand. "Don't look so shocked. She still cares about you. She's been here half a dozen times since they brought you in."

She'd probably been here while I was asleep...

Was she the brown-haired woman in the business suit I'd glimpsed before? Or the black-haired woman calling out for me in the lush green meadow?

I couldn't remember. I still couldn't speak, so there was no way I could ask Lexi about anything. My throat felt like it was stuffed with cotton.

Lexi was watching me. I sensed she was trying to pick up on my thoughts. I could tell by her clear blue eyes and dead-steady gaze that she was extremely perceptive. After all, it hadn't taken her much to figure out I was thirsty just a few minutes ago. I could tell she had a lot on the ball. As I stared at her, I caught another fleeting memory of the brown-haired woman. But this time, Lexi was following her as she walked away. Lexi's face was streaked with tears.

Then the image faded.

The brown-haired woman was probably my wife, and also Lexi's mother. But what was the significance of her walking away, with Lexi in tears, following her?

"She still cares about you."

Did that mean she'd left me? Were we divorced? Did it mean Lexi hadn't wanted that to happen?

Divorce. The word instantly brought about a flurry of hazy, disjointed memories. I saw the clouded image of a desk, a strange office. A middle-aged red-headed woman in a dark suit sat behind the desk, shuffling papers. I sat in a chair, facing the desk. Another woman sat a few feet from me. I couldn't see her face. The red-headed woman handed me a sheet of paper. It was a list of items, but everything on it was blurry and indistinguishable. I had the feeling I was supposed to read it, sign it and hand it back.

I tried very hard to visualize the other woman, but all I could make out was the strong smell of lavender, reading glasses, and--

"Do you remember anything that happened?" Lexi asked suddenly.

I didn't know what she meant, so I shook my head. I was still wondering about that other woman. And, of course, the paper I was supposed to read and sign.

"Do you remember *anything* while you were in your coma?" Lexi asked. "Anything at all?"

Again, I shook my head.

Lexi gently held my hand for a few moments. Then she looked into my eyes and took a deep breath. "Wanna know why you're here?"

I could tell by her serious expression that I might not want to hear about it. But I nodded anyway. Hearing the details might possibly help me remember other things.

90

"Everyone said it was a really bad wreck. Your car was hit almost head-on by a truck, and there were three other cars and a pickup involved."

I figured something like that must have happened. It explained the blackness, the coma, this room, my intense pain, the bandages, and Lexi being so attentive and worried. She probably thought I was going to die.

It also explained my amnesia. Judging by the bandages covering my head, I'd suffered a serious head injury, which meant my brain had been injured as well. I'd read something about a coma causing amnesia, but once again, that tidbit slipped away quickly, like a puff of smoke.

"Fortunately, no one was killed," Lexi said. "The Audi's gone, though. It was a mess. Totaled. Sorry..." She squeezed my hand.

I drove an Audi. I couldn't remember if they were nice cars, but the name sure sounded impressive. It made me wonder if I had money. Once again, the image of that desk drifted back.

"You were the only one in the accident who suffered a coma." Lexi gently stroked my hand. "Everyone else got away with minor stuff, even the trucker who slammed into you. There's a traffic cop who wants to talk to you about it when you're feeling better. He said he was pretty close when it happened and even saw it. Mom and I already talked to your insurance agent, and he wants to talk to you about the lawsuit as soon as you're feeling up to it. The doctors also want to talk to you about it. They said they need to tell you a few things about your condition, as well as therapy. The accident happened on Semoran Boulevard, while you were on your way to work. It happened not far north of Colonial Drive, close to the Toyota distributorship."

Semoran Boulevard. Colonial Drive. Toyota distributorship. None of it rang a bell. I closed my eyes and hoped something would rise amongst the senseless clutter filling my consciousness--a street sign, a familiar eatery...

Nothing came.

I was on my way to work when all this happened. I struggled to grasp at anything that would tell me where I lived. Again, nothing. A brief blur of heavy traffic and a crowded parking lot popped up, vanishing just as quickly.

This was getting old. My frustration level continued to rise. I could hardly remember anything. My home, my job--it had all become a blank. I couldn't even remember the faces of anyone I knew or worked with. Even that image of my desk had grown hazier. The only thing that remained clear was the framed photo of this sweet, beautiful young girl.

"I know you can't talk," she said, "but maybe you can tell me what it was like if I ask the right questions. Sound all right to you?"

Rather than let my depression take hold, I figured this might get my mind off my troubles. It might also help me remember. If nothing else, it would keep Lexi here with me. I'd been growing more and more comfortable in her presence. It somehow kept the darkness from taking over. So I nodded.

"When you were comatose, were you sleeping? Was it sort of like...a dream, maybe? You can nod if I'm right. Or squeeze my hand."

I nodded.

"It *was* like a dream, then?"

This time I squeezed her hand. She smiled, so I decided to keep doing it.

"I didn't start talking to you when I first started coming to see you. They told me I could. They even encouraged me to do it, but I didn't want to. Not at first, anyway."

I managed a smile.

She rubbed my hand. "It wasn't that I didn't *want* to... It was just that, well, you looked so totally at peace, and I didn't want to disturb you. But when I started thinking about it, I realized that maybe you'd hear me, and if you did, it might help you come out of it. And it wouldn't be that hard for me at all. You know how I totally talk a lot." When I gave no reaction, she said, "You'll remember, eventually. I so *totally* talk a lot." She laughed.

"Anyway, this gave me a chance to see what I could actually do--besides jabbering away, I mean. You were like a captive audience, so I knew you couldn't go anywhere. I know that sounds mean, but that's how I looked at it. I even thought about reading you one of my math assignments, but I got to thinking about it and decided that would be really cruel, ya know? I know math isn't your thing, and I didn't want to

93

keep you from coming out of your coma. All that math might make you wanna slip into a deeper one, so I decided not to subject you to any of that. They said you'd hear everything, and I didn't wanna say anything that might bum you out. Did you? Did you hear me at all?"

Math isn't my thing. Another blank.

My eyelids began getting heavy again. I wanted Lexi to stay right here with me, but I knew I couldn't last much longer. I just sighed and let my eyelids turn everything dark again.

Lexi moved her face closer, and I smelled her hair again. She whispered, "It's okay, Dad, we can talk later. Just rest, okay? I'll be here when you're awake again."

I didn't have the chance to nod. The blackness had already swallowed me up.

***

As I walked through the woods, I sensed someone--a woman--walking beside me.

She was very close, and our hands nearly touched as we trudged through the grass...

But when I turned to talk to her, no one was there.

"Jack?"

I could hear her voice quite clearly. She sounded like she was only a few feet away. I could also hear the panic in her voice, the fear. I knew she was right there beside me. I could hear her, feel her presence, sense her fear. But my eyes had betrayed me; they wouldn't let me see her.

I stopped walking and forced myself to concentrate until I could see her. For a moment, I thought I actually saw someone standing there. But as I waited for the image to materialize, darkness rushed over in a giant wave, covering my surroundings. And when the darkness came, the woman's voice returned. It was just as close and as clear as it had been moments before. "*Jack, please don't leave me…*"

"Dad? You all right?"

Startled, I opened my eyes. Lexi stood over me in a sleeveless lavender blouse and designer jeans. Her hair hung loose, gleaming in the harsh lighting of the room. It looked like she'd just brushed it.

"You okay?" She sounded worried.

A cursory glance told me I was lying in the hospital bed in the same small, white, sanitized room. I nodded.

"You sure? You were seriously restless."

I nodded again. My headache was almost gone; the darkness in my head didn't seem quite so thick or heavy. I suddenly remembered that my Audi was a charcoal gray and that it was pricey and stylish. I also remembered my office desk again and saw the name DRAYSON INDUSTRIES printed in white block lettering on a black wall directory in a lobby, above a group of potted plants.

She smiled and said something else, but I wasn't paying attention. I was still trying to remember the black-haired woman. Her face seemed to blur and fade away whenever I tried visualizing it. It made me wonder what kept obscuring her from my view. Was it guilt? Sadness? Or something else?

And why did I keep thinking about that pine forest?

"You slept a long time. Did it help?"

I smiled and realized that it didn't feel quite so awkward. Apparently my facial muscles had finally decided to cooperate. Or maybe my memory had stepped in to remind them how to do their job.

She bent over and kissed my forehead. Her hair fell onto my forearm. It was warm and made my flesh tingle. Just as I began to enjoy the sensation, she straightened, pulling it back and flipping it over her shoulder. Then she turned, dragged her chair closer and sat down. She reached through the metal rail and took my hand. "Wanna talk more about what happened when I was talking to you last?"

I nodded. My mouth was dry. With my free hand, I pointed to my face.

Lexi immediately got up and went over to the table. She picked up the pitcher. "Wanna try actual water this time?"

I nodded.

"Fantastic." She poured an inch or so into the cup, set down the pitcher, came back and gently pressed the rim of the cup against my lower lip. "Squeeze my hand when you've had enough." She tilted the cup a fraction of an inch at a time and coaxed a few drops of the cool liquid into my mouth.

It tasted like the world's sweetest elixir, and I eagerly swallowed every bit of it.

Lexi asked if I wanted more. I shook my head, licked my lips and enjoyed the sudden coolness in my stomach. She took the cup back to the table, came right back and sat down. My mouth felt a little better. When I cleared my throat, it didn't hurt quite so much. I wondered if I should try to speak. I could at least give it a whirl, couldn't I? It wouldn't kill me. I gathered up my strength and managed a weak, "H-Hi," in a throaty whisper.

Lexi jumped out of the chair. "Hi, Dad!" She leaned over me and kissed me on the cheek, and I felt the wonderful sensation of her hair tickling my skin again. She smiled at me; her eyes were wet. "It's so *totally* amazing to hear your voice!"

I cleared my throat again. So far, so good. And since it hadn't seemed to hurt anything, I decided to try something a little more complicated. "Maybe tomorrow...I'll sing...a light ballad..."

She laughed and kissed me again. "I'll go tell the docs you're able to talk."

I held on to her hand. "Please...no..."

"What's wrong?"

I didn't want anyone ruining this. I felt that I was improving much better and faster with Lexi around and wanted to hold on to these treasured moments as long as I could. "Not wild about doctors..."

She grinned and lowered her voice. "All right, then. We'll keep this our little secret for right now. 'Kay with you?"

I nodded.

"Okey-dokie." She sat back down. "Wanna go back to what we were talking about yesterday afternoon? Remember any of it?"

I shook my head. I remembered a little but wanted her to start talking about it again in case I'd forgotten something.

"The stuff that happened when you were in your coma. We were talking--at least, I was-- about what you saw, what you heard. I was talking to you when you were unconscious. You said heard me. Did you actually hear my voice?"

The pine forest came right back. I saw the tunnel, and I was approaching it. I had no idea why. I wasn't even sure why I saw a tunnel in the middle of a pine forest.

Was the dark-haired woman with me? I tried hard to remember, but whenever I tried focusing on her, she blurred into the darkness.

"Yes," I whispered hoarsely.

She bent closer. "What did you hear me say?"

I remembered Lexi's voice coming from inside the tunnel. "*Dad*," it had said. "*Come home*."

"You...told me...come home."

She nodded eagerly. "I *knew* you could hear me. I just *knew* it. Terrific!"

"H-How...did you know?"

She shrugged. "I just knew. It was a feeling, I guess. When you were in the coma, your eyes blinked faster each time I started talking. I read something about it while I was doing research on comas. Rapid Eye Movement. REM, they call it. I read that dreams occur most frequently during these stages. So are they right? Were you dreaming when you heard my voice?"

I nodded.

"Can you remember what you were dreaming?"

The image of the tunnel came back, but nothing else. When I closed my eyes and tried to remember more, everything turned blank again. When I stopped trying to remember, the dark-haired woman appeared. She was standing in front of the tunnel entrance, blocking it. I still couldn't see her face. "*Jack,*" she said, "*don't. Please don't.*" Then my head started hurting again. I groaned and closed my eyes.

"That's enough for now." Lexi bent and adjusted my pillow. "I wouldn't have asked you any of this if I'd thought it would make your head hurt."

"I'm...all right."

"Can I get you anything?"

"I would like another sip of water...if you don't mind."

"I so *totally* don't mind." She poured more from the pitcher, came back, pressed the rim of the cup gently against my lower lip and coaxed another couple of teaspoonfuls into my mouth. "Enough?"

I nodded. My mouth and throat tingled, and I immediately felt better. "You're a great nurse, kiddo…"

She laughed. "Mom would *so* love hearing that." She sat in the chair and crossed her legs. She was wearing jeans, but I could tell she had nice legs. She was probably around five-four, but her legs seemed abnormally long, and this made me wonder how much more she'd grow. It also made me wonder how tall her mother was. "She talked about you yesterday, said she's happy you're doing okay."

"Really?" I still couldn't remember the woman, but the fact that she hadn't come here with Lexi, at least while I was awake, gave me the impression Lexi could be embellishing things.

Lexi frowned. "Please don't act like that. You know she still cares."

"Sorry…" I knew then I'd been right that she was so perceptive. I hadn't even realized what she'd seen on my face.

Lexi started telling me about some of the classes she wanted to take when she started college in the fall.

It suddenly made me curious. "Lexi, how old are you?"

"You really don't remember?"

"I will. I promise I will. I just don't right now…"

"I'll be eighteen in three months."

"And you're starting college in September?" As soon as I said it, I wondered if we'd discussed this before.

100

"I skipped seventh grade, remember? Oops, sorry." She giggled. "Pretty soon, when you're back to being your loveable old self, you'll remember how gifted I am." She tilted her head and fluttered her lashes.

I forced a smile. "Old?"

"Figure of speech, silly."

Silly. Yes, sometimes I am pretty silly...

Where had *that* come from?

Lexi laughed. Mindful of my bandages, she playfully mussed my hair. Then she went back to talking about her new classes again.

While she talked, more hazy images swam past my vision. The meadow returned, along with the pine trees. I didn't see the tunnel, but I caught another glimpse of the dark-haired woman. She was standing in front of one of the pines, crying.

CHAPTER NINE

Several days passed.

As usual, Lexi came to see me on her way to school. She stayed for about half an hour, then left. She was happy that my voice was much stronger and that I was able to reach up to adjust my pillows myself. I didn't tell her about the pain in my back that flared up as soon as I shifted my position. I didn't want her to worry, and was careful that I didn't make any groans or gasps in the process. I even took the paper cup from her and drank the water by myself, but when I saw sadness in her eyes, I purposely let the cup slip in my hand. She caught it before it could spill, then helped me finish my drink.

Starting at around eight o'clock on the fourth day, two different doctors and three different nurses came in every hour or so, checked my vitals and left. One of the doctors, the tall, white-haired guy I'd seen before, stood beside my bed and told me a few things about my condition and what I'd been through. I had a pretty good idea of what I'd been through. The fact that I'd been lying in a hospital bed covered in bandages for nearly two weeks told me I'd been through something pretty bad. But I knew this was just a matter of routine. I vaguely remembered how doctors liked to give the impression that they ran things. I'd always known that the nurses were the people who actually made the process work. This, of course, would explain why the doctors treated them so badly.

"You were in a coma for five days," the doctor told me. "The injuries you sustained in the traffic accident were severe, but you're recovering quite well. The injury we were most concerned about was the head trauma you sustained when your car was struck. The evidence--as well as your injuries, and how you were found when the emergency unit arrived--suggests you were knocked out of your seat. Your seatbelt complicated the situation. The harness cut into your left bicep and kept you from being tossed into the passenger seat, but it also kept your pelvis fastened to the seat, causing a severe twisting of your spine in the lumbar region."

That would explain the excruciating pain in my lower back and how the nurses had been careful when moving me and adjusting the tilt of the mattress. "How bad...is it?"

"A couple of compressed discs, but with traction and regular manipulation, you should be good as new in a couple of months. I've set up a schedule with a chiropractic doctor in your area. Six to eight weeks of weekly visits should correct the problem."

"What about my head?" I was more worried about my brain than my back.

"The right side of your skull slammed into the headrest on the passenger seat, and you sustained a severe concussion as a result."

"Was there...brain damage?" My voice had trailed off toward the end, becoming a whisper.

The details of all this were unnerving enough, but what concerned me most was my memory. I knew the coma would affect it. I also expected to be confused and forgetful for a while, but I was very frightened that I wouldn't get it all back.

"It's too early to tell right now. However, going by the results of the tests we've run, we're optimistic that you'll eventually fully recover."

"Eventually?"

"These things take time. There's no other way to say it."

"I...can't remember a lot of things."

"That's to be expected. The brain needs time to recover in order to resume its processing."

"A lot of other things don't make any sense." I was thinking of the meadow, the pine forest, and the tunnel--and, of course, the dark-haired woman.

"Following a coma, especially one lasting several days, the patient typically experiences confusion and frequent periods of PTA, or Post-Traumatic Amnesia. Complete memory recovery often takes place over a period of several weeks, many times several months following a longer coma. Since yours was relatively short, we're optimistic that recovery should only take a few weeks, at most."

I wanted to ask him more questions but I was getting tired. Besides, I had the strong feeling that he was growing restless and wanted to be somewhere else. Doctors didn't like spending too much time with a patient. They didn't want to get to know them too well. He didn't sit down and kept glancing at the doorway. This was okay with me. I was nervous about this visit and greatly relieved when he stopped talking about my injuries. To me, this meant he'd told me everything, so I didn't have to worry about anything else. My accident had been serious, but I'd been very lucky. Things could have been much worse.

I let my eyelids lower. I hoped this would give him the strong hint that I was too tired to talk anymore, and that he should just leave.

After about half a minute, once the sustained silence told me he'd finished talking, I opened my eyes.

He'd already gone. I closed my eyes again and tried to relax, but I couldn't stop wondering why I'd been dreaming about a meadow, a pine forest, and a dark-haired woman.

I caught another glimpse of the tunnel. The woman reached out for me and called out to me moments before she disappeared in the darkness. I heard nothing else and saw nothing else.

After a few minutes, my tired brain went blank, and I fell asleep.

***

Lexi came back at around noon, followed by the brown-haired woman I'd seen in my bits of memory.

The resemblance in the two women was strong, particularly in the nose, chin, and lips. Based on that evidence, I decided this was Lexi's mother, who was also my wife--or, more likely, ex-wife. I didn't remember much about her, but the name Claire had popped up a couple of times in my head during the last few hours. When she came in, she slipped past Lexi and placed her large tan leather handbag on the chair in the corner, next to a portable table.

She was slender and small-breasted, and her hair was thick and chestnut-colored, brushed straight back. She was dressed in a light-blue jacket, matching skirt about an inch shy of the knee, white blouse and black open-toed high heels. Her calves were small and shapely. She was obviously dressed for work, so I assumed she'd come over during her lunch hour. I couldn't remember any details about her or where she worked, but judging by her wardrobe, she did quite well. A couple of shiny silver rings adorned her long, slender fingers, and a silver bracelet encircled her left wrist. The watch on her right wrist looked pricey. Her nails were manicured and painted a glossy red. The top button of her blouse was open, and a small glittering silver necklace embellished her tanned neck. She came closer and the smell of lavender grew stronger, reminding me of that recurring image of the two women sitting at a desk. Judging by the lavender smell, Claire might have been the woman sitting beside me. I wondered if the redhead was her divorce lawyer.

She smiled, but it lacked brightness. It suggested she was uncomfortable, or embarrassed.

I found that I didn't care if this woman was uncomfortable or embarrassed. I didn't feel any warmth for her and was pretty certain the feeling was mutual. But I knew not to make waves. I was relieved Lexi had come back and looked forward to our visit. She was dressed in a dark-blue tank top, tan Capri's, and white athletic shoes. She was carrying an enormous textbook and two paperbacks. And, of course, her laptop. I hoped she intended to stick around.

"I'm glad to finally see you awake," the woman said.

Since I still wasn't one hundred percent certain who she was, I decided to take a wild shot at it anyway. "Claire?"

"I see your memory's coming back." Her smile appeared genuine this time, more relaxed.

As soon as my brain absorbed her voice, a few memories trickled back. I knew as soon as they flashed by that I could have lived without them. Claire had cheated on me with someone she knew or worked with. The affair had been brief, but it had destroyed both the relationship and the marriage.

I quickly found that I felt no animosity for this woman. After surviving an accident, I now realized that such trivialities no longer mattered. Life was much too short to burden it with past failures and torments.

"You have to go back to school in a little while?" I asked Lexi.

"I'm finished for today." She plopped her stuff down on a table. "I've already gone through enough classes to graduate. I'm just coasting for the next few weeks."

I turned back to Claire and wondered why she'd come. Was it guilt? Curiosity? Or did she still have feelings for me?

"Something wrong?" Claire asked.

I shrugged. "I guess I'm just a little surprised you're here."

I could tell by the sudden glare that she hadn't liked my statement. "I've been here to see you several times, Jack. When I first got the call, I called my office right away and told them I wouldn't be in. Then I rushed right over."

"I guess I was out cold at the time. Sorry."

"I'm sure you've been told that you were out cold for five days. And we were really worried. Both of us."

"I appreciate it."

"No problem. And I'm glad to see you getting better."

"Lexi's been a genuine angel."

"Oh, stop, Dad."

I smiled at her. I could tell she knew I was speaking from the heart. "You know I'm sincere. And I hope you realize how much I look forward to your visits."

Lexi's eyes gleamed; she pushed her hair away to cover her embarrassment. "Dad, I *love* coming to see you..."

Claire was frowning. Apparently my earlier remark had really bothered her. "Why wouldn't I come, Jack? We were married nearly eleven years."

Eleven years. Once again, I drew a blank. No memories of the courtship, wedding, or honeymoon. *Was* there a honeymoon? Did it matter?

Of course it didn't. Not now, anyway. Why should anything matter now that the marriage was over? All that should matter was that my daughter loved me, and my ex-wife still seemed to care enough about me to come to the hospital during her lunch hour to check on me.

But as I began processing all this, I realized something didn't quite add up. Lexi was seventeen. Claire and I were married eleven years. Did this mean Lexi wasn't my daughter? Confusion quickly set in again, but I didn't want to ask Claire anything about the marriage. This wasn't the right time. Besides, I wasn't comfortable with her here. I wanted to be alone with Lexi, and hoped Claire wouldn't stay very long.

"I appreciate the visit, Claire." I hoped that would pacify her.

"I wanted to come, Jack. You were my husband, after all. And you almost died."

"I guess it just wasn't my time."

She didn't reply, but I could tell she was just as edgy about this visit as I was.

"I got the curriculum for Rollins in the mail today." Lexi opened her leather binder. "They offer a really good Math program. Statistical Consulting sounds good, and I'm gonna look into their Software Engineering program for my second semester. Their Operations Research program also sounds totally right."

"Actually…well, it sounds pretty complicated," I said.

Lexi laughed. "That's what you always say, Dad."

"I do?"

"Math has never been one of your strengths," Claire said.

Where had I heard *that* before? I struggled to remember. *Math isn't your thing.* Lexi had said that to me, hadn't she? I just couldn't remember when.

"What is, then?" Since they'd brought it up, I was suddenly curious. This could be the perfect opportunity to learn a few things about myself.

"What is what?" Claire asked.

"My strengths. I still can't recall much. I remember a desk and an office. I can even remember Lexi's photograph on the desk, but not much else. Does Drayson Industries ring a bell?"

"It should. You've been with them since you graduated college." Claire went silent and stared at me. "You honestly don't remember?"

"I can remember *some* things, but most of the other stuff is blurry, or just one big blank."

"You're their Personnel Director. Bill Ziegler is your boss. He's the CEO of the company."

"He was here, by the way," Lexi said.

"Here? At the hospital?"

"He and three others came in. They wanted to see how you were doing, but one of your nurses said it would be too much activity, and that they should come back later."

"I probably wouldn't have known who they were anyway."

"They were concerned, of course," Claire said. "So was your secretary. She came, too. In case you don't remember, her name is Alice Sommers. She's..."

I didn't hear the rest. The name instantly registered something in my head. Before I realized it, I was thinking about the pine forest and the tunnel again.

Alice Sommers.

Alice. Alice Somm--

Alison.

Why did that name suddenly jump into my--

"Jack?" Claire tapped my arm. "Are you all right?"

I pulled myself out of it and turned toward the sound of her voice. It took me a few seconds to find my way back into the hospital room. "You did say Alice Sommers, didn't you? Not Alison, but Alice Sommers?"

"Alice has been your secretary for several years. I don't know any Alison who works there."

My pulse had quickened. I strongly felt I might be on to something. I decided to try a long shot. "What does Alice Sommers look like?"

Claire's forehead wrinkled. "You honestly can't remember?"

"If I could, do you think I'd be asking all these questions?"

"Alice is in her mid-fifties. She has white hair and hazel eyes. She's tiny--about five-four, I guess--and thin as a rail. She's a dynamite secretary, as you've always said, and she's been with Drayson the last thirty years. Are you sure you're all right, Jack?"

"I'm fine." I let my head fall back and stared up at the ceiling. My brain had apparently had too much excitement for one day.

Many of these memories just weren't making any sense.

CHAPTER TEN

Three days later, the traffic cop Lexi had told me about came to see me at around three in the afternoon.

His nametag said *DANNEK*. He was around thirty-five, six-two or so, broad-shouldered, and probably went around two hundred pounds, all of it solid muscle. He introduced himself, took off his service cap and stood beside my bed, looking uncomfortable.

Earlier that day, they'd removed my head wrappings. After carefully cleaning the wounds, they'd replaced the dressing with a large Ace bandage that covered the gash just above my right temple, where my head had slammed into the passenger seat. I didn't think I looked too bad--or nearly as bad as I did when they'd first brought me in. I felt better, anyway. Lexi had been shaving me the past week, when she came in for her visits. She'd shaved me this morning, so I figured I looked fairly presentable. But apparently Officer Dannek saw something he didn't like.

"I haven't grown an extra ear, have I?"

There was no humor in his smile. "You look fine under the circumstances, Mr. Clarkson."

"Why do I suddenly feel like a circus oddity, then?"

"It's not you at all. I'm just a little peeved." He sighed. "I don't know if you've been told this, but the trucker who hit you was texting at the time of the accident."

"I didn't know."

"He's presently in custody, facing several major charges. He also tested positive when we gave him a breathalyzer. It wasn't much, but enough to put him over the legal limit."

"This should be a slam-dunk for me, then." I didn't want to face months and months of a lengthy court battle.

"Legally, I imagine you're pretty much in the winner's box. Physically?" He shrugged. "That's another story, isn't it?"

"I'm doing fine."

"Good to hear." But he looked skeptical.

"Yesterday morning, one of my fleet of doctors said the test results that had come in were very encouraging. He also said I should be healthy enough to leave the hospital in the next couple of days."

"That's good news. I'm happy you're recovering."

"So tell me about the accident. My daughter gave me the impression it was a doozy."

"It was pretty bad. A total of six vehicles were involved and nine people. Fortunately, no one else suffered major injuries. Just minor stuff apparently, but the insurance companies and the courts will be involved in wrongful injury and reckless driving charges for the next few months. It happened during morning rush, and nearly a dozen vehicles were involved by the time the emergency units and tow trucks showed up."

"Well, judging by what I'm finally able to remember about morning rush hour, I'd say OPD got off pretty easy that day."

Officer Dannek nodded grimly. "It definitely could've been much worse." Then he lowered his head and began playing with his service cap.

"Something's still bothering you."

"Texting. It's the latest scourge, and unless serious legislation is done about it, it'll continue. In my opinion, it's the worst new development that's happened to highway driving since I started with OPD nearly fifteen years ago."

"I can imagine."

"It's made things ten times worse for law enforcement. It's given us another epidemic of crimes that we're just not equipped to handle--not with our present manpower. Normally, more than twenty-five percent of everyone we pull over for a minor traffic violation test over the legal limit for alcohol, and an even higher percentage test positive for drugs, either pharmaceutical or recreational. Now we've got to be on the lookout for texters, who present an eighty-plus percent chance of causing a major accident. And as you well know from what happened to you personally, texters are much more dangerous than drunk or spaced-out drivers. Texters frequently take their eyes off the roads for up to thirty seconds at a time--which can translate into more than a quarter of a mile, or the length of five football fields. And it's much harder to prove--unless, of course, eyewitnesses are readily available. Otherwise, phone records must be accessed and sent over to the Department, as well as the courts."

"Thank technology for that." I couldn't help sounding bitter. My returning memory bits reminded me of my contempt for modern technology and computers.

"Well, once again, I'm glad you're doing okay. I gave your attorney my phone numbers and how I could be reached when your case comes up. If you need to talk to me at any time, for any reason, I'll leave my card with you." He took it out of his shirt pocket and placed it on the table next to the bed. "It was nice talking to you."

I thanked him. He smiled, tipped his hat and was gone.

About twenty minutes later, a lawyer Claire had sent came in to see me. He was tall and thin, had a buzz cut and looked like he was around twenty-five years old. I wondered if he was the guy Claire had had her fling with but decided he was too young. Even if he was the one in question, I no longer cared. The marriage was over, and I'd obviously gotten over it. Now I was anxious to leave the hospital and resume living again.

We talked for about fifteen minutes. He said a bunch of things that sounded like complicated legalese gibberish, and my brain zoned out and I found myself counting the smudges on the ceiling tiles, as well as the number of switches on the monitor facing my bed. After a few minutes, he sensed he was losing my interest and asked if he could come back when I was feeling better. I would have agreed to anything by then. I wanted my peace and quiet again--which could happen only with his immediate absence.

He picked up his briefcase, got up, smiled faintly, and left.

I relaxed for the next hour or so while waiting for Lexi to come for another visit. I waited until around six. Then I began getting tired. I soon found that I couldn't keep my eyes open. Lexi was obviously too busy to come over, so I closed my eyes and dozed off. I surrendered to the soft darkness, and in just a few minutes found that I could no longer hear gurneys squeaking by, or the swishing of orthopedic shoes on the tile floor...

"*Jack?*"

The harsh whisper woke me. I raised my head and looked around.

I lay in bed in the hospital room, just as alone as before. I let my head fall back onto the pillow and listened but heard no one. Then I tried analyzing the voice. It was a woman's voice, but I couldn't recognize it. For a moment I thought I'd heard it before, but after sifting through the wreckage of my mind for more details, I came up empty.

Was it the dark-haired woman? What if it was? I still had no idea who she was. Even if she was here in this room, I wouldn't know her.

But she wasn't here. No one was here. I was all alone.

"No one is here," I whispered to myself. "No one. The voice was just my imagination. I'm going back to sleep now."

117

I closed my eyes and in no time dozed off again.

CHAPTER ELEVEN

Four days later, I was allowed to leave the hospital.

Lexi picked me up at around ten that morning. It was Saturday, and she had the weekend free. She told me as soon as she came into my room that she wanted to spend the whole day with me.

She drove me to Winter Park in her three-year-old Challenger, which Claire and I had apparently given her for her birthday. I couldn't remember any of the details but knew she wouldn't lie about something like that. I knew I'd probably remember the occasion soon enough, so I didn't give it further thought. I had more important matters to work out at the moment, such as trying to recognize things we passed on our way back to my home.

"Anything look familiar?"

The endless stretch of shopping malls, car distributorships, parking lots, restaurants and fast-food places had become a massive muddle of sparkling glass and color. It wasn't too long before my eyes glazed over. "Not yet."

"You've been living in this area ever since you and Mom split up. Your accident happened at the next intersection."

I focused my attention on what loomed straight ahead, just beyond the windshield. The long, straight stretch was lined with shops, eateries, mini malls and garages. If my subconscious had latched onto something, it kept it well under wraps. Nothing registered at all.

"Nothing's coming back." Once again, I felt myself slipping into a mild depression.

"Don't worry. It'll happen."

I just sighed.

"According to what the doctors said, you suffered a pretty severe blow to your head. You're doing better than they expected."

"I apparently have a hard head."

"Good thing."

We were silent for about a minute. During the silence, I tried putting together my next question as carefully as I could. I wanted to bring up something that had been bothering me for the last couple of weeks. It was a sensitive matter, and I hoped I could approach it intelligently, without letting it turn unpleasant. Lexi was extremely mature for her young age, but that didn't mean she couldn't be hurt.

"I need to ask you something."

"Sure."

"I'm a little hesitant…"

"You can ask me anything, Dad."

"I know, but I'm still a little reluctant about this…"

"Is it about you and Mom?"

I nodded.

She smiled. "You split up about six months ago. Is that what you wanted to know?"

I nodded again but didn't say anything. This girl was even more perceptive than I'd thought.

"Anything else?"

"How bad was it? I mean, for you?"

She grew silent and stayed this way for a little while. I could tell she'd turned inward. I cursed myself, realizing I'd gone too far. I wanted to apologize, to blame my stupidity on my condition. I'd had no intention of hurting her or bringing up horrible memories. But before I could say anything, she said, "It was bad."

"Lexi, I'm so very sorry I brought it up…"

"I know why you split, so I totally understand. You don't owe me any explanation. Besides, you already apologized for it."

"I did?"

"A few weeks before you moved out, you took me aside and explained everything." She smiled. "Actually, you took me to the Mall for an ice cream cone and we spent the afternoon there. It turned out to be a nice day, considering what you told me."

"I'm sure the day or the ice cream cone couldn't really do much…"

"It couldn't fix things, but I knew right then that even though life would never be the same, you weren't going far. You told me you'd always be in my life."

"But I really think I should've somehow kept us from splitting--"

"Mom hurt you. I know it, and so does she. I was right there when it happened, and I don't blame you one bit. She was clueless about the whole thing and didn't realize how good she had it."

"I'm sure she probably didn't actually *plan* something like that."

"Mom can be flirty at times. I've known that since I was little. I've seen her when she's had a few drinks and some nice-looking guy in a good suit smiles at her and tells her how great she looks."

I decided it was time to move on. Lexi was obviously angry at her mother for the divorce. I didn't want her taking it home to Claire and having Claire call me and ask what I'd done. "None of us is perfect, Lexi."

"I know."

I sat back and tried to visualize what had really happened. The arguments. The tears. My storming out of the house. The slamming of doors. It still hadn't come, but this was something I wasn't too concerned about. It shouldn't have happened but it did, and now was the time to leave it in the past, where it belonged. But I had to know a couple of other things before I laid the subject to rest.

"How are you and her?"

"You mean how are we getting along?"

"That's what I mean."

"I'm pissed at her for it, of course. I mean totally. She knows it, but she's my mom, and knows what she did. She also knows how close you and I are."

"Then she's okay with our spending so much time together?"

Lexi laughed. "She has to be."

I realized right then that Lexi was one strong-willed young lady. I was very proud of her, and knew she'd go far in life. "I feel very badly that you went through that."

"Dad, I'm all right. Really." She rested her hand on my shoulder. "Almost all my friends have gone through the same thing. I'm just glad I still have you."

I placed my hand over hers. "I'm really happy you're in my life."

She squeezed my shoulder. "I wouldn't have it any other way."

About five minutes later, Lexi pulled into the sprawling grounds of condos, went down the long private road and parked in front of what looked like a complex of four condos. She got out, went to the rear of the car and opened the trunk to get out my walker and the suitcase she'd packed for me a month earlier, when I'd first been admitted.

I sat in the seat, staring at the condo straight ahead, at the end of the walk. It looked familiar, but in a very strange way. It seemed to be a place I'd seen a long time ago. A place where someone I'd once known lived. So did the cars parked along the curb. For all I knew, anyone could be living here now.

But even though my brain was obviously trying to trick me, I knew it was my home. Despite what happened to me, I lived here.

I stayed in the passenger seat, taking in everything. Shrubs spanned the long row of buildings, with flowers adding color to the lush greenery. The place had a small front porch, shutters, and a green awning over the living room window. The awning looked fairly new; it wasn't faded, and gleamed in the sun. I'd probably replaced it or had it painted recently. In either case, I had no recollection.

Lexi wheeled over the walker and set it about a foot or so from the opened passenger door. All I had to do was grab the padded handles, let my legs drop, and pull myself into a standing position.

But I didn't *want* to pull myself into a standing position. I didn't *like* the idea of using a walker; it reminded me too much of old people in baggy pajamas and fuzzy pink slippers, shuffling down the corridors of hospitals and rest homes. I wasn't old, nor was I crippled or paralyzed. But the doc had said I should use it for the next few days in case of blackouts, dizziness, or periods when my coordination failed me.

I still didn't like the idea and planned to use the damned thing only when totally necessary.

"Dad?" Lexi was staring at me. The toes of her tennis shoes pressed against the front wheels so it wouldn't roll when I grabbed it.

I looked up at her. I didn't want her to think I was angry at her, so I managed a weak smile. But when my eyes went back to the cursed walker, the frown took over my face again.

"It's only for a little while," she said softly.

"I know..."

"I'm keeping it steady, so it doesn't move. I'll step away when you're ready to kick butt and tear up the walk."

"This is humiliating."

"No one's looking."

"I'm only--" Damn. I couldn't even remember how old I was. Since I hadn't seen myself in a mirror lately, I had no way of telling. I didn't think I was much older than Claire, and she looked around thirty-eight. Besides, I didn't feel old, and even with my injuries I sure didn't feel helpless. "I'm not old."

"I know." She batted her lashes. "You're a good-looking guy in the prime of his life."

"That *really* makes me sound old."

"You're hot and sexy and--"

"Now you're telling me things no father should hear from his daughter."

"Dad, you're making *way* too much out of this. As soon as we're inside, you can leave this stupid thing out on the porch if you like."

She was right. I *was* making too much out of this. But as I stared at her, another matter had taken precedence, something much more important than my grabbing onto the stupid walker. "You know how old I am, don't you?"

She smiled. "Of course I do."

I waited. She just stood there, smiling impishly.

"I guess you're gonna make me ask, aren't you?"

"Ask me what?"

"You're having way too much fun with me, you know."

"I don't know what you mean. But since you asked, I guess I'll tell you. You turned thirty-nine this past March."

Good. At least I was still on the right side of forty.

"I just wondered if you remembered."

Lexi was giving me one of her knowing looks. "Of course I remembered."

"At least I'm not over forty yet."

"No, you have several months until that happens."

"Just don't keep reminding me, and I'll be just fine and dandy. For a while, anyway."

"See? Not everything has to be bleak. Now grab this stupid thing so we can get you inside."

With a grunt, I took hold of the grips and pushed myself up and out of the seat. While Lexi followed close behind me, carrying my suitcase, I pushed the cursed thing up the walk, to the front porch.

***

Lexi fixed supper for me that evening.

She put four thick burgers in the broiler, cooked them until they were dark and juicy, placed thick slices of cheddar cheese on each and sprinkled bacon bits on the works. She also heated up a can of bourbon-flavored baked beans. Lastly, she added a large vanilla cheesecake to the table, which she'd bought at the local supermarket and brought over to the condo before picking me up at the hospital.

I sat facing her at the kitchen table, admiring her. I was truly grateful that she'd brought me home and went to all this trouble for me. Everything looked and smelled heavenly. My mouth was watering, but I didn't know if this was because I craved these foods or was simply tired of what they'd been feeding me at the hospital.

Lexi went to the fridge, took out a bottle of Guinness Stout, opened it, poured the contents into a large glass mug, and placed it in front of me. It was foamy, dark, and thick, and my mouth began watering even more.

Lexi sat back down and smiled at me. She was obviously waiting for some sort of reaction.

I felt like an idiot. Surely I could remember my taste in food and drink. But I quickly found that my mind, once again, was filled with questions and totally devoid of answers. "Do I like dark beer?"

"Are you serious? You totally *love* it. It's the only kind you drink."

"Really?"

"Try it."

I picked up the glass and sipped. I was still on meds for my back and the headaches, but I didn't care. When the cold, tangy brew rolled over my tongue and slid heavily down my throat, I realized how great it tasted, and found myself relaxing in the chair. A slew of memories rushed back. Business luncheons in Orlando with bottles practically covering the table. Coming home after a long day, marching over to the fridge, and opening a bottle. Driving down to the 7-Eleven at the corner and picking up a couple of six-packs for the weekend.

"Anything coming back?" Lexi was still watching me.

I nodded and had another slug. "Ya done good, baby doll."

"Terrif…" She looked relieved.

I put the glass down and studied my plate. "I like cheeseburgers and baked beans?"

"You like cookouts, too. You even have a barbecue grill outside, on the patio in back."

Cheeseburgers. Baked beans. Guinness Stout. Cookouts. I lived in Winter Park, worked as Personnel Director at Drayson Industries, had a boss named Bill Ziegler and a tiny white-haired secretary named Alice Sommers. I also once owned an Audi.

Did all this sum up my life before the accident? What else was I? What else did I do? Did I have any hobbies or interests? I saw myself as boring and predictable.

Lexi slapped a huge dollop of ketchup onto her cheeseburger, arranged a group of sliced pickles in a smiley face pattern onto the works, and placed the toasted bun carefully over it. She picked it up with both hands and bit into it. She watched me as she munched eagerly. "Something wrong?"

"What else do I like?"

She swallowed, grabbed her glass and had a slug of Pepsi. A blot of ketchup had gathered at the corner of her mouth. She noticed it right off and swiped it with the tip of her tongue. "You mean food?"

"Food. TV shows. Music. Clothes. What did I do when I wasn't working? That kind of stuff."

"I thought you said some things were coming back..."

"They're trickling in, but not steadily. A ripple here and there, then nothing for a while."

"They said at the hospital that it would take--"

"I know." I rubbed my eyes. "They said it would take weeks, maybe longer. My short-term memory seems to be working well enough."

"They also said you're recovering very well."

"I know that, too."

"Then what's the problem?"

I wanted my life back, but it wasn't happening fast enough. It also wasn't happening the way I wanted it to. I'd expected the memories to come back in a violent, mind-blowing avalanche when we'd pulled up to the condo. I'd expected a slew of images bombarding me when I pushed the walker into the living room foyer and saw familiar surroundings. I'd expected disjointed flashes in the kitchen, the hall, the bathroom. Had I entertained Claire or some other woman in the kitchen? The bedroom? What kind of music did I listen to when I was with a woman? What did I listen to when I was alone? Had something earthshaking happened to the country--or to the world--while I was watching TV? It irritated me that I couldn't remember. I felt my frustration growing as I ate the cheeseburger and didn't experience the flood of fond recollections I'd hoped for.

I kept recalling things that made no sense. The meadow. The pine forest. The tunnel. And, of course, the dark-haired woman. Each time these images rushed back, they brought about a sense of sadness, a sense of loss. Most of all, they brought about a heavy sense of guilt. I strongly felt that if I didn't soon piece all this together, something horrible was going to happen.

"Dad?"

I noted her worried expression and suddenly realized we'd been discussing something. What was it? Once again, I found that I was at a total loss. Now I began to wonder if my short-term memory had been injured in the accident as well. "Yes?"

"You suffered a head injury and you're doing very well. You know it and I know it. So *please* tell me what's really wrong."

Then I remembered what we'd been talking about. "It's just not happening as quickly as I'd like it."

"It'll happen, and I'll be right here with you when it does."

I blinked. "You're gonna...stay with me? Here?"

"If you want me to."

"What about your mom?"

She blinked. "You want *Mom* to stay here, too?"

I couldn't help smiling. Lexi had the unique gift of lifting my spirits in an instant. "That's not what I meant, smarty."

"What *did* you mean?"

130

"I know we discussed this on the way over, but I really need to know if that'll be all right with her. I don't want her causing any trouble between us..."

"Dad, I'll be going to Rollins in the fall anyway. That's just down the street, on Holt. It's five minutes from here. From Mom's apartment, it's at least half an hour. The traffic factor alone will be the deal-breaker. Of course it'll be all right with her."

Rollins didn't ring any bells. Neither did Holt. "Holt?"

Lexi laughed. "Holt Avenue, Dad. You don't remember that, either?"

I sighed. "I guess not."

"Don't worry, it'll all come back. But anyway, since I'll be going to Rollins, and since you're living all alone in this really huge two-bedroom condo with that totally ginormous spare room you've been using to store a bunch of boxes you haven't even opened yet..."

"Are you asking me if you can stay here while you attend classes?"

Lexi's smile lit up the kitchen. "I was *so* hoping you'd offer. Of course, Dad. I'll gladly stay here with you if you really want me to."

I realized once again just how lucky I was to be in her life.

***

That night, a woman's voice came to me in a dream.

"Jack, why did you leave me?"

With a loud gasp, I opened my eyes and pushed myself up on an elbow. My back throbbed, my pulse raced, and I was in a cold sweat. The digital clock on the table said 3:55.

I lay back down and waited for my heart rate to settle down. For the next few minutes, I stared at the darkness of my bedroom ceiling and struggled to understand what was happening to me. But when I found that I could not make sense out of any of it, I decided to get up.

I pushed the covers aside, slipped on my robe and slippers, and tiptoed down the hall. Lexi lay sleeping in the spare room. I wanted to talk to someone about this but didn't want to wake her. Even if she'd been awake, I wouldn't know how to talk about it without sounding insane. *Lexi, I'm hearing voices. It's the same voice, and it sounds like a dark-haired faceless woman I've never seen before.*

A stranger would suspect I was losing my sanity if I told them that. Lexi loved me, but something like this could easily shake her confidence in me. I couldn't bear it if she thought I was going crazy.

I felt horribly alone and vulnerable. The darkness of the condo clung like a dark veil to the air, making me feel claustrophobic. The nightlights generating tiny halos of orange haze in the hall above the living room baseboards did little to help.

I switched on the kitchen light and shuffled into the room, sat down at the table and studied my surroundings. Snatches of memory flickered back, and the familiarity of the room made me feel more comfortable. I got back up and went over to the pantry. Shelves stacked with Tupperware, paper plates, rolls of paper towels, boxes of rice, oatmeal, a case of bottled spring water, a twelve-pack of Dr. Pepper, half a dozen cans of Sprite and two twelve-packs of Pepsi suggested I might possess a hoarding gene or two. On the top shelf, bottles of Kentucky bourbon, brandy, and several small bottles of Puerto Rican rum gave me the impression that I wasn't too keen on sobriety.

I picked up a bottle of brandy, grabbed a clean glass from the drainer and went back to the table. I poured an inch of the coppery-colored liquid into the glass and coaxed a few drops into my mouth. Then I sat back and waited for the fire to start up in my gut. Once it began spreading into my limbs, I closed my eyes and tried to interpret my dream.

Who the hell was that woman and why couldn't I stop thinking about her? What was the significance of the meadow? The pine forest? The tunnel? Was it some place I'd been to? Some place I'd visited? Memories of my childhood had popped up intermittently the day before, and I recalled the times neighborhood friends joined my older brother and myself to explore the woods behind our subdivision.

Why did I keep agonizing over a meadow and a pine forest?

Had I seen that tunnel before? I was almost certain we'd never explored a tunnel in those days. There was a boarded-up tunnel that had been used many years earlier by miners, but none of us had gone near it. It had been sealed off long ago; we couldn't have gone inside unless we'd had the tools to tear down the boards sealing the entrance. We were stupid, lazy teenage boys; none of us had been industrious or ambitious enough to attempt such a task.

Had an unpleasant memory of our entering the tunnel escaped my consciousness? Did we, in fact, enter the tunnel after all? Had something frightening or traumatic happened while we were in the shaft? Had it been frightening enough to force my subconscious to use my traffic accident to hide it from me?

If so, what did all this have to do with a dark-haired woman who kept calling my name?

What significance did the name "Alison" have with all this?

Why did so many feelings of intense guilt gnaw at me whenever I thought about this woman?

Who in heaven's name *was* she?

CHAPTER TWELVE

During the next seven days, my memory steadily improved.

I began remembering things that had been nothing more than shadows just days earlier. Details of my eleven-year marriage to Claire that had escaped me before had suddenly become clear. I recalled the times Lexi's father had neglected to visit her on his scheduled days, and the many times I'd driven Lexi to junior high school on my way to work in Orlando.

But even though I began feeling more like my old self, my nights didn't go so smoothly. I continued having dreams about the meadow, the pine forest, the tunnel, and the dark-haired woman. I even remembered someone else in the dream, a large, broad-shouldered man with fair hair and no face, but when I struggled for the details, his image and all other recollections of him vanished. In one dream, this man stood in front of a pine tree and disappeared just as he opened his mouth to talk. Where he'd once been standing, the dark-haired woman appeared briefly, but vanished moments later as well.

On the third day of that week, my boss Bill Ziegler, Alice Sommers, and a man I vaguely remembered as Tom Gilmore, who also worked at Drayson, came to see me after lunch. I'd hoped the visit would brighten my spirits, perhaps even help me forget my troubled dreams by bringing back more memories. However, it wasn't long before I realized my spirits were the least of my worries. Halfway through the visit, as Ziegler began talking about certain events that had happened at Drayson during my absence, I actually heard the dark-haired woman calling my name.

"*Jack? I know you haven't forgotten me...*"

Startled, I turned very subtly in the direction of the voice. I didn't want to say or do anything to alarm my visitors. Everyone seemed uncomfortable anyway. I couldn't blame them; I probably would have also been uneasy under the same circumstances. I didn't want to give them any reason to think I could be suffering from a mental condition. So I moved as inconspicuously as possible and hoped no one noticed.

Her voice sounded like it had come from the direction of the stereo system, which had been playing one of my old Foreigner albums at a very low volume. But as soon as I focused on the voice, I heard nothing. Still, I was certain I'd heard it, and was convinced it was in the room with us.

"Jack?" Ziegler's voice snapped me back.

"Everything okay?" Alice asked.

Apparently I hadn't been as subtle as I'd hoped. All three were watching me closely. Ziegler and Tom both looked uneasy. Alice was clearly worried and sat frozen in her chair.

I grinned sheepishly and fidgeted in the recliner. I was embarrassed, but more disturbed than anything else. I tried to convince myself I was hearing things. I told myself that it was time to stop this hallucinating and return to the real world. "I'm fine."

"You...look sort of pale." Alice hadn't moved.

"Every once in a while, I hear things." I decided to bring it out into the open and see where it went.

"Like what?" Tom asked. "Voices? That sort of thing?"

Their confused stares made me feel like some sort of oddity. I knew right then that I had to downplay this. Otherwise, they *would* think I was suffering from a mental condition and wouldn't want me to come back to work.

I shrugged. "Different things."

"Like what?" Tom asked.

"I don't know. I think I heard Foreigner sing something I hadn't heard before. My doc said things like that are normal after a head injury."

"Of course." Ziegler was nodding, agreeing with himself. I suddenly remembered that he did that quite a bit--especially at meetings. He'd make an important statement, and if no one said anything right off, he'd qualify what he'd just said and nod in approval.

"He said it's related to the confusion I suffered when I finally woke up," I added. "I think he said it's the brain's special way of acclimating itself to its old environment, or something along those lines." I hoped I sounded like I knew what I was talking about.

"We're pleased you're making such progress," Alice said. "And after just six weeks."

"I was planning to give you at least three more weeks of recovery before asking you to come back," Ziegler said.

"That would be nice," I said. "But can you spare me?"

"Tom, here, has taken in some of your workload temporarily. How's that going, Tom?"

"Just dandy," Tom said, grinning at me.

"You were supposed to stay with me," the strange voice said, and I stiffened in my chair. This time I forced myself not to budge or even turn around. Besides, the voice sounded like it had moved a few feet closer to the living room archway.

Fortunately, none of them had noticed. They'd begun talking about someone named Collins, an old colleague of Ziegler's. Apparently Collins had also suffered a head injury a while back, but hadn't been able to work for a full year.

As they chattered away, I focused on the area of the room directly to my left and hoped I wouldn't hear her voice again.

All I heard was their chatter.

***

Sunday night, I had a very strange dream.

Darkness surrounded me, and I was looking for a way out of it. I could see a tiny distant light flickering hazily amongst the darkness. I didn't know how far away it was but knew I had to get to it, no matter what.

With slow, cautious steps, I began moving toward it. The darkness was impenetrable; I had no idea what lay on the ground directly ahead of me. I didn't even know if I was in a tunnel or mineshaft. I kept moving. The light straight ahead began to grow. I guessed that it was an entrance, and that I'd reach it in no time.

But as I drew nearer, I heard a harsh whisper close behind me.

"Why did you leave me?"

Gasping, I spun around.

I saw only darkness. I squinted at it, hoping my vision would eventually adapt. For the longest time, all I could see was the darkness, but soon I was able to distinguish a shape moving around inside it. "Who's there?" I whispered.

"You know who I am, Jack." It was a woman's voice, and she sounded upset.

"I don't know..."

"You do know. Don't tell me you don't because you do."

"I can't even see you. Not very well, anyway..."

"Close your eyes, Jack."

That made no sense. How could I tell who she was if I closed my eyes? "How can I see you if--?"

"Close your eyes and you'll remember. You have to, for both of our sakes. Once you remember, then you'll see me."

What she said was strange and made no sense, but I wanted to know what was going on, and did as she said. The darkness quickly faded, and a woman's face appeared quite clearly in the picture screen of my brain. Her face was beautiful and sharp-featured, with large, piercing dark eyes

139

and long, flowing black hair. Her full lips opened and mouthed the words, "Can you see me now?"

"Y-Yes..."

"Now do you remember?"

I struggled, but nothing would come. *Think. There's got to be a reason why she'd just said I knew her.* She looked familiar and sounded familiar--shouldn't *that* tell me something? I'd seen this woman before--I was sure of it. I'd talked to her, laughed with her, cried with her. There *had* to be a reason why I should know her...

But I simply couldn't remember!

The meadow. I'd met her in the meadow. I know I did; I just couldn't recall any of the details. But somehow I had this overwhelming feeling that I really should know her, and that there was a logical reason why I didn't.

Just as something began squirming out of the chaos of my mind, the woman faded, and the darkness returned.

"I *can't remember you!*" I screamed at the darkness.

"You remember, Jack," she whispered back. "Tell me you do."

"I *thought* I did, but--"

"You remember, Jack..."

"B-But--"

"You remember!" Her whisper had become a hysterical shout. "You *must* remember!"

"What's your name?"

"You know my name, Jack..."

"Why can't I remember?"

140

"*Please* remember…" The voice sounded farther away. "Please…try very hard!" Still farther away. "You must! You *have* to…"

"But I can't…"

"*Force* yourself, Jack!" The voice was now so far away, I could barely hear it. "I'm trapped in your mind… *Please* bring me out… *Please* remember me…what we did…what we shared…"

I opened my eyes.

I was lying in my bed in a cold sweat.

CHAPTER THIRTEEN

Lexi and Claire came over at around one-fifteen the next day to fix lunch.

Still somewhat shaky after my strange dream the night before, I was a little uncomfortable when they arrived, but managed to smile cheerfully and exchange brief pleasantries when Lexi kissed me lightly on the cheek before following her mother down the hall to the kitchen.

I'd wanted to mention the dream. I didn't know why; I guess I wanted someone else's opinion--or maybe some reassurance that my recovery was giving me side effects. But I didn't know how I could bring it up without sounding disturbed or causing them worry. Claire and Lexi were in very good spirits; I didn't want to darken what would be an otherwise pleasant visit.

I went down the hall and watched them from the kitchen doorway as they busily set the table and collected things from the fridge. I was delighted that Lexi had come to see me again but suspected this was some sort of "mercy" visit, and that they felt sorry for me.

"I appreciate the company, but it's really not necessary to go to all this trouble..."

"You're hungry, aren't you?" Claire asked.

"I had to bring over some stuff anyway." Lexi took the coffee out of the fridge. "I might as well start fixing up my room for this fall."

Claire placed a Tupperware dish filled with lettuce and sliced tomato on the table and glanced at me. "How are you feeling, by the way? You look better. Your face has more color than last time I saw you."

"I feel much better, thanks."

"Fantastic." Lexi took the coffeepot to the sink to rinse it out. "I'll bet you remember a batch of stuff you couldn't remember before."

"Yep. A truckload of the suckers." I went back down the hall and relaxed on the living room couch. As I listened to the clattering of dishes and silverware, I recalled similar memories of Claire and Lexi fixing breakfast years earlier, when we lived in Casselberry. This invoked the memory of Lexi spilling a full carton of milk one Sunday morning, when she pulled it out of the fridge. She'd been about eight at the time and managed to cover most of the tile floor when it slipped from her hands just as she was about to put it on the table. She'd been so embarrassed by the accident that she rushed to her room, sobbing hysterically while Claire and I painstakingly cleaned the mess with paper towels and a wet mop. As soon as I'd finished helping Claire with the cleanup, I went to Lexi's room to console her, and told her about the time I'd spilled half a can of yellow paint on the trunk of my father's light-blue '72 Thunderbird when I was nearly twelve. It brought her out of her depression immediately.

I smiled at the memories and was relieved and grateful that my brain was returning to normal. But as I faced the TV screen, which was showing an ancient Humphrey Bogart movie on Turner Classic Movies, I couldn't stop wondering if I'd ever be able to interpret the dream I'd had the night before.

The woman's face was familiar, but I had no idea why. I tried bringing back faces from my past but realized almost at once what a fruitless endeavor that would be. One encounters hundreds of people in thirty-nine years. Relatives. Friends. Acquaintances. Faces I'd seen on TV and in movies. People who came to the house to do electrical work...or plumbing...or to fix the gutters, or mow the yard. People I'd seen only once, just briefly, and forgotten almost immediately.

But no one I could think of resembled the beautiful, fine-featured woman I'd seen in my dream.

How did I know this lady? And why had I been agonizing over her since my accident?

I muted the TV just as Bogie and Mary Astor got into a somewhat breezy exchange on the deck of a ship. Then I sat back and closed my eyes. Lexi and Claire had gotten quiet in the kitchen; the silence was relaxing. I hoped that by emptying my mind of all distractions, I might remember *some*thing. I sat rather still for the next couple of minutes, trying to turn my brain into the same blank screen it had been for the first few weeks after my accident. But this time it just wouldn't work, and I wanted to curse myself when my thoughts kept looping.

I needed to stop doing this. Once again my brain refused to cooperate. It seemed to be trying to convince me that I didn't know this woman and had never met her before. For a moment I wondered if my imagination had created her. If I didn't stop agonizing over this and tried focusing on reality, I'd make a total shambles out of the visit.

With a huge sigh, I opened my eyes and--

The meadow loomed just a few yards straight ahead.

My heart sputtered. I rubbed my eyes and kept them shut. I hoped that when I opened them again, I'd be back where I belonged.

After about a minute, I opened my eyes and looked around. I was still in the meadow, sitting amongst lush grass, flowers, and bushes. The pine forest loomed in the distance, a towering fortress of trees and wild brush.

What the hell had just happened? Where was my living room? My condo? My sofa? How did I get here?

I closed my eyes and struggled to focus again. *I'm not here, but in my living room, sitting on the couch. On the widescreen, Bogie and Mary Astor are exchanging banter on the deck of a ship. Whatever happened before was nothing more than a product of my imagination, brought on, possibly, from my recovering mental processes. When I open my eyes again, I'll be exactly where I was before.*

My heart thumped erratically as I slowly opened my eyes. I was back in the living room, sitting on the couch, as before. The meadow was nowhere to be seen.

What the hell?

"Dad?" Lexi's voice.

I jerked my head toward the hall and felt something pop in my upper back. Lexi was standing in the living room archway, gawking at me. She was looking around the room suspiciously.

"Something wrong?" It took me a moment to find my voice.

She raised a brow. "Were you here a moment ago?"

I swallowed. "I've been here the last ten minutes or so. Why?"

She crossed her arms; her sandy brows slid together. "I looked in just a minute ago and didn't see you. Then I went down the hall, to your bedroom. You weren't there, either. You weren't in the bathroom. I thought something happened, so I came right back. Now here you are." She smiled impishly. "You're not playing games with me, are ya?"

I grinned and felt my cheeks flush. "I'm a little old to be playing games, Lexi…"

"That doesn't answer my question."

"No, I'm not playing games. Better?"

"Care to explain why I didn't see you the first time around, then?"

My thoughts reeled as I frantically thought of something. The fact that I could have disappeared from the room had already sent the chills racing up my spine. But I knew I had to stay calm--at least, for now.

146

"I…might have been on the floor while you were walking by the first time. The back of the couch obviously hid me from view."

"Why were you on the floor?"

"I dropped some change when I was going through my pockets."

She thought about that for a few moments. "Okay, I guess that's reasonable. Anyway, lunch is ready. You coming? Or are you gonna trust Mom and me not to eat all the good stuff while we're waiting for ya?"

"Coming, dear."

She giggled and disappeared down the hall.

I gave the room one last quick scan before getting up. It was still the living room. There was no sign of a meadow anywhere in my line of vision.

But something weird had just happened. Lexi had looked in the room only minutes ago and hadn't seen me. This told me that I'd somehow returned to the meadow I'd been dreaming about since I'd come out of my coma.

Had this really happened? Had I actually gone back there?

How was this possible? How could I transport myself to another place?

What the hell was happening to me?

***

Claire left around three.

Lexi stayed until six, watching my DVD of *I, Robot* with me. It was one of her favorite sci-fi flicks. She said we'd seen it together once before. I believed her but couldn't remember the details.

147

We spent the afternoon together and enjoyed the movie over a big bowl of buttered microwave popcorn.

We didn't talk during the entire movie. Lexi rarely spoke when she watched a movie; she liked to concentrate on the action, even if she'd seen it all before and knew what was going to happen. I appreciated the silence and relished being with her. It reminded me once again how close we were and how much she meant to me.

Once the movie ended, she got up from the sofa, took the empty bowl and her empty glass to the kitchen, came right back, and picked up her stuff from the living room chair. She'd brought along her laptop and handbag but hadn't opened either. As I watched her getting ready to leave, I experienced a strong sense of sadness building up within me. I always felt this way just before she left. I reminded myself that she wouldn't be far. Besides, she'd be living with me in just a few weeks.

But it still saddened me to watch her gathering up her things.

Just as she turned to leave the room, I asked when she'd be back.

She looked at me and laughed, and I realized just then that I must have looked really pitiful. "I'm only twelve miles from here, Dad. That's half an hour, tops, with heavy traffic."

"I know." I felt like an idiot. I was supposed to be the adult here, but here she was, less than half my age, consoling me as if I was her pet puppy she was leaving all alone in a strange place.

She came over, gave me a kiss on the cheek and mussed my hair. "I'll probably be busy for the next couple of days. I'm finishing up some research I've been doing for one of my teachers, but that only takes up a couple of hours of my time in the early afternoons. Make me a promise?"

"Sure."

"Call if you need me, no matter when-- okay?"

I assured her I would, and she smiled and waved as she went out the front door. I stood at the door and watched her get in her Challenger. She waved again, pulled out and coasted down the street.

I closed the door, went back into the kitchen, poured myself a small brandy, returned to the living room and put on the local news. The brandy relaxed me almost immediately. I stretched out, closed my eyes and let the darkness sweep me away again.

Once again, I found myself in the lush green meadow. I was walking down the sloped grassy path when I saw her standing in front of a pine tree, watching me. She was fairly tall and slender, with long, flowing black hair and dark eyes. Her hair slid across her shoulders when the breeze touched it. She wore a maroon V-necked short-sleeve shirt, jeans, and white open-toed high-heeled pumps.

The high-heeled pumps struck me as odd. Strange footwear for walking around in the woods. But when I looked down at myself, I saw that I was wearing a suit.

This was beginning to have even more of a dreamlike feel.

As I approached her, she moved away from the tree, and we walked through the wild brush. I could feel her eyes on me. When I turned, she said, "Aren't you gonna ask me my name?"

I had a very strange feeling that I already knew her name. But I didn't say anything. If I said anything she didn't want to hear, I suspected she'd bristle. I could tell by the fiery intensity in her eyes and the way she held herself that her blood ran hot.

"Well?" she asked. "Are you gonna ask or what?"

"I think I already know."

"What is it, then?"

I didn't speak.

"Go on, take a chance. Who knows? You might actually get it right."

"Is it...Alison?"

She almost smiled. "I didn't think you'd remember."

"I didn't think I would, either."

We trudged leisurely through the grassy path. I began wondering if she knew my name. Part of me didn't want to ask. She probably knew a lot about me, although I had no idea how.

But I had to ask--just to make sure.

Just then, she said, "Of course I know your name, silly."

I froze, gawking at her. How did she do that? How could she possibly know what I was thinking?

"I know everything that's going on in your head, Jack."

It took me quite a while to find my voice. When I was finally able to speak, what trickled out of my throat sounded weak and pitiful, like the gasp of a man suffering from emphysema. "H-How do you know my name? What I'm thinking?"

"I'm living in your head, Jack. You should know that by now."

"H-How did you get…in there?"

She smiled. "I'll let you figure that one out by yourself."

Just as I was about to ask my next question, the darkness swallowed her up, and I saw someone lying in the grass beneath the tree directly behind where she'd been standing. But just as I began to approach it, the vision faded.

Then the woods faded away.

My eyes shot open; I sat up abruptly. My lower back protested, and a sharp jolt of red-hot pain shot up to my neck. I gasped and lay back among the cushions, hoping I hadn't re-injured my vertebrae.

I lay perfectly still for several minutes, willing my back to stop hurting while struggling to remember every single detail of that dream.

Why did I return to that meadow again? Where was this place?

Most important of all, who was that woman?

The pain in my back gradually subsided. I sighed and relaxed. It suddenly dawned on me that I was remembering things I hadn't been able to remember before.

Then I began to wonder if any of this had really happened.

152

CHAPTER FOURTEEN

That night, I found myself back in the same place.

My surroundings were identical to what I'd experienced on the living room couch earlier that day, but this time everything was much clearer and more detailed, suggesting that all this might have actually happened.

I trudged down the grassy path. Alison stayed a few feet behind me, mindful of her pumps as she stepped over exposed roots and fallen tree limbs. As I approached a bend in the path, I saw something lying in the grass beneath a tree. I drew nearer, and the object became much more distinct. My gut tightened with each step, my pulse quickened, and I instantly realized what was lying in the grass.

It was the body of a man.

"Wait." I turned around and moved toward her, blocking her view. I had a feeling she'd freak if she saw the body. In fact, I *knew* she'd freak. I also knew *why* she'd freak, and even what she'd do when she freaked. I knew I had to somehow soften the blow and warn her, but I had the strange feeling that my efforts would be wasted. Even so, I knew I had to do it. "I think we should--"

"Oh my God!" She gawked at the sight. Her hands flew up to her mouth. "L-*Larry*?"

My heart raced. I'd been right about everything. I had no idea how I knew all these things. To keep my sanity, I kept reminding myself this was a dream, and things rarely made sense in dreams.

She rushed past me through the thick brush and stopped near the figure lying at the base of the tree. She stood there shaking. Sobbing quietly, she dropped to her knees.

My thoughts spun wildly as I knelt on the other side of the body, facing her. I knew I was going to feel for a pulse, turn the man on his side and examine him for injuries. I also knew I wasn't going to find anything, and neither was Alison. Again, I didn't know how I knew these things. It was almost as if everything had been all mapped out. As if I'd dreamed all this before.

What the hell was going on?

More memories swam past. I realized right then that I knew many things about the man lying on the ground between us. I knew he was Alison's ex-husband. I also knew they were married for nine years and lived in Flagstaff until their divorce. Larry moved to Orlando and began working at Disney as some sort of industrial engineer, or designer, specializing in animation. He was an intelligent, articulate man who went fishing in his spare time. He and Alison had a child--a daughter, whose name was Kendra. She was eight, was very bright and liked reading stories such as the *Wizard of Oz* series, as well as Harry Potter, and the *Narnia* books. She was devastated when her dad and her mom divorced, and hated her dad for moving away.

I also knew that even though Larry *appeared* dead, he was still alive. In just a few moments, he'd open his eyes and start talking. He'd attempt to sit up. Alison and I would help him to his feet. He'd walk around for a few minutes, asking questions, trying to get his bearings. He'd start an argument with Alison, and I'd walk away, but I wouldn't get very far. When I was halfway down the hill, Alison would join me. We'd resume our walk through the woods but would soon notice that Larry wasn't with us. We'd stop walking and turn around. Larry would be standing in front of the tree, clutching his gut. Alison would call him, but he wouldn't answer. He'd simply stand in front of the tree, clutching his gut in both hands. A moment later, he would disappear before our very eyes.

How did I know all this?

Why was everything so damned clear?

Why did it all feel so real?

***

I spent the morning and afternoon of the next day sitting in the living room.

The TV was on, but I wasn't paying attention to it. I didn't even have the volume turned up. I was certain that I was going insane, that something bad had happened to my brain while I was in my coma. I feared my head injury had done some nasty rewiring to my memory banks. As a result, I was suffering from a growing state of dementia no one could have foreseen or expected.

Was it dementia? Or was I remembering things that had actually happened? If so, when did all that happen? And where?

My thoughts began looping again, the images whirling past like film spinning free of a projector. As it all sped by, I glimpsed the meadow, the woods, the tunnel, the woman named Alison, and the red-headed man named Larry.

Sounds accompanied the images, making everything frighteningly real. The woman spoke to me once again. I heard her voice just as clearly as I had the day Bill Ziegler, Alice Sommers and Tom Gilmore came to see me. What was truly terrifying this time was not so much that the voice had returned, but that it had returned in the same room, in almost the same spot.

"Do you remember me now, Jack?"

I stiffened in my seat and waited anxiously for my heart to stop hammering before I decided to move. Once I realized that I might survive this moment, and that my heart might not thrash out of my chest, I looked carefully around the room.

The voice sounded like it was about five or six feet away, to my right, in the space between the TV cabinet and the small antique walnut table that sat against the wall about three feet from the living room archway. I stared at this area the longest time, waiting for her to materialize right there. I expected to see her standing there, scowling at me with the same contempt I'd just heard in her voice. I expected to see her flowing black hair, her dark piercing eyes. The firm set to

156

her mouth. That same expression of utter betrayal that I'd seen in the dream.

But I saw no one and felt no one's presence. The carpet was clean and free of all visions and images.

Despite my fears, my suspicions, I was the only one in the room. I was reasonably certain I'd heard a voice, but I refused to believe I was hearing things that might be nothing more than a product of my imagination. I had to believe that I was alone in the room. If I thought even for a moment that I was *not* alone, I really was crazy. There could be no other explanation. Dementia had apparently followed me the moment I'd recovered from my coma. I was afraid it would stay with me until I finally decided to do something about it. If I tried to ignore it, it was certain to earn me an immediate trip to the rubber room...

"What's my name, Jack?"

Her voice, this time, had come from an area on my left, near the bay window.

Once again I froze.

I realized at that moment that if I *was* hearing a voice, whoever belonged to it was moving around. Some invisible being was in my living room, walking around. This epiphany was like a spike through the heart. I had visions of her walking past the widescreen, the coffee table and the bookcase, looking at things, inspecting them. I could almost see her glancing out the window, turning around, then coming over to the sofa and standing behind it, looking down at me.

Eerie, to be sure. But I could think of nothing else.

"What's wrong, Jack? Nothing to say?"

"Wh-Who *are* you?" My words came out painfully, as if they'd become shards of glass slicing into the soft tissue of my throat. I was surprised I was able to talk at all. I was even more surprised my brain could still function.

"You tell me," came the curt reply.

The voice had moved a few feet to my left. I wondered if I'd been right--if she actually *was* coming around to the back of the sofa. I imagined her standing there, looking down at me, frowning, shaking her head.

"Why do you sound so angry?"

"Like I just said...you tell me..."

I swallowed a thick, gooey lump. "You're Alison?"

"You know I am..." The voice sounded much closer.

"You have black hair...and dark eyes."

"Your memory betrays you, Jack."

"H-How do you know me?"

"You *couldn't* have forgotten me. Not this soon."

"I *can't* remember you...no matter how hard I try..."

"You betrayed me, Jack." The voice sounded like it was just a foot away. "You betrayed me. You promised me you'd stay with me!"

"Please... Tell me who you are, what I did... Why do you...hate me so much?"

Silence.

158

"Please...*tell* me!"

Silence.

"Please!"

Nothing.

I lay back and closed my eyes. I remained in this position for what seemed like hours. When I sat up and opened my eyes again, I was almost totally convinced I'd been sleeping.

CHAPTER FIFTEEN

I spent the next morning pacing the hall, thinking about the dark-haired woman, and wondering how I knew her and why she was so angry with me.

I also wondered how she was able to get into my mind so much that she was ruining my life.

At 10:45, I glanced at the kitchen clock during one of my many trips down the hall and realized that I'd skipped breakfast. Disgusted with myself, I went in and grabbed the skillet from the cabinet. I opened the fridge, got a loaf of bread, butter and two eggs, put everything on the kitchen counter, and immediately began thinking about my mystery woman again. In that same instant I forgot all about my plans for breakfast, shuffled out of the kitchen and resumed pacing the hall.

At two, my stomach began protesting loudly. I stopped in front of the kitchen doorway and glanced stupidly at the cluttered kitchen counter. It took me a few moments to realize the reason for the mess and another few moments to remember what I'd done. I felt like an idiot. I went back into the kitchen, hurriedly fixed a scrambled egg sandwich, and stood at the counter, eating it. But just as I returned the bread and butter to the fridge, my thoughts wandered again, and before I realized it, I was out in the hall, pacing again.

At two-thirty, when I found myself growing tired and sluggish, I decided to fix a pot of coffee. I got a pot going, went down the hall and sat in the recliner in the living room, staring at the blank TV screen until I felt some of the tension inside me easing up. I closed my eyes and enjoyed the silence and the peace and quiet for a few minutes. Then I had the strange feeling I'd forgotten something again. The tangy smell of freshly brewing coffee drifted into the room, and my eyes snapped open.

I went back to the kitchen, picked up my coffee cup, approached the pot and placed the cup on the counter. All I had to do was grab the spoon and dump a tablespoonful of sugar into the cup. Then I could pour the coffee into the cup. Nothing involved or complicated about that, was there? Any idiot could do it. But as soon as I reached for the spoon, I zoned out again and began wondering if I'd ever eaten with the dark-haired woman. If I'd shared drinks with her, gone on a date with her...

If we'd slept together...

This was getting ridiculous. I'd wasted most of my day zoning out and moving around like a zombie. It had accomplished nothing, and I was getting tired of it.

I could no longer function. I was vegetating, plain and simple. The doctors would probably call it "very little productive brain activity," or something more complicated and much more medical sounding. But whatever they called it would be right on the button. Except for my ability to walk around without help, I was one step away from being comatose again. That in itself was a scary thought. It told me that if I didn't do something about this soon, I was going to need to talk to a psychiatrist.

"Dad?"

The voice sent a tingling shock wave through me. I dropped the spoon on the counter and spun around.

A woman was standing in the kitchen doorway. My eyes wouldn't focus at first. I thought I saw long, flowing black hair but realized right off that the darkness of the hall had added a slight cast to the figure, making her hair darker. I had to squint to get my eyes to focus. I hoped they'd soon start functioning and tell me what was going on.

It only took them a few moments. The blurred figure in the archway gradually cleared and turned into Lexi.

I sighed in relief. It was Lexi out there in the hall; she'd come to see me. This was a good thing. Actually, the concept of Lexi coming here was a *great* thing, and I suddenly found that I felt much better.

But even though I felt greatly relieved that Lexi had come to see me, I still couldn't rid my mind of the dark-haired mystery woman who, for some reason I could not understand, hated me and continued haunting me. The woman I'd been agonizing over. The woman I'd been dreaming about but simply could not remember.

"Dad? What's wrong?"

I couldn't reply. There was nothing I could say to her that would make any sense. Even if I'd wanted to tell her what was going on, I had no

162

idea where to start. How could I possibly tell her any of this? How could I tell Lexi what I couldn't understand myself? How could I tell this lovely young girl something that made no sense?

"Dad? Are you okay?"

I wanted to say something just to let her know that I was still among the living, but when I opened my mouth, my brain blanked out again, and I felt just as useless as I did when I first came out of my coma.

"Dad? Please say something..."

"Lexi, there's something wrong with me." It gushed out of my throat before I realized it. It was a vague, obvious statement, one she no doubt already knew, but as soon as I'd said it, I felt a flush of warm relief filling me. But then I found that I was angry for admitting it to her. Now that it was out in the open, she'd want to know everything. And once I started telling her about it, there would be no turning back.

But before I could say anything else, she said, "I know," and gave me an awkward smile.

Of course she knew. She was a bright, perceptive young lady and could figure me out at a glance. It made me wonder what else she already knew. I tried reading her expression. I could see only worry on her face, and fear in her big blue eyes.

"I guess it shows, doesn't it?"

She stepped into the room carrying her laptop, a textbook and a large black handbag. She set the laptop and textbook on the kitchen table, draped the thick strap of the handbag over the

163

back of the chair and gave me a quick smile. "You're standing there, staring at an empty cup. You're pale, bummed out, and look kinda freaky. It's sort of a total slam-dunk--ya know?"

I couldn't help smiling. After what she'd just said, I felt foolish for not confiding in her earlier. Of course she could tell something was very wrong. But what worried me was how I could explain this unbelievable strangeness to her. How could I tell her what was happening to me without sounding like an idiot? And even if I did manage to sound fairly sane, how would she react? Would she dismiss it? Consider it some side effect from my long recovery? Would she tell me that my coma might have caused brain damage, and that we should see the doctor and have tests done to make sure?

Or would she just think I was reading too much into this and tell me to take it easy and try not to worry about it?

"Well?" She was waiting for a reply. "Am I right or what?"

"You've pretty much nailed it."

"'Kay..." She got a can of lemon-flavored tea from the pantry. She came over to where I stood at the counter, grabbed a glass from the drainer, gave me a quick kiss on the cheek, and went back to the fridge. She opened the freezer door, scooped up some ice, dropped the cubes in her glass and sat down at the table. She poured the tea into the glass and had a slug. "So what's weirding you out?"

There. She'd started the ball rolling and now I had no choice but tell her what it was all about. If I decided not to, or tried changing the issue entirely, she'd really worry, and I didn't want that. But if I decided to tell her, I'd have to tell her everything. I knew I couldn't lie about it. Lexi could tell when something didn't sound right. I could just give her some bullshit and say I was having trouble with my memory again. There would be no shame in that. I'd been in a serious traffic accident, lay in a coma for five days and almost died. No one would expect me to be one hundred percent recovered in seven weeks. I could probably tell her anything and she'd have to accept it.

But I wanted to be honest with Lexi because I wanted her to be honest with me. And she had been. Even though my memory was still cloudy about some things, I did remember that she'd always told me what was on her mind. She'd shared things with me when she was growing up and finding things out about herself and about boys. She'd asked me things she couldn't ask her mother, and I told her what I knew. I'd told her because I knew she could handle it. She was a very bright, sensitive, intuitive young lady, and I was confident she'd be successful at whatever she chose in life. I trusted her, and because of this, I could find no reason why I shouldn't tell her what was happening to me.

"This has something to do with your memory, doesn't it?" She hadn't taken her eyes off me since she'd sat down.

I watched her as she had another sip of iced tea and wondered how she'd figured that out. Once again, it was probably a no-brainer for her. I hadn't gone through anything like this before my accident--it didn't take a genius to decide something unusual was happening with me.

A little nervous, I poured coffee from the pot, added sugar and brought it over to the table. I set it down and sat facing her. She continued watching me, waiting for my explanation. I remembered that she'd always been a good listener, so I knew she wasn't going to do or say anything until I'd told her my story. Normally this would be a good thing because the silence would help me decide how I would begin. But somehow, the silence right now only served to remind me that I had no idea how I'd begin. Or what I'd say.

"You know you can tell me anything, right?" She smiled and reached across the table to touch my hand.

"I know." It made me feel a little better, but it still didn't give me a clue about how I should begin.

"Then just tell me."

I had a sip of coffee and thought about what I'd say to get this issue out in the open. Whatever I said had to be something she could understand-- something that sounded reasonable. That was my big problem with all this. It was so fantastic, so weird. I didn't understand any of it and didn't think anyone else would, either.

So how could Lexi be any different?

"You didn't *kill* anyone, did you?" She was smiling.

I smiled back at her. Once again, this beautiful, insightful young lady had instantly brightened my mood, reminding me once again why I loved her so much.

"No, I didn't kill anyone, Lexi."

"Then tell me. I promise I won't laugh."

I sighed. "I wish it *would* make you laugh. I wish it would make *me* laugh, too."

Her smile vanished, and I hated myself for doing that. I wanted to go back in time just a few minutes and undo what I'd just done but knew I couldn't. If I *could* go back, I'd change a lot of other things as well.

"What *is* it, Dad?"

"Lexi, something really strange happened when I was in my coma, but I have no idea what it was, or what I can possibly do about it."

"All righty..." She sat forward and placed her elbows on the table. "Then tell me what you *think* happened."

"All I know is that I've been plagued with weird dreams since I came out of it."

She shrugged. "But that's normal, Dad. The doctors said--"

"This has nothing to do with what the doctors said."

"Then what *does* it have to do with?"

"Like I said, I'm having weird dreams. They're all the same, and they seem to center around something that happened to me in some strange place I don't ever remember visiting before."

"What sort of strange place?"

"It happened in a meadow somewhere near a pine forest."

"And you don't think this is just some dream you made up when you were in your coma?"

"I did at first…"

"What about now?"

"Like I keep saying, I have no idea."

"What makes you think this isn't just post-coma stuff?"

"There are others involved. People I've never seen before."

"Others?"

"There's a woman named Alison."

"She's in your dream, too?"

"Yes."

"And you're sure her name's Alison?"

"Yes…"

Lexi frowned; she seemed to be trying to remember something. I honestly hoped she'd come up with something that might help me. She had a sip of her drink and set the glass down. "Isn't that the name of your secretary?"

My hope deflated. "You're thinking of Alice Sommers."

"You're right. Sorry. So what were you and this Alison woman doing?" She watched me for a moment and then smiled. Her cheeks reddened. "This wasn't…one of *those* dreams, was it?"

"I wish it was. Then I wouldn't be so worried about taking it so seriously."

"Then…what *were* you two doing?"

"I think we were looking for a way out."

"Out of what?"

"The meadow. The woods."

"Let me get this straight. You were both there and didn't know how you got there?"

"Exactly."

"You were trapped? Like in one of those old *Twilight Zone* episodes? I'm thinking of that one where some people were trapped in that dark, circular room, looking for a way out, and found out they were all in hell. Is this anything like that?"

"That's a pretty good analogy, actually."

"And you'd never seen this Alison person anywhere before?"

"Not that I can remember."

"And you're sure you saw all this when you were in your coma?"

"Yes. No. I don't know *what* I saw when I was in my coma. I only know that I've been reliving this same dream, over and over, ever since my memory started coming back."

Lexi had more iced tea and watched me closely.

"Something coming to you?"

She put down her glass. "I'm trying to remember if this sounds like one of those sci-fi flicks we've watched together--"

"This isn't a *flick*, Lexi!" I regretted my flare of anger the moment it slammed through me. Lexi was trying to help me. She was my best friend-- perhaps the only person in the world who could

169

guide me through this. The worst thing I could do was upset her or push her away. I didn't want to be alone right now and I certainly didn't want to figure this out by myself. "I'm sorry, baby." I patted her hand. "I'm just on edge."

"I can tell. You're wearing your mad face."

I sat back and sighed. "The whole thing...it just makes no sense. None whatsoever. And it's really doing a number on me. I can't think of anything else, and when I try to, my mind automatically goes right back to it. Just yesterday I was thinking about it in the living room. I was wide awake, and then I closed my eyes for a few seconds and realized I'd been sleeping, but when I began thinking about it, I wasn't sure if I'd been awake or asleep."

"It really *is* getting to you, isn't it?"

"Big-time." I didn't want to tell her that I thought I'd actually transported myself out of the living room when she and Claire had come over to fix lunch.

"It sounds like you've been doing some heavy-duty drugs."

"I wish it was that simple. With drugs, you expect reality to become distorted and make no sense. This thing--whatever it is--comes and goes when I least expect it."

"Your pain medication...are you still--"

"I haven't taken any in a couple of days."

"Why not?"

"My back's been feeling pretty good lately."

"That's good."

"It's the only good thing happening to me right now, actually."

"But you do know you're supposed to be going to the chiropractor, right?"

"As you can see, I've got other things on my mind."

"But it's your back, Dad…"

"I promise I'll start going once I figure out what's happening to me." I wasn't in the mood to get into an argument about something as stupid as a weekly visit to a back doctor--not when more urgent things were going on.

"I'll hold you to that, ya know."

"I know you will."

"So let's get back to this dream… That's all there is to it? You and this strange Alison woman walking through the woods, looking for a way out?"

"That's how it was at first. Yesterday more details came out--things much too real to be mere figments of my imagination. Alison's ex-husband turned up in the dream. Alison has a young daughter named Kendra, who's eight, and her ex lives in Orlando."

"Were these other guys in the dream, too?"

"Just her ex-husband. Kendra wasn't."

"How do you know about the daughter?"

"Alison told me about her."

"And this other dude--her ex… He was in the dream, too?"

"Briefly. We found him lying under a tree."

"Why was he lying under a tree?"

171

"At first we thought he was dead, but a little while later, he started talking and sat up."

"What did he say?"

I thought about it for a moment. It was hazy at first, but as soon as I focused on it, the details rushed back. "He said something about picking Alison up at the airport. Apparently she flew to Orlando for a convention. He said he picked her up and was going to take her to breakfast before dropping her off at her hotel at Disney Village."

"I guess they're still civil to one another because of their daughter."

"Actually, I felt a lot of tension between them."

Lexi had another sip of tea. "This sounds much more detailed than your average dream, Dad."

"I know."

"In fact, it sounds like it actually happened."

"That's what's bothering me. It *feels* like a dream but isn't. And when I try analyzing it, it fades away."

"So what happened with her ex? What else did he say?"

"He talked a few minutes about picking her up. Then he looked around, and when he realized he didn't recognize anything, he wondered how we'd got there. We told him we were going to explore the woods and see if we could find something. Alison and I began walking away, but he stayed where he was."

"Then what?"

I shrugged. "He vanished."

172

Lexi blinked. "You mean--"

"Just like that." I clicked my fingers. "He was there one moment. Then he was gone."

She frowned. "Now it's beginning to sound like a dream."

"That's why I'm so damned bummed out about the whole thing. Just when I try convincing myself it's a dream, I remember something else about it, and this tells me it might have actually happened."

"Tell me more about this dude. Her ex. What's his name?"

I picked up my coffee cup. "You think his name might clear something up?"

"I think anything you tell me will help. The more details you remember, the faster we might figure it all out. So what's his name?"

For a moment I'd forgotten. "Let's see... A moment ago, I knew what it was, but now it's a little fuzzy. I think it's--"

"Larry," the disembodied voice a couple of feet on my left said. "Larry Grant."

Gasping, I jerked my coffee cup and sent its hot contents splashing the side of the sink cabinet and halfway across the tile floor.

PART TWO

THE JOURNEY BACK

CHAPTER SIXTEEN

While Lexi cleaned up my mess with paper towels, I sat at the kitchen table, gawking at the space where I'd heard the voice.

I heard nothing else, but that didn't matter. The damage had been done. The mysterious woman named Alison had spoken to me again, her voice coming out of thin air, like the whisper of someone hiding in the shadows.

But this was my kitchen. The lights were on; there were no shadows for someone to hide in. And what I'd heard wasn't a whisper--it was a clear voice.

Someone nudged me. I nearly jumped out of my chair. It was Lexi. "You okay?" she whispered.

It was only then that I realized she'd finished cleaning up.

"Yeah. I guess."

"What happened?"

"I...heard a voice." There was no use keeping this from her any longer.

"I figured you heard *some*thing. Still hear it?"

"No, and if you don't mind, I need to lie down."

"I *so* totally don't mind."

I tried standing, but my legs were unsteady. Lexi quickly stepped in to help me up. I felt silly at first. Lexi barely tipped the scales at a hundred pounds to my one-eighty, but was obviously strong enough to support my weight. She put her arm around my waist, guided me down the hall and led me into the living room. When we were just a couple of feet from the sofa, she turned me around and I collapsed onto the soft cushions.

I stayed there, staring up at the white popcorn ceiling, and thought about the voice. All I knew was that it was the same voice I'd heard the day before and that it had come back to haunt me once again, this time with Lexi right there in the same room.

Lexi knelt on the floor beside the sofa and held my hand. She looked terrified. I couldn't blame her. I was a little terrified myself, and wanted to close my eyes and make the last few minutes disappear.

There was no way I could fix this. The voice had come back and I had to deal with it. But now I knew that it had come back while I was fully awake--not like before, when I wasn't sure if I was awake or asleep.

But somehow that didn't give me much consolation. It made me realize I could be hallucinating. And if I was, I needed therapy.

"Talk to me, Dad."

"I'm okay, baby."

"No you're not."

"I'm all right. I just need a little rest..."

"You're *not* all right." Lexi let go of my hand. She looked angry; there were tears in her eyes. "Anyone could tell by what you just did with your coffee cup that you're not all right."

"I told you I was having weird dreams, didn't I?"

"Dad…" When she spoke again, her voice was softer, gentler. "I don't know exactly what happened in there, so why don't you just tell me so we can do something about it?"

"Lexi…"

"Who was in the kitchen with us?"

I found that I couldn't speak. I could only stare at her and wonder what she'd heard. It occurred to me that if she'd also heard the voice, I might not be going crazy after all.

"Lexi…what did *you* hear in there?"

"Nothing."

"Then why did you just ask me--"

"You heard something. You told me you did."

Now I began wondering if I'd actually heard it in the first place. I hadn't heard it since. It could have been my imagination stepping in again, for all I knew. And something told me that I might be making entirely too much out of it than I should.

"I thought I did. Maybe it was my imagination--I don't know."

"Don't do this, Dad. You totally heard something in there."

"How can you be so sure?"

"You jerked your head around like anyone else would when someone sneaks up on you. Tell me that didn't happen."

I just sighed.

"Was it that woman? That Alison lady?"

My pulse raced. Once again, she'd nailed it perfectly.

"It was, wasn't it?"

I nodded.

"You actually heard her in there? You heard her speak to you?"

Again I nodded.

"What did she say?"

"She told me her ex-husband's name."

"You're not serious."

"She said, "Larry Grant.""

"And that's all?"

"That was more than enough, wasn't it?"

"And where was she? Could you see her?"

"I only heard her voice. I heard it about three feet on my left, in front of the sink."

"Wow." Lexi's eyes grew. I expected her to tell me that she wanted to take me back to the hospital, or at least call my doctor. She just sat there, shaking her head.

"Now do you see why I've been so bummed out lately?"

She didn't reply, just kept shaking her head.

"Lexi? Do me a favor?"

"What's that?"

"*Please* stop shaking your head like that."

"How would you *like* me to shake my head?"

"Just stop doing it and tell me what you're thinking."

"I'm thinking that this Alison lady was in the kitchen, listening to us, only we couldn't see her. And when you couldn't remember her ex-husband's name, she stepped in and helped you out...but you were the only one who could hear her."

"That's basically what happened."

She sat back and watched me. I could tell she was deciding if her explanation was something she really wanted to believe.

"You're not thinking of taking me to the local mental ward, are you?"

"No, but you do need help."

"I know, but I have no idea where to go or who to ask about it."

"I know you don't like doctors."

"I don't trust them and have absolutely no confidence in them."

"Psychiatrists, too?"

"They're doctors, aren't they?"

Lexi sat in silence and stared at me.

"You're obviously thinking of something."

"Yeppers. I could be."

"Does this have to do with taking me back to the hospital anyway?"

"Dad, I'd never take you somewhere if I knew you really didn't want to go there."

"I honestly don't think they could help me with this."

"I don't think so, either."

"Then what *are* you thinking?"

178

Lexi got up. "I might actually have something else that could work."

"You mean something other than a hospital?"

"Maybe..."

Her vagueness was beginning to make me nervous. "Lexi, this thing is weird. I can't imagine anyone who can help me with this."

"We've got to do something, don't we? This wasn't the first time you heard her, was it?"

"No. It wasn't."

"Then we've got to face the fact that you'll probably be hearing from her again."

I didn't even want to think about that. "You're right. I probably will."

She looked down at me grimly but said nothing for several moments. I suddenly feared she actually had some idea how to handle this. A moment later, she nodded and said, "I've got to make a call. I'll be back in a minute."

Her dark expression made me extremely nervous. "Lexi, I wish you'd tell me what you've got on your mind."

She'd already turned and dashed out of the room.

***

"Why won't you tell me where you're taking me?"

Lexi didn't reply as she drove. She hadn't said much during the half-hour trip. She'd hardly said anything since she came back into the living room just a few minutes after she'd left to make her mysterious phone call.

I'd quickly grown apprehensive about the trip. Just a few minutes after we got in her car, she pulled onto Semoran and headed north. A few miles later, we crossed 17-92, where Semoran led to Altamonte Drive. I suspected we were heading into Longwood, but since she hadn't given me the slightest hint where we were going, I had no idea what she had on her mind.

"You won't even tell me who you called, will you?"

She just smiled.

"This is kind of unsettling, you know."

"Just sit back and enjoy the ride."

"How can I enjoy the ride when I have no idea where you're taking me?"

"You'll find out soon enough."

"Don't be cute, now."

She laughed. "I thought you liked it when I'm cute."

"Don't change the subject. You've been extremely quiet since you made your mysterious call. A guy gets nervous when a girl gets extremely quiet and starts thinking about something. It makes him wonder what she's up to."

"Even when he knows she's trying to help him?"

"How can I possibly know that? You haven't told me anything."

"Have I ever done anything bad to you?"

I didn't like it one bit that a seventeen-year-old was making mincemeat of me. I was the grownup here; I even had a college degree and more than twenty years of life experiences over her. "That isn't the point and you know it."

"What *is* the point?"

"The point is this: a guy tends to get pretty nervous when a girl tosses him in a car and doesn't tell him anything else. Guys don't like being taken for a ride."

"Even by young girls like me?"

"*Especially* by young girls like you."

"Thanks, Dad. I'll remember that when I'm a year or two older and have hordes of guys after me."

I didn't want to think about that. But then I discovered that she'd just made me forget my present problems. And when I realized what she'd just done in the blink of an eye, I knew I shouldn't have to worry about her. Lexi would have no trouble handling herself in the real world.

"Well, whatever you do, don't bring them to see me without first warning them. I don't want to be responsible for scaring a kid to death."

She winked. "No need to worry about that. I'll tell them every single thing I know about you."

Her wink made me feel even more uneasy. "For some reason, that doesn't make me feel any better."

"You're not gonna be totally possessive about every guy I ever date, are ya?"

"I haven't up until now, have I?"

"I've only been on a couple of dates, Dad. Don't tell me you've forgotten that."

"Even if I did forget, it doesn't take a rocket scientist to see that you don't exactly have a legion of guys following you around."

"Well, to refresh your memory, I told you and Mom that I didn't want to get serious with anyone until after I graduated from college."

"That explains the lack of an entourage, I guess. But thanks for the refresh. The old brain ain't exactly firing on all cylinders. Not yet, anyway."

"You'll remember, eventually. I told you and Mom that right after I turned sixteen, when you began teaching me to drive. I know half a dozen girls who've already been pregnant, and I don't want that happening to me. It'll mess up my plans."

"How'd you get so damned mature for such a young age?"

She laughed. "It's in the genes, Dad."

"Yeah, I guess your mom had a hand in that."

"My dad, too."

"I wouldn't give him too much credit for--"

"*You're* my dad," she said. "You always were, and you always will be."

I could tell she meant it, and for a moment didn't know what to say or how to react. It took me totally by surprise, and I had to struggle to remember what we'd been talking about before that.

"Nothing to say?" Lexi was smiling.

"Nothing that could top that."

She reached over and patted my hand. "Once I do start dating, you're probably gonna act just like everyone else's parents. You'll wanna lock me in my room until I'm forty."

"Now you're saying I'm just like everyone else?"

"No. You're really not."

"Then where's this fiercely protective obsession idea coming from?"

She laughed. "That scary vertical crack between your brows is bigger than ever. Your happy face is gone, and there's that vein in your neck that's *so* totally out there, it's really creepy..."

"All right, all right. You've made your point. You can't blame me, can you?"

"You do trust me, right?"

"I sure do."

"Then what's the problem?"

"I just don't trust *guys*--especially if they're anything like I was."

She laughed. "Don't sell yourself short. You're pretty amazing, actually."

"Thanks, and by the way, I've noticed that you've managed to avoid the subject for the last ten minutes. I admire that."

"Good. My work is done."

"So...where the hell are you taking this amazing but obsessive and obviously mentally unstable guy?"

"You'll see in just a few minutes."

We crossed the road leading to the dog track. She made a right on Ronald Reagan Boulevard and pulled into the winding drive leading to the long, one-story brick building that was Lyman High School.

"You're bringing me to your school?"

She laughed. "I'm *so* glad you finally figured it out…"

"The sign gave it away. You're not gonna make me sit through one of your boring math classes, are you?"

"Dad, how would one of my boring math classes help you?"

"Good point."

We coasted down the two-lane road that led to the main lot, where several vehicles were parked. Lexi turned left, and we went down the bus lane that spanned the front of the building. At the far end, she parked at the curb behind a black utility van, a tan Honda Accord and a red pickup. Then she switched off the engine, turned to me and gave me one of her bright, reassuring smiles.

"Now what?" I felt even more uneasy than when we'd left the condo.

She pulled the keys out of the ignition and grabbed her bag. "We go inside."

I sighed and opened my door. "I guess I should've known we weren't going to just sit here and wait for something to happen."

184

CHAPTER SEVENTEEN

It was past dinnertime, but the halls were far from deserted.

Small groups of sloppy-dressed students sat cross-legged on the tile floor, their backs pressed against the long string of lockers behind them. Two girls around Lexi's age pored over their tablets while several other students engaged in garbled conversation. Three of the girls and two of the guys glanced blankly at us as we went past.

"Hey, Lexter," one of the guys said.

"'Sup, girl," another said.

"Guys," Lexi said without slowing her stride.

"Lexter?" I whispered.

She shrugged. "I've got a ton of nicknames."

I vaguely remembered the old days, when I went weeks without hearing my first or last name uttered without clever embellishments or derogatory labels, or rhymes. I didn't know why I expected things to be different for Lexi's generation. "I guess I should have expected that."

She smiled and gripped my arm. We turned right at the intersection and went down another long, dimly lit corridor, where a dozen or more students had congregated. Two sat facing one another in a small alcove in front of the *SCIENCE* door, making out. I couldn't be certain, but I assumed they were of both sexes,. Both had short hair--which didn't mean much these days. Two others glanced at us as we passed. A tall, athletic-looking guy with a dark buzz cut said, "'Sup,

185

Sexy Lexi." He didn't acknowledge me at all as we went by.

Despite my concern for being here, I found myself jealous and slightly offended, and wanted to tell him to put his eyes back into his skull. Lexi looked up at me and smiled.

"Am I that obvious?" I asked.

She patted my arm. "You look like that Terminator guy about to kick a heavy batch of serious butt."

"I didn't like his name for you."

"Like I said, I've got several…"

"Sexy Lexi?"

She moved her face closer to my chest. "Dad, you really need to chill."

"I don't think I can do that right now."

"It's nothing. Brad's a flirt."

"Brad? It just figures."

"Huh?"

"He even looks like a damned Brad. What's his last name? Manly? Granite?"

She laughed. "*Please* amp it down a little, 'kay?"

"If you insist…"

"You don't wanna embarrass me, do ya? I've still got a few more weeks of school left."

"I'll just concentrate on my own problems, then."

"Don't worry. We're gonna see what we can do about 'em."

We turned left at the next corner and passed several more doors and classrooms, until we reached another dimly lit hall. A door stenciled

LIBRARY awaited us about halfway down. When we were about five feet from it, Lexi stopped walking. I stopped with her. As she reached for the door handle, I stared at the door and tried hard to let my logic take over.

A library. At least, that's what the sign said. Why had she brought me here? Research? About what? Dreams? Hallucinations? Could research really help me in this case? And why was it necessary for us to come here in the first place? Nowadays, anyone could do research with their laptop in the privacy of their own home. That's what Google was for, wasn't it? Or any other of the countless search engines that had been cropping up on the Internet during the last few years...

She grabbed the handle and began to pull. Suddenly tense, I whispered, "You have one last chance."

She stopped moving. "For what?"

"To tell me what you're up to."

"Dad, trust me, okay?"

The brightness in her big blue eyes instantly dissolved my fears. I knew Lexi wouldn't do anything that would hurt me or put me in danger. If she sincerely thought this visit was going to help me, I saw no reason to doubt her.

"I trust you."

"That wasn't so hard, was it?"

"A little."

She smiled and pulled open the door.

A man around forty years old sat behind a desk in a corner of the room, reading a magazine beneath a small table lamp. He wore a white shirt and tie. His dark-brown jacket was draped rather neatly over the back of another chair. He had a black buzz cut and didn't look our way when we came in.

Once again I wanted to ask Lexi what was going on but decided to wait. I'd just told her that I trusted her. In fact, I trusted her more than anyone else I knew. If she thought this was a good idea, it probably was.

I hadn't been in a high school library in years. I don't know what I'd expected, but I was glad old-fashioned hard-bound and paperback books were still in existence. Most of the tables were equipped with computers and monitors, but anyone could tell it was a library.

We went down the long, carpeted aisle, to the other end of the room. Endless rows of books on shelves extended from the center of the area, falling short of both ends of the room by just a few feet. Several students browsed the books while others sat at tables, studying, or working their laptops or tablets.

Once we reached the end of the aisle, four doors faced us at the far wall. One door was marked *SUPPLIES*, while the two next to it were unmarked. The fourth displayed the sign *LIBRARIAN* in its center. Lexi approached this one and knocked softly on the door.

"Lexi?" Despite my confidence and trust, I began growing uneasy again. I found that I was a little frightened when I imagined who was going

188

to open that door. I hardly thought a librarian could find a solution to my problem.

"Don't worry, Dad," she whispered. "This'll be okay."

"All right, but just so you know, I'm a little nervous about this…"

She smiled, and I could tell she was about to tease me again. "Really?"

"Yes."

The door eased open.

A small, slight woman appeared in the dark doorway. She was about five feet tall, very slender, and looked to be between fifty and sixty. She had curly gray hair, a small, fine-featured face, and large, deep-set steel-gray eyes. She had a long, pointed nose and did not smile. She wore no makeup. Her mouth was a severe line, which gave her a permanent scowl. I wondered if she ever smiled at all. She wore faded jeans, a light-blue sweatshirt and black tennis shoes. She took us both in--first Lexi, then me. Her cold, intense eyes settled on me and stayed there for so long, I began getting even more uncomfortable. Finally, she broke the connection and turned to Lexi.

Lexi smiled. "I'm glad I caught you before you left for the day."

Her steel gaze returned to me. "I am usually here until late. I had a feeling you were going to call." She spoke softly, her voice low-pitched and gravelly.

Lexi smiled at me. "Dad, this is Melina."

I nodded but didn't extend my hand. This woman didn't look like the type who did much handshaking. If she did, I expected her grip to be cold and brittle, like a block of ice. Besides, her hands were busy holding a hardcover edition of Raymond Bayless's *The Other Side of Death*. I had no knowledge of the book, but the title alone made me a little nauseous.

Lexi turned back to Melina. "This is my--"

"He is the man you've told me about."

"He's my dad. His name--"

"Your name is Jack." She took two steps toward me. A strong coffee odor emanated from her. Her eyes focused on mine. Although she was a foot shorter than me and much narrower than I was, I felt overwhelmed by her presence.

"Dad? You okay?"

I continued staring at the woman. "I'm fine, Lexi." I couldn't let her intimidate me. I took a breath and straightened. It seemed to help a little that I'd made her a couple of inches shorter. "Apparently Lexi told you about me, am I correct?"

"Alexandria told me only that you have a problem I might be able to help you with." She didn't seem bothered at all by my slight increase in stature.

"Listen...Ma'am..."

"I am known as Melina."

"I don't know what you think this is all about, but I'm not so sure Lexi should have brought me here."

"Dad..."

I patted Lexi on the shoulder and gave her a quick smile. "I've got this, Lexi." I turned back to

190

Melina. "It's true, I'm having problems, but I don't think you'll be able to--"

"You have a very large problem. I can see it in your aura. I can see it in your face, your eyes."

Aura. Disappointment raged through me. This was just great. Lexi had brought me to one of those charlatans who should be in a carnival, rather than a high school library. I'd never taken much stock in con artists of any sort. Why Lexi had wasted her time bringing me here was something I'd have to ask her on the trip back home. She did ask me if I trusted her, and I did. But what could this woman do? How could she possibly help me? Other than her intense gaze, her intoxicating presence and her rather morbid reading material, I didn't see the point.

I had a feeling this trip was a huge waste of our time.

But I didn't want to hurt Lexi's feelings. If I turned around and left, Lexi would be hurt, embarrassed, and angry. She might not want to speak to me, and I couldn't blame her. I'd be alienating my only friend and ally. I'd be forced to go back home and face the same problems that had been driving me crazy the last few days. But this time, I'd be facing them all by myself.

No, turning my back on this wasn't the answer. At this stage of the game, I had no desire to spend the rest of my life being haunted by strange voices and strange dreams. I had to be willing to look into everything, even if it meant spending fifteen minutes with this part-time fortune-teller.

However, I saw no reason to make this easy for her.

"All right, so you can see my aura. I guess some people believe in what you do, but unless you're a doctor..."

"You are skeptical."

"I guess you saw that in my aura, too?"

She ignored my sarcasm. "I see it in your eyes. You are disappointed in Alexandria's choice. You think coming here to see me is a waste of time, and you consider me nothing more than a part-time fortune-teller. I find it strange that someone who hears voices and has strange dreams would so quickly dismiss someone who might actually be able to help him."

My God. This woman had just read my mind. That freaked me out, and I found myself fighting the urge once again to turn around and leave, but this time for a much different reason. I glanced at Lexi and could tell that she was freaked out as well. Her grip on my arm had tightened, and she pressed herself more snugly against me.

But I refused to admit that this changed anything. These people were experts at reading expressions, body language, even smells--and their unusual skills helped give them an idea of their victim's state of mind.

"That was impressive," I said.

Her expression did not change. "I did not say that to impress you. I said it because that is what you are thinking."

"You can...read minds?"

"I sometimes possess such abilities."

192

I wanted to ask her why she was working as a high school librarian when she had such incredible abilities that could be used elsewhere.

She was watching me closely. I could feel her evaluating me again. "People in this country choose to regard my abilities as something that belongs in a carnival, or some other freak show act they regard as entertainment. They are ignorant and stupid because they cannot understand how such abilities can help them in life. This is why they do not hold such gifts in high regard and prefer instead to ignore them entirely. It is of no importance to me. I happen to love books and am quite content spending my life among them, rather than wasting my existence looking at cartoons or reality shows or watching people acting like imbeciles on the computer."

My God. She did it *again*.

"Listen, Miss...Melina...you obviously have many talents, and many of them--at least the ones I've just seen--are extremely rare and quite impressive...but I still don't think you have any idea what I'm--"

"You are wrong, Jack Clarkson. I know exactly what your problem is. I might even go so far as to tell you that I probably can help you overcome it."

How the hell did she know my name? As far as I knew, Lexi was still using Taylor--which was Claire's maiden name as well as the last name of her biological father. And if Lexi didn't tell her what was wrong, how did this woman know about my problem?

I struggled to keep my composure. "All right, then. What is my problem?"

Her gaze still did not falter. "You are a man who has recently been to hell. You've obviously brought back some of it with you and have no idea how to get rid of it."

***

The room was small and dimly-lit.

The opposite wall, a solid bookcase, ran from the floor to the ceiling. A five-foot-tall metal filing cabinet stood against the wall next to the door. An ancient desk, two chairs, and a long table covered with more books sat in the center of the room.

Melina gestured for Lexi and me to sit. She then slipped behind the massive desk and lowered herself slowly into the high-backed black leather chair. A green blotter covered the desk surface. There was also a telephone and a stack of hardbound books, among them, *Glimpses of the Beyond*, *Excursions of the Spirit World*, *Between the Gates*, *Incarnation*, *Love in the Afterlife*, *777*, and a few others. Two other smaller stacks of books sat off to the side. I saw several printed names, among them, Edgar Cayce, Dr. John C. Daniels, Martin Ebon, and Arthur Ford. On the second stack, I noted *The Power of Your Subconscious Mind*, by Joseph Murphy; *Hypnotic Techniques*, by David Calof; and four other books about hypnotism. She placed *The Other Side of Death* very gently on the blotter in front of her and sat watching me, her hands resting on the cover of the book.

I felt extremely uneasy. This woman was small and slight, but as intimidating as anyone I'd ever met. Her eyes were cold and hypnotic, pulling you into them. She'd already been inside my head and read my innermost thoughts. I strongly suspected that, due to her obvious interests in the occult and hypnotism, she possessed even more frightening abilities.

She'd mentioned my trip to hell. Although I hadn't associated the beautiful meadow and the pine forest with an excursion into the Dark World, what had been happening to me since could be considered a reasonable assessment.

But how could she possibly help me? She was obviously quite capable of reading my thoughts, but did that mean she could fix my problem? What could she do to rid me of those dreams? Could she do anything to prevent me from hearing the dark-haired woman's voice again? How about the constant guilt I felt whenever I thought of the woman? The nagging fear consuming me, suggesting that I'd somehow hurt her in some way?

The fact remained: Lexi had brought me here for a reason. Now I had to struggle through this and put my faith in this strange, frighteningly perceptive woman who could do things I'd never experienced before.

"If you want me to help you," she said, "you must tell me everything."

"I shouldn't have to. You actually saw what happened for yourself."

"I didn't see it as much as I sensed it."

"What did you sense?"

"Your turmoil. Your darkness. And, of course, your fear."

"What else?"

"A meadow. A pine forest. Most of all, I sensed the strong presence of a woman. A young woman with dark hair and large dark eyes."

My God. She went in there again. I gripped the padded arms of my chair.

Her gaze didn't waver. "Your eyes tell me I am correct. About everything."

It took me a few moments to find my voice. When it finally came out of my throat, it was a mere whisper. "Maybe you are."

"I know I am."

"What did you mean about my bringing some of it back with me?"

"I think you know exactly what I meant."

I turned to Lexi. "Did you tell her that I was in a--"

"Alexandria told me nothing about you," Melina said. "I know about your accident. I know about your coma. And I know why you are here. So tell me the rest."

"The rest?"

"Tell me what you would like me to do about this problem that has been troubling you so much."

"You already seem to know, so I can't imagine what you expect me to add..."

"As I just said, I know about your accident, your coma, and your dreams. I know about the

196

meadow, the pine forest, and the woman. What I need to know is what you would like to change."

She'd just mentioned my dreams. My God-- was there anything this woman could not see in my head?

"You are easy to read," she said flatly. "You are very vulnerable right now, very troubled. Your thoughts are in the forefront of your mind. And since you are desperate enough to seek help, you are not attempting to hide anything."

"You mean there are some whose thoughts you can't read?"

"There are fools and skeptics everywhere. There are others whose thoughts are too muddled to read. And, of course, there are those whose thoughts are not much more complicated than those of a beetle, or fruit fly. I won't waste a moment of my time with them, for obvious reasons."

"I'm still skeptical about...about this."

"Even after all I have told you about yourself?"

"If I truly believed what you've just done, I'd have to think you were some sort of supernatural being."

She didn't reply for several moments. "I am not supernatural. I am merely a mortal being who has been aware of the gifts I have been given and the knowledge of how to use them. Where I come from, such gifts are not so rare."

"Where are you from?" I couldn't tell by her accent. She spoke perfect English, with just a trace of something that might have been Russian or Croatian. Since I was no expert, I couldn't tell. I suspected she'd learned English as a second language and used it exclusively once she came to this country.

"I was born and raised in a place where people live much simpler lives--where the Divine One is not so far away or so unattainable. A place where television sets, laptops and cell phones are not essential for the growth and development of the mind and the human spirit, where society is not obsessed with athletic events or the gluttonous, self-indulgent lifestyles of celebrities and politicians." She paused for a moment. "So tell me why Alexandria has deemed it necessary to bring you here for my help. Tell me why these dreams are concerning you so much."

"I'm also hearing voices."

"They are voices from your dreams."

Her expression told me her last statement hadn't been a question. "How did you know?"

"I just know. What I don't know is how you wish me to remove them."

"You can *remove* dreams?"

"I cannot remove anything from your mind or your spirit without changing or damaging your psyche. The soul is a heavenly gift and must never be tampered with. Tampering with it in any way would be against the Divine One's plan."

"Then what *can* you do?"

"I can attempt to make your dreams harmless. Once this has been done, you will no longer be plagued by them, and this will help you on your journey toward complete recovery."

"How can you make them harmless?"

Melina remained silent for a few moments while staring at the book on the blotter in front of her. She slowly raised her eyes and said, "It is very simple. I guide you through them."

I didn't like where this might be going. "How can you possibly do that?"

"I must take you back to them."

"Take me back? How can I possibly go back? I was in a coma."

"I can guide you."

"How? Through hypnosis?"

"Something like that. Once we return, the healing will begin. With my help and guidance, understanding will help you through the process, and you will recover and no longer fear the dreams or hear the voices."

Once I fully understood what she'd just said, I had the feeling that this woman was about to make me go through something horrible. "You just said return, didn't you?"

She nodded.

"What exactly did you mean by that?"

"You must go back."

"You mean back to the dreams?"

She didn't reply.

"If you want to hypnotize me and make me dream about all that again, I can probably do that, but I just don't know what it'll accomplish..."

"It will accomplish nothing."

"Then what exactly are you talking about?"

"You must go back to that place and experience it all over again."

CHAPTER EIGHTEEN

You must go back.

The words sliced into me like razor wire. If I'd just been told I had cancer and had only weeks to live, I wouldn't have been more frozen with terror than I was right now.

Was this woman crazy? There was no way I could sit here and listen to her anymore. I had to get away from her. I had to get out of this room. I could no longer breathe in here. I was suffocating. Without a word I got up stiffly and turned for the door.

"Dad?"

I said nothing as I passed Lexi's chair. The door was just a few feet away. Beyond it, freedom awaited me. And air--cool, fresh air. But what was even more important was that this steel-eyed, evil bitch wasn't out there, and once I closed the door behind me, I'd never have to look at her or listen to her nonsense ever again...

"Dad, *please...*"

The panic in her voice immediately dissolved the anger and the shock eating at me. I stopped cold just as I reached for the door handle. Damn. With just two words, Lexi had turned my utter terror into guilt and humiliation. I turned and looked down at her. She sat stiffly in her chair, looking frightened and hurt, her eyes gleaming with tears. I felt like I'd just kicked a puppy.

I had to stop this. I hadn't kicked a puppy. I just didn't want to go through this again. Lexi had to understand. I knew she was trying to help, but she had to realize that I couldn't go back to that place. Judging by what it had been doing to me already, going back there would destroy me. I went back to her chair and placed my hand on her shoulder. "Lexi…"

"Please, Dad… At least hear her out."

"Lexi, I feel like I'm suffocating. I have to get out of here."

"Dad, the dreams…that voice… If you'd seen yourself in the kitchen just a couple of hours ago…"

"I can't, baby. I can't go through that again."

Melina looked me right in the eye. "If you do not, you will never be free again."

The mere thought of going back sent a barrage of ice sliding down my back. More than anything, the horror of what happened--of where I might have actually gone--made my flesh crawl. I feared that if I returned, I wouldn't be able to come back.

I focused on Melina and forced myself to keep my voice as calm as possible. "Do you have any idea what I've been through?"

"Yes."

"Then you must know what these dreams have done to me."

"I know that as well."

"And you still want me to go back?"

"It is the only way you can purge yourself of your problem."

"Dad…" Lexi grabbed my arm. "You're hearing voices, and they're driving you crazy.

You're not the same anymore. You're scaring me, and this is destroying you. You have to *do* something about it."

"I know, baby… But if you knew what I've been through…"

"Dad, you don't remember what you've been through. All you remember are bits and pieces of what you thought was a dream."

She was right. Even so, what I'd experienced was more than enough

to keep me from repeating this. "Maybe, but judging by what it's been doing to me, I know that it must have been awful. Melina herself said I've been to hell."

"She only saw what it's doing to you. She didn't really see the place itself. From what you've told me, it was beautiful. There was a meadow, and a pine forest--"

"It's not the actual place that's scaring me…"

"You don't really *know* what's scaring you, Dad…"

"You cannot know for sure unless you return," Melina said.

I rubbed my eyes. "I just don't think I can go through it again."

Lexi gripped my arm even harder. "Dad, whaddya think it was like

when I came to see you in the hospital? I came every single day. I sat by your bed as long as they'd let me, holding your hand, talking to you, hoping that one day you'd hear me and would come out of it." More tears gathered in her eyes.

I despised myself for what I was doing to this wonderful young girl. I'd had no idea what it had done to her; I'd been thinking only of myself. I'd been selfish and stupid. If I'd had any idea what she'd been going through, I would never have acted this way.

I squeezed her hand. "Lexi, I had no idea..."

"I didn't mind, Dad. I wanted to because I thought it would help. And it did, didn't it? It brought you back, and I was so glad, I prayed for the first time since I was a little kid. I don't know if my prayers did it, but something obviously helped. You'd not only survived your coma, but you also came back. But then I realized that you'd changed, and you needed my help even more than before, when you were in the hospital. You're still broken, and I have to watch it all over again. I want to help fix you. Melina can help. I know she can."

A tear had drifted down her cheek. I gently wiped it away and turned to the tiny, cold-faced woman behind the desk. "Do you really think you can help me?"

"Yes. But only if you wish it so."

With a deep sigh, I returned to my seat. Lexi clasped my hand, and when I looked at her again, she was smiling. I smiled back. Then I turned to face Melina. "I'm in your hands."

Melina stared at me for a long time. I had a feeling she'd gone in there again, checking the layers of my brain to see if I'd just told her the truth. "This is good. But you are right. It will not

203

be easy. However, it is the only way I can help free you."

"Just do it before I change my mind."

"Look into my eyes." She sat forward and put her slender elbows on the desk blotter. "Look at nothing else. From now on, nothing exists for you but these eyes. They have become your universe, your world. You now live in them."

I did as she ordered. The rest of the room gradually faded away. I no longer felt Lexi's hand grasping mine.

"How do you feel?"

I swallowed. "Scared." My voice sounded muffled.

"What else?"

"Foolish. Intimidated. Helpless. Depressed."

"Good." The steel-gray eyes enveloped me, and I suddenly felt warm and numb. "And now?"

"Warm. Numb."

"What else?"

"A little tired."

"Very good. Now close your eyes."

It was difficult at first. They wanted to stay focused on the woman's eyes. But I finally let my eyelids drop, and the resulting darkness was warm and comforting.

"Relax." Her voice became a whisper. "Take your mind, your body, your spirit. Release them, let them go. You are now a free spirit, light as a feather. You are flying, and as you fly, you are growing lighter and lighter…drifting in the air, weightless, with nothing to hold you down…"

The darkness grew softer, warmer.

204

"Relax…" Melina's voice sounded farther away.

I'd drifted away, through the darkness, and after just a few moments, the darkness lightened, becoming gray, then silver…then finally a soft shade of white…

"Fly…" I could barely hear Melina's voice. It sounded miles away. "Be free. Fly like the wind…through the trees…"

Lighter… Softer… I was consumed by a gentle calm I'd experienced before, in another place I once knew…a place I'd been to before…

"Soft. Calm. Gentle… Nothing can harm you… Soon you'll be back there…and everything will be explained…"

"Any idea where we are?"

The strange voice startled me. I opened my eyes and found that I was standing in a pine forest. My thoughts immediately disintegrated, as if they'd been swallowed up by the same dark emptiness that had taken over my mind earlier.

"I'm here again," I whispered, not believing my own eyes. "I've somehow…come back…"

"You must live through it again," another voice said, not very far away. The voice was low-pitched and raspy. I vaguely remembered hearing it before, not so long ago. "Let it happen again…"

Yes. For some reason I could not remember, I had to let it happen again, or it would never go away. I wanted it to go away, didn't I? Yes. I had no choice. I didn't know what exactly it was that I wanted to go away, just that it was destroying me. It was beautiful and peaceful here in the woods, but I knew I couldn't stay here. The dark-haired vision walking with me down the grassy path was also beautiful. Any normal guy would want to stay here with her.

But I knew I couldn't.

As we walked, I wanted to tell her what was going on, but I had no idea. I knew something was wrong, something really bad, and that I'd been here before, but my thoughts were cloudy and muddled, and I couldn't tell her anything even if I tried. For a moment I thought my mind had cleared, but as soon as I tried sorting things out, my thoughts muddled again, turning dark, and I knew that if I said anything at that moment, nothing would make sense, and I'd sound crazy and frighten her even more. Just moments ago, when she'd asked me if I knew how we'd gotten here, I'd told her I didn't have a clue. I thought I did, but something inside me told me that I should tell her I had no idea, because that was the way this was supposed to play out.

She'd then thought about this for a few moments and said that this had obviously happened quickly, before either of us knew what was happening. I'd asked her how she knew that, and she pointed to me and said, "You're wearing a suit."

Even before I looked down, I knew what I was wearing. But I looked down anyway because something inside me told me I had to.

I knew a lot of things. As my mind cleared, I realized that I even knew why she was wearing heels. I wanted to tell her. I also wanted to tell her why I was wearing a suit, but as soon as I started to, I found that I wasn't quite sure. Once again, my mind clouded up and my thoughts vanished.

What was happening to me?

"Do not fight it," that strange voice said, coming back from the darkness in my mind.

"My memory…"

"It will come back when the time is right."

"Damn, this is scary…" The dark-haired woman was shivering, and I knew she was scared.

I was scared, too, but for a much different reason. What scared me was that I was back, reliving it as if for the first time. I had to tell myself that this couldn't be real, that I was just imagining that I'd been here before. This was merely a shadow of a former dream I'd once experienced.

But just then, she began growing clearer and more vivid. Soon everything else faded away, and I knew right then that this was an actual place.

"Concentrate," whispered the strange voice in the back of my mind. "You are there, and nothing else exists anymore…"

Her name is Alison, I thought, remembering, although I had no idea how I could remember someone I'd just met. *Alison Grant*.

"Concentrate on being there, and nothing else. Let it happen…"

We continued trudging through the thick brush. Everything looked familiar, yet I couldn't figure out why it should. I hadn't been here before, had I?

Or had I?

Yes. I had been here before, although I couldn't remember when. But I could remember that the last time I was here, something terrible happened as we went around the next bend. I couldn't remember exactly what it was, but I knew that I didn't want to go through this again.

This time, I stopped. I struggled hard to determine why I stopped, why I didn't want to go through this again. Once again, my mind wouldn't cooperate. Was it my imagination creating something bad? Or was this nothing more than a gut feeling?

"What's wrong?" She turned.

"I don't...want to..."

"You must," whispered the mysterious voice.

"I have a strange feeling of what might happen."

"You must do it."

"But--"

"You must *do* it."

"You're coming, right?" Alison looked worried.

Reluctantly I joined her.

Something lay in the grass beneath an oak tree about a hundred feet down the grassy path. I had a strong suspicion of what it was. This suspicion told me that this was going to turn out horribly. I didn't know how I knew that, but I was afraid to question myself. I closed my eyes and tried changing the outcome, visualizing something else. A log. Broken branches.

But I knew it wouldn't change.

208

"Don't do it," the voice warned. "Don't try to change anything."

"What is that?" Alison asked.

"I don't know…" I didn't want to tell her what I thought it was. If I was right, it would make all of this much worse.

"You cannot change what has already happened," the voice in my head repeated.

"I know."

"A-Are you going over there or what?"

I managed to get my legs moving, coaxing them through the heavy brush. Behind me, I could hear the crunching of dead leaves as Alison followed close behind me. I wanted her to trip, to stumble. I wanted her to fall off her heels so I could help her back down the hill and protect her from what I feared would happen.

Just a few steps later, I saw the body.

"Oh my God!" She'd sidestepped and gawked at the sight. Her eyes filled with tears. A raspy squeal squeezed out of her throat. "L-Larry?" She rushed past me through the thick brush and stopped a few feet from the figure lying at the base of the tree. I could hear her sobbing quietly as she dropped to her knees next to the fallen man.

A strong sense of *déjà vu* slammed into me. I knew this would happen. I knew it, yet I couldn't stop it.

"Larry and I were married for nine years." Alison sat there, gazing at him. Moments later, she bent over and put her hand under his neck. "Larry?"

I knew that I'd feel for a pulse, but there wouldn't be one, so this time I didn't bother.

"Is this what you did before?" the irritating voice asked. "You just sat there and watched her?"

"No…"

"Then do what you did the first time."

"But I already know what will happen--"

"It does not matter. Do it."

Sighing, I felt for the pulse at his neck. As expected, I felt none.

Alison watched him for a few moments then raised her head and looked around. Once again she asked me where we were, and once again I told her I had no idea. And even though I knew some things now that I didn't know then, I still had no idea what this strange place was.

"Why is Larry here with us?" Alison asked. "What happened to him?"

"You don't remember anything?"

"Not really."

"I picked you up," Larry said, his head rolling in the grass.

Alison gasped. I knew I should have gasped as well, but I didn't. I just stood there, watching her as I had the first time.

The man's eyes opened, and he struggled to sit up.

"Larry? D-Did you…say something?"

"I just said I picked you up." He took a few deep breaths and rubbed his eyes. Then he began asking the same questions the two of us had already asked ourselves.

I reached out to help Alison pull him into a sitting position. He noticed me and asked who I was. I told him, and he found that he was too weak to stand. He sat back down and rested, and then we helped him back up a few minutes later. He swayed a little, so we held on until he could stand on his own. He said he felt better and began looking around again. He talked about picking up Alison from the airport and said he was going to take her to the Vista Resort. Alison didn't remember any of it. She only remembered that she'd flown to Orlando from Flagstaff. He asked if she remembered his phone call. She said yes, but nothing about the conversation.

They began arguing, so I turned and went down the grassy slope. As I walked, I heard them doing exactly what I'd expected. I also suspected that it wouldn't be very long before Alison came back after me.

About a minute later, I heard the crunching of twigs. I turned and saw her catching up with me. Larry wasn't behind her. At first I wondered why, but after a moment, a dark image flashed in my head, and I didn't want to speak. I knew that if I said anything, something awful would happen, and I didn't want Allison to go through this again...

"Ask her what you were going to ask," urged the cursed voice in my head.

"But if I do, something bad will happen…"

"It has to happen. You know this."

"Still, I'd rather--"

"*Do* it!"

I sighed. The voice was right; there was nothing I could do to change any of this. "Did you leave him back there?"

Alison stopped walking and turned. "Larry? Why are you still back there? Is something wrong?"

He was still standing in front of the tree, watching us.

"Larry?"

Another dark image flashed past my vision. Once again, I struggled to keep from losing my sanity.

"Say it," the strange voice urged.

"I can't."

"You must!"

I sighed deeply. "He...doesn't look too good."

"Larry?"

Just as that last dark image had dictated, he began fading. His eyes opened wide, his jaw dropped, and he looked like he was about to scream.

Then he vanished.

Alison stood there, frozen. It took her long, agonizing moments to find her voice. "Where did he go, Jack? Where in heaven's name did Larry go?"

"He's gone," I said, "and I think we ought to--"

"Say nothing else," urged the nauseating voice.

Alison dashed up the hill and stopped where Larry had been. She began circling the tree and

212

yelling his name. Then she screamed and disappeared in the woods.

"I can't watch her go through this again," I said.

"You have to."

"It's horrible."

"I know."

I ran after her as before, found her crouched in front of a deadfall as before, and sat down beside her, as before. I listened to her, talked to her, consoled her, and stayed with her. I knew exactly what she was going through and I also knew what was happening. I just couldn't tell her. I wanted to, but--

"You cannot tell her anything you didn't say before."

"I know, dammit."

"These are images. You cannot change them."

Just then, Lexi's voice drifted inside my head. "You're gonna be okay, Dad. I love you, and you're gonna be okay."

"*Please* don't make me go through this again..."

"You must."

"What's wrong?" Alison was watching me.

"I just...heard a voice. It sounded like Lexi. She's my stepdaughter."

I forced myself through the next exchange, and before I knew it, we began walking down the familiar grassy path.

Once we reached the clearing, I saw the glittering doorway and knew the very worst was about to happen.

"*Jack? What's wrong?*"

I didn't reply.

"*Jack?*"

"You must answer her."

"I can't."

"Yes you can."

"This time, I refuse--"

"You cannot refuse! If you refuse, you both will die!"

I forced myself to turn away from the doorway. And from Alison.

CHAPTER NINETEEN

"I *can't* go through this again!"

I had a strong feeling that if I left, Alison would perish. But I also knew that I couldn't stay here and let the same thing happen again.

"You must," the voice in my head replied flatly.

I wanted to continue to protest but felt myself being pulled back into the dream.

"Jack?" Alison was shaking my arm.

I backed away from her and looked around. Trees surrounded us. A clearing loomed straight ahead, but the doorway blocked it. It wasn't a doorway but a rectangular walkway with glittering light radiating from its center.

"Jack? Talk to me, please?"

Alison looked worried as well as frightened. She wasn't staring at the doorway, and I knew why. She wasn't staring at it because she didn't see it. She saw only a space between two trees. But to me, at the end of the clearing, standing boldly between two pine trees, a sparkling doorway blocked our path.

Alison asked why we weren't seeing the same thing, but before I could reply, I heard Lexi's voice again, saying, "I'm right here, Dad. I love you, and I'm waiting for you to come back."

It sounded like it was coming from within the doorway.

"Jack?" Alison was shaking me again. "Are you all right?"

No, I wasn't all right. I wasn't all right the first time I'd been through this and I sure as hell wasn't all right now. But it was much worse now because I had an idea of what would happen, and if I wanted to change it, I had to do it before I did anything else…

"You cannot do anything about it," the horrible voice in my head told me.

"I have to."

"You can only fix this later, after you fully know what actually happened."

"*Jack?* Talk *to me…*" *Alison trembled as she held onto me.*

"*I heard her voice again. It was just as clear as your voice.*"

"*Jack, I know this is getting to you. It's getting to me, too. I mean, a doorway glittering with light? In the middle of a* pine *forest?*"

She said she was having a big problem with this and needed my help. She said I had to force myself to keep my head clear. She said she knew that I loved Lexi, but that Lexi wasn't here.

"*Did you hear me, Jack? Lexi's not here, but I am.*"

Even though I'd been through this before, I began having doubts once again if Alison was real. This time, my doubts were even bigger. If she wasn't real, this was all unnecessary. If she was a dream, or illusion, I'd been agonizing over nothing.

But something told me Alison was real and had somehow followed me long after we entered the glittering doorway.

I reached out and touched her face. It was warm...and smooth...and soft...and most of all, real.

"I'm real, Jack." She moved closer and put her hands on my shoulders. "You touched me before. I was real before, and I'm still real. Can't you understand that?"

"Yes. Of course I understand."

Her right hand came up and gently touched my cheek.

"If I wasn't real, you couldn't touch me and I couldn't touch you, right?"

"You're real. You have to be real."

"I am real, Jack."

"Then why can't you see the doorway? Why can't you hear Lexi's voice?"

I didn't know why I asked her that. A small part of my mind knew why she couldn't, but I found once again that I was incapable of rationalizing any of this.

Alison didn't know why she couldn't hear Lexi or see the doorway. She had no idea why because there was no reason why she should know. I thought I knew but didn't know how to tell her. I also knew that the right words would not come to me--not now, anyway. Something in my mind told me that the right words would come only after I'd gone through this nightmare once more.

She reached up and placed her hands at the back of my neck. Then she kissed me, hard and passionately.

She'd just kissed me to prove she was real. I knew it the first time, and realized that even now, after she'd done it again, she was just as real as I was, and that I had to find some way to tell her what was happening.

She broke the kiss and pulled away. "Convinced now?"

I sighed, closed my eyes, and waited for the familiar tingling to ebb.

"What are you doing now?" the voice asked.

"Trying to get over that kiss."

"Get over it quickly."

"That's easier said than done."

"Why is that?"

"It was a really good kiss."

"Snap out of it, Jack Clarkson. Focus!"

"Alison's real."

"Yes. Of course she is."

"And she's alive."

"And you must do whatever you can to save her."

I reluctantly turned back to the doorway.

"What happened back there?" Alison asked.

It took me a few moments to remember. I was still thinking about that kiss. Focus, I told myself. Listen to the voice. It will help.

"Yes," echoed the voice. "Focus."

"I heard Lexi's voice coming from within that doorway."

"What did she say?"

"She said she loved me. She said she was waiting for me."

"Dad..."

"I just heard her again. She called my name."

Alison moved closer. "Did it sound like it was coming from the same place?"

"Yes. The same--" I turned back to the doorway. It had disappeared. Only an oval doorway of darkness remained.

But I knew this would happen, didn't I? I also knew that when it did happen, it meant my time with Alison was rapidly coming to an end.

I felt as if someone had just reached inside my chest and ripped out my heart.

"Wh-What's wrong?" Alison stared straight ahead, looking very confused.

I couldn't tell her my feelings--or my fears. I couldn't tell her anything that I really wanted to tell her. If I did, that cursed voice from hell would invade my head and tell me to shut up.

"The doorway...it's gone." It was the only thing I was permitted to say.

Alison turned back to me. "What exactly do you see?"

"Darkness."

"You mean, where you once saw the doorway is now just darkness?"

"Between those two pines trees. The glittering lights are gone. Now it looks like...some sort of dark entrance. Don't tell me you still don't see anything."

"I see that same space between those two pine trees, Jack. There's grass growing there, a mound of pine needles, and a few broken twigs. Nothing else."

"Dad, please come home..."

I glanced at Alison. *"You still don't hear it, do you?"*

"No. Where did you hear it that time?"

I turned back to where the doorway had once been and pointed. I cringed when I realized that it had now become a tunnel. *"There's a tunnel there now."*

Alison turned sharply and gawked at the area between the two pines. *"You mean...you see a tunnel now?"*

"And you still don't see anything?"

She stared at the area and shook her head.

"Dad, I'm right here, and I'm not leaving until you come back..."

"Lexi?"

"What do we do, Jack? Something's obviously happening to us right now, something that hasn't happened before."

"I know." Once again I sensed something horrible coming and wanted to do something-- anything--that would stop it...

"You can't," the voice said, interrupting my thoughts.

"I know, but it's very difficult to go through this again, knowing something bad is about to happen and being unable to do anything about it..."

"As I said before, it has to be this way."

"I'm no scientist," Alison said, *"but I kind of think we should be seeing the same things. We're both here in the same place, looking at the same trees, the same meadow, and the same sky. If*

220

everything's the same, it should be the same for both of us. That means I should've seen the doorway, the darkness, and the tunnel. But it isn't happening like that, is it?"

"No."

"Dad?"

Lexi's voice was louder, clearer, and sounded much closer.

"Lexi?"

"Dad?"

My heart raced. "Can you hear me, Lexi?"

"Dad, I'm right here…"

"Jack, please talk to me."

"Talk to her, Jack. Tell her what you told her the first time."

"I can't."

"Why not?"

"I have this feeling that something bad will happen if I do…"

"You are right. It has to happen this way because it always *has* happened this way."

"Then I won't say anything."

"Don't you realize that you must tell her? That you must do everything you did the first time? Don't you realize that if you don't, if you try and change anything, this will turn out very badly for her?"

"It's going to anyway, isn't it?"

"Yes, but at least we'll be able to fix it if you know exactly what went wrong. If you change *anything*, we won't be able to help either of you because we won't be able to tell what really

221

happened from what you tried to prevent from happening."

I knew she was right, but I still didn't want this to happen again.

"*Jack? Please talk to me…*"

I struggled to keep from saying anything, but my resistance quickly trickled away, and I realized that even though this would be really bad, it had to be done. "Alison, I've got to go in there and find out what's going on. I have a feeling Lexi's in that tunnel."

Alison said nothing. She was staring at the tunnel, possibly trying desperately to visualize it.

"There is *a tunnel there, believe me."*

She turned back to me. "I believe you, Jack. I may not see it, but I believe you're seeing a tunnel."

"Thank you. And since I don't know what's in there, I think I'd better go in there…alone." I tried to keep from saying that last word, but it came out anyway.

"No! We're going in together, *understand?" Alison's face had become tense, triggering my memory and reminding me of the horror that was going to happen. "I don't know what's happening, Jack, but I won't let you leave me. I won't let us split up!"*

"It'll…only be for…a second…"

"I don't care!*" She moved closer. "I've got this horrible feeling that if we split up, we'll never be able to get together again!"*

"My God. She was right." A sharp blade of ice penetrated my heart when the realization sliced through me. We'd separated. This was where the darkness had swallowed me up and brought me back to the other world, where Lexi patiently awaited me. "Alison was absolutely right. No wonder I feel the guilt, the shame. How could I have doubted her? How could I have--"

"Go back to the dream."

"I deserted her! I--"

"Go back. Now!"

"Please don't leave me, Jack! Please!"

The white terror on Alison's face shocked me the first time I saw it. Now I wasn't surprised at all. Since I now knew what was going to happen, I knew exactly what she was feeling.

Holding hands, we cautiously approached the tunnel.

"Whatever happens," Alison whispered, "I'm right here with you."

"I'm right here with you, too." I felt like a traitor as soon as the cursed words slithered from my throat.

"Don't let go of my hand."

"I won't."

"Promise me with all your heart and soul that you won't under any circumstances let go of my hand."

I was a traitor--a lowlife. I'd abandoned her. I'd never turned my back on anyone before in my life, but I'd abandoned this beautiful lady, and was about to do it again...

"Jack?"

"I promise." This time, I'd keep it. If it was the last thing I ever did, I'd stay with her, even if it meant staying here...

We crept closer to the darkness. I could feel the cool air coming from within the tunnel. We took two more steps, then three, our feet moving unsteadily over the tall grass. The tunnel awaited us just ten feet away. The cool air grew cold and much stronger, and a distant smell of antiseptic assaulted my nostrils.

This time I knew what it was. It was the hospital awaiting me as Lexi called me.

"Dad?" Lexi's voice, louder than before, came from within the tunnel.

I'd replied to her the first time, but now I found myself resisting, keeping quiet as I gripped Alison's hand.

"Tell Alexandria what you told her the first time," the voice insisted.

"I didn't say anything--"

"You are lying!"

How did she know? It didn't matter; I intended to remain silent.

"Tell her, Jack Clarkson. Tell her this instant!"

Once again my spirit intervened, and despite my resistance, I heard myself shouting in reply. "I'm coming, Lexi!"

Three more steps and we were just a few feet from the threshold. The cool air enveloped me, as did the antiseptic smell.

Alison began pulling me back from the opening. I turned around and tugged at her. I knew what was happening and refused to let it happen this time.

She pulled harder, gritting her teeth. Her eyes filled the sockets; she gawked at her hand as it gripped mine. She was staring at our hands as if she had no idea what they were. "What's happening? Why am I pulling away from you?"

I'm gonna do it this time, I promised myself. I'm gonna bring her with me if it's the last--

"Do not try to change this," the cursed voice reminded.

"Dad, I'm right here..."

"Jack, please don't let go of me!"

"I'm holding on to you as hard as I can!" I couldn't let her go this time. I had to bring her with me...out of the tunnel...out of this strange world...and into the hospital...

"Hold on harder!"

One more step and I was inside the darkness of the tunnel, enveloped by cold and that sweet antiseptic smell. Alison's grip tightened, but I could no longer see her. The darkness had thickened, enveloping us, and she'd quickly faded.

Dammit. It was happening *again!*

"Alison! For God's sake, hold on!"

"Jack! Don't let me go!"

"Alison? Where the hell are you?" I held on tightly, but I still couldn't see her in the darkness. *"Alison, come closer so I can see you!"*

"Jack!"

Dammit! Damn, damn, damn!

"I *can't* let her go again!"

"It must happen just as it did the first time."

"If I let go, it'll happen all over again!"

"It *has* to happen all over again."

"I can't--"

"Dad?"

"Jack!" *Alison's voice sounded much farther away.*

Her grip grew even tighter. A moment later, she stopped pulling away. The darkness thickened and I could no longer see anything--not even the hands locked around my own.

"Dad, I'm right here..."

"Lexi, I love you, baby, but I've got to stay here with Alison and try and find a way out of here!"

"Jack! Please!"

The darkness gradually lifted. I kept my eyes tightly shut. I didn't want to lose her again.

"Open your eyes."

"I don't want to--"

"Open them!"

My heart thrashed as I opened my eyes...

I could finally see her face. But this time was different. Just as Lexi's face appeared before me, it faded, and for a moment I saw Alison again--

"Yes!"

--but her image lasted only a moment...

And then the darkness swallowed me up.

"No! No! NO!"

Lexi's image appeared and then faded, disappearing in the darkness. Alison's image returned, hazy at first, then much clearer as it emerged from the darkness.

"Alison?"

"Come back to me, Jack... Don't leave me...
You promised you wouldn't leave me..."

"I'm here." I was looking directly at her and reaching out, but something was wrong. She was looking around frantically but could not see me and was just out of reach of me. Our hands groped for one another, our fingertips coming within inches of touching. Although the darkness had swallowed me up, I could still see her clearly.

"I can't see you, Jack!"

"I'm here! Right here in front of you!"

"The darkness is so thick...where are you, Jack? Where did you go?"

It finally occurred to me that she couldn't hear me, either. I began shouting. *"I'm right here, Alison!"*

"Dad? Come back!"

"Lexi?" Her voice sounded like it had come from somewhere behind me in the darkness.

I had to get back with Alison. I knew I wouldn't have any trouble finding Lexi again, but if I didn't stay with Alison, I'd lose her forever. I turned back to the frightened image just a few feet in front of me. "It's me, Alison. I'm right here, and I promise I'll stay right here until you find me, and this time I won't--"

"Jack, you promised you wouldn't--"

I reached out for her. My hands went right through hers. I could no longer feel her. The darkness had turned me into a ghost.

"Dad?"

"Jack Clarkson," shouted the raspy, low-pitched voice. "You must open your eyes this instant!"

"The darkness...it's swallowing me up...help me out of this--"

"Dad?"

"*Jack? Where are you?*"

"Alison, I'm gonna stay here until you can see me, and we're gonna find a way to get out of--"

"Wake up...wake *up*..."

"*Jack, please!*"

I felt myself being jerked away from Alison. "Who's there? Who just grabbed me?"

"Dad, it's me, Lexi... Please *wake up!*"

The darkness grew lighter...then gray...then silver...then a hazy white...

228

CHAPTER TWENTY

Lexi stood over me, shaking me.

Her eyes were wet, her face a taut mask. Her hair danced in front of me as she shook me. "Dad?"

I closed my eyes and took a few deep breaths. My heart was thumping so violently, I thought it would leap out of my chest. My neck was wringing wet, the back of my neck cold with sweat.

"Dad?" Lexi shook me again. "Are you back?"

"I think so..." I wiped the back of my neck. "What happened?"

Lexi's glistening eyes were enormous; her lower lip trembled.

"Lexi?" I had the strange feeling I'd done something that terrified her. "Tell me what happened."

She took a breath. "You...faded." Her voice was a mere whisper.

"I what?"

"You almost disappeared!"

I stared at her, trying to analyze her expression, to decide if what she'd said was the truth. I knew she wouldn't lie to me, but what she'd just said made no sense--none whatsoever. I recalled the time Lexi and Claire came to my place to fix lunch. While they were busy in the kitchen, I went into the living room, sat down and, before I knew what was happening, found myself in the meadow again. I hadn't realized anything strange had happened until Lexi appeared in the hall and asked where I'd been. At the time, I hadn't the foggiest notion what she was talking about, and thought she was playing a game. I still didn't understand any of this, but at least now I had an inkling of an idea.

I turned to Melina. "It's true, then?"

"Yes. You almost left."

"Left?" I still couldn't comprehend any of this.

"You almost went back to the place where you once were."

This still didn't make sense. "But you *wanted* me to go back. You told me I *had* to go back. And I did, didn't I?"

"Yes."

"Then what did you just mean? And what did Lexi mean when she said I faded?"

"Your physical essence almost joined you there."

"You mean, back *there*? When I was with Alison?"

A nod.

"Please tell me what happened."

"It is complicated, and I cannot expect you to fully understand what

this is unless I explain the whole concept."

"Then tell me what I need to know."

"I can only say you must go back again."

Had I heard her correctly? "Did you just say…what I *thought* you

said?"

"Yes."

Lexi gasped. "*No*."

Melina nodded. "You must return to the tunnel. You must go back for Alison."

"But I already went back, and it was just like what happened the first time. It was almost like a recurring dream. I can't see how I can possibly help her at all—especially since you told me I couldn't change anything."

"You must not go back that way."

I never felt more confused than I did at that moment. "Which way are you talking about?"

"The way I just led you--through hypnosis."

"Why not?"

"You crossed realms."

"I *what*?"

"Our world is very complex. It is comprised of several different spheres, or realms. Some intersect while others do not. This realm--the world we experience with our senses--is our conscious world. Our *real* world. The one in which you just visited, the realm of dreams, can be inhabited only by the subconscious. It is the world of the mind, the imagination. Only our most wonderful thought processes choose to exist in this realm. We can visit it briefly, but it cannot be crossed over unless the spirit has actually abandoned its physical body."

"What happened when I faded?"

"It was your spirit struggling to leave your physical essence. For a brief period of time, your spirit eclipsed your body."

"And if I do this again, I might succeed?"

"Yes, and since it almost succeeded, it is highly likely that it will surely succeed after another attempt."

"But you want me to go back to the same place that almost killed me just a few minutes ago."

"I am almost certain it is your destiny."

"You're not making any sense."

"I totally understand that you are unable to grasp the concept. Most cannot understand the existence of different worlds. But it is true. There are several we know of, and several that are completely unknown to us. The only world most of us can accept is the one we see--the one we live in, in which all things are visible and attainable to us. The world of the five senses. But the others? Those where our dreams and fantasies flourish? They are known only to those who believe in them and wish to see them."

"That makes no sense," I said. "I've always been a very logical person. To me, logic and science are the only things in this life that make sense."

"You do not believe in the spiritual world? The world of dreams? Of the imagination?"

"Of course I believe in the imagination. I've read a book or two in my lifetime, and I've seen a ton of movies. I've also had my share of dreams."

"Then despite your opinions, you are indeed a believer of the other realms."

"This still doesn't explain why my spirit is the weak link here."

232

"As mortals, we are not permitted to enter these other realms at will. The physical body has been assigned to exist in this realm and no other. There is a high cost for entering other realms, and the spirit is the one that will suffer."

"But you're not giving me a choice."

"You have two choices."

"What are they?"

"The solution here is very simple. You can either return or you can choose not to."

"And if I choose not to?"

"You will live, but in your present condition, your guilt will consume you, and you will gradually lose your mind."

"And if I choose to go back?"

"Once you enter this realm, your spirit will eventually decide that it belongs there, and will not wish to come back. You wanted to stay this last time, correct?"

"I wanted to stay long enough to bring back Alison."

"Can you remember the first time? Did you wish to stay then?"

"I was looking for my way back when I bumped into Alison."

"If you hadn't encountered her, you would have decided to remain there."

"But I did encounter her. She's still there, and she wants to come back."

"She wants to come back to be with you again. And she does not want to be alone in the realm."

Once again I felt a stab of guilt for leaving her. "These choices really suck."

"They are the only ones you have. Alison has no choices. She is trapped in this realm of dreams."

"I was trapped, too."

"Alexandria brought you back. She could connect with you physically as well as spiritually and emotionally."

"But I was just there. Why couldn't I bring Alison back?"

"Alison's spirit needs a physical connection to take her out of this realm."

"What about Lexi? She's right here. She could--"

"Alexandria has no connection with Alison. This is why Alison couldn't hear her or see the tunnel. You are Alison's connection to this world. Your physical being needs to bond with hers to enable the spirits to reconnect. Otherwise, she cannot come back."

"I don't know where her physical body is."

"This is why you couldn't bring her back. If you'd stayed with her, she would have eventually kept you with her. As I have said, the spirit is much happier in the realm of dreams and will instinctively choose to stay there. If it had not been for Alexandria and myself contacting you, you would have stayed in the realm with Alison and deserted your physical essence completely."

"So Alison needs me physically to help bring her back?"

"Yes."

"Why me?"

"Obviously no one else has tried bringing her back. At least you know where she is."

"I know where her *spirit* is."

"Yes."

"And when I last saw her, she really wanted to come back."

"She obviously still has reasons to return. Otherwise, she would choose to remain in the realm."

"And you're sure she can't survive if I don't go back for her?"

"You are correct."

"And if I don't go back, I'll also die, but much later? After I lose my mind?"

"Yes."

I thought about this for a few moments. Lexi sat close to me, her trembling hands grasping my arm. I could feel the cold terror emanating from her. I couldn't blame her.

I had to go back and find Alison. I could stay here and eventually go crazy from the guilt, or return to that strange world and die trying to save a woman I'd deserted, a woman who was alone and terrified.

"So how do I go back?" I asked Melina.

"You must first find her physical body and connect to it."

"I was in an accident. I suffered a coma. That's probably how I entered the realm."

"I suspect it was."

"So how do I find Alison's body? I have no idea how she entered the realm."

"You must find out quickly. There is not much time."

"Are you sure?"

"I was with you when you entered the realm. I saw her, too. She'd already begun fading. It will not be long before she fades completely."

I swallowed a lump in my throat. "And when she does?"

"Her spirit gains entrance into the next realm. This realm is one from which there is no escape."

"Which realm is that?"

"Where the spirit goes for eternal rest."

"You mean…?"

"Yes. Alison will be dead."

***

It was dark by the time Lexi and I drove back to Winter Park.

I didn't say anything for the first five miles of the trip. I was still numb by what happened in Melina's office and couldn't get past anything else. I gazed at the heavy flow of headlights penetrating the windshield but could see only the darkness of the tunnel in which Alison was trapped, alone and scared, calling for me and wondering where I'd gone and why I'd abandoned her. It was the same tunnel I'd returned to just a few hours ago and, judging by what Melina had told me, the same tunnel I had to find once again.

Although I knew my returning to the realm could mean my death, I realized that it didn't matter. I couldn't go on living like this. Ever since I'd come out of my coma, my existence had been little more than disjointed dreams and Alison's cries of anguish and betrayal. I knew that as long as this situation remained unresolved, it would continue. My guilt and regret would eventually destroy me.

I had to do something but had no idea where to start. How could I possibly find Alison? I only knew that if I didn't find her physical body, her spirit would eventually die as well.

"I know what you're thinking." Lexi's voice snapped me back.

I hadn't even noticed that we'd stopped at a busy intersection, or that Lexi had turned in her seat and was watching me.

I imagined I was pretty much an open book right now--especially now, since Lexi knew what had been going on. But after that session with Melina, I supposed anyone would have been able to figure it out.

"It seems hopeless, doesn't it?" I finally said.

"Everyone else would just forget about it. They'd consider Melina a fruitcake and laugh the whole thing off."

"I guess I'm not like everyone else, am I?"

I could see her smile in the darkness of the cab. "You're not like anyone I've ever known."

"I hope that's a good thing."

"Normally, it would be a great thing."

"Normally?"

She sighed. "Like I just said, most everyone else would forget about it and just go on with their lives. I can't imagine you not doing anything about it, not trying to fix it."

I went back to staring at the windshield. I couldn't look at her right now. I couldn't find the courage to meet the gaze of this bright young girl, whom I loved and respected. She was right-on about me, and I could tell how she felt. She probably hoped I could be like everyone else.

I had to let her down and do what I had to do.

"*Please* tell me what you're thinking, Dad…"

In spite of my intentions, I knew I couldn't keep anything from her. "You know I have to fix this, don't you, Lexi? It's bound to be impossible, dangerous, frightening, and a dozen other things that are just as bad. Like you just said, it would be very easy for anyone else to walk away and forget about it. The guilt wouldn't consume them because people rarely feel guilt or responsibility anymore. They just don't care about one another-- not as much as they used to. They walk away from highway accidents and close their eyes to anything they don't want to be involved with. It's much easier now; they have cell phones and iPads and all those other high-tech toys that can keep them safe and isolated in their own little world. But it doesn't matter what other people would do. Not to me. I have to do whatever it takes to help her."

She didn't say anything right off. Then the light changed, and we started moving again. "Do you remember the time I found that stray puppy on my way home from school?"

I tried recalling the incident, but it wouldn't come. I vaguely remembered driving her to the vet with a puppy in her lap one evening, but not much else. "Sorry, Lexi, but my head is still foggy about a lot of things."

"I was seven or eight at the time. You and Mom weren't married long, and we'd just moved into that three-bedroom in Casselberry. Anyway, I found it huddled behind some garbage cans in someone's driveway. It was skinny and scared, and it whimpered when I picked it up. I was gonna bring it home and ask you or Mom to take us to the vet so we could get it checked out, but before I made it home, it jumped out of my arms and ran away. I chased it for a while, but it moved really fast, and after a while I couldn't find it. Then I got all freaky and upset and ran home. I told Mom about it but she said I should forget about it because it was probably sick and would die before I found it again. I hated her for that and didn't talk to her for at nearly a week afterward. But I knew you wouldn't feel the same, and when you came home, I told you about it. Mom came in and told you what she'd already told me--that someone had dumped it because it was sick. But you didn't care. You said it would be a crime to let it die all alone in the street. We went right back out and found it. It was only about a block away and was hiding in someone's bushes. As soon as we found it, you scooped it up in your jacket and we ran home and got in the car, went back out and drove to the vet. It died that same night, but it died in our arms, while the two of us were petting it and talking to it."

I still couldn't remember but guessed she was probably telling the truth. It sounded exactly like how Claire would have reacted to the situation.

"You couldn't turn your back on it."

"Everyone deserves a chance--especially dogs, who have no control over their destiny. They seldom get the chance to pick their owners."

"He was a sweet little guy. He would've been a good pet."

"Dogs usually are."

"I know you, Dad. You don't turn your back on anyone. That night was a perfect example. You'd just gotten home, you were tired, and you wanted to relax, have a beer and listen to some old music. But you didn't. You knew a sick puppy was out there, alone and scared, and it bothered you."

I thought about what she'd just said. But that alone wasn't what convinced me to go back and find Alison. I'd formed a connection with her. And it wasn't the kiss--although that was something else I couldn't get out of my mind. I'd promised her I wouldn't leave her there, and I knew I wouldn't rest until I'd gone back and found her.

I could tell Lexi was thinking of what might happen if I did return to the realm. "You don't want me to go back there, do you?"

"I know you have to, Dad."

"That's not what I asked you."

"I only know that I don't want to lose you. You're my best friend, the only father I ever really had, and I love you very much."

"I love you, too. But you're right; I have to do this. And going by what your friend Melina said, I've got no choice. I stand a good risk of dying, no matter which way I choose to go. I think it's simply a matter of how I choose you to remember me."

"I don't wanna think about that for a long time, Dad..."

I could tell I'd upset her, but I knew she was strong enough to handle all this. It was the truth; like it or not, she had to know how I felt. "She's all alone, Lexi. Alison's trapped in that tunnel all by herself, with no one to help her, and she has no idea where she is, where I am, or what's happening."

"I know."

We were both silent for the next couple of miles.

"Now I'm not really sure if I did the right thing by taking you to Melina," Lexi said, almost to herself.

"You did the right thing, kiddo."

"Then why doesn't it feel so right?"

"If it wasn't for Melina, I wouldn't have any idea what happened or why I've been having these dreams or hearing these voices. And I wouldn't know about Alison or even that she's in trouble."

"I guess there's that. But it still feels all wrong."

"It only feels all wrong because of what has to be done."

"Maybe..."

241

"Tell me about her, Lexi. Melina."

"What do you wanna know?"

"How do you know about her? I know she works at the school, but how could you possibly know about her abilities?"

Lexi smiled. "I didn't."

"You must have known *some*thing about her to bring me to her…"

"Well, it's kind of a weird story."

"Really?"

She laughed. "I know. She *is* pretty strange, isn't she?"

"I've never met anyone remotely like her before."

"Neither have I. She always keeps to herself and rarely talks to anyone. She only started working there a couple of days before your accident. Our regular librarian was out on maternity leave for the last month or so. I don't know where they found Melina, but one day she was just there, gathering up books and putting them back on the shelves. She's always reading, too. Whenever she's not working, she's in that little office, sitting behind the desk, reading. I'll bet she's read every single book we saw piled on that desk."

"And you haven't seen her talking to anyone else? None of the other students?"

"Only when they ask her to reference something or want to know about a certain author. She seems to know about every author in that library. They call her "Ghoul.""

"The nickname's cold, but it somehow fits. So, how'd you meet her?"

"She came over to my table in the library one afternoon during one of my free periods. I was having a bad day, and was sitting by myself, staring out the window. This was the day after your accident. I was waiting for the bell so I could leave early and drive to the hospital to see you."

I didn't reply.

"Anyway, I felt someone really close behind me and when I turned, there she was, standing right there, looking down at me. I wanted to ask if something was wrong, but she just bent over and whispered, "He'll like it when you go see him and talk to him.""

"She knew about me?"

"Evidently."

"How did she know about the accident?"

"That's just it. I have no idea. I never told her *anything*. As I just said, that was the first time I ever really noticed her."

"And she just came over and whispered that to you?"

"I didn't know what she was talking about at first, so I asked her. She said, "I know someone very close to you is very ill. It is important for you to visit him and talk to him." I told her you were in a coma and wouldn't even know I was there, but she said, "It does not matter. He will hear everything you say.""

"Did you ask her how she knew?"

"That was the strangest part of all this. She said she saw a heavy darkness clouding my aura that day. She said the darkness didn't appear to be permanent--which was a good thing--and that if I talked to you, you'd get better, and the darkness would go away. Isn't that about the freakiest thing you've ever heard?"

CHAPTER TWENTY-ONE

We got back to my place at around 8:30.

I went into the kitchen, got a can of lemon-flavored tea for Lexi and grabbed a beer for myself while she placed her laptop on the table, opened it and sat down. I put the beer on the table and slid the can over to her. Then I got a glass and some cubes and placed it near the can.

"Thanks, Dad." But she didn't take her attention from the laptop as she logged in and started whacking away at the keys.

"Hungry?" I figured she'd be starved. I didn't think she'd eaten since lunch.

She didn't reply.

"How about if I fix some sandwiches?"

"Not just now, thanks." She still didn't pull her eyes away from the screen.

I popped open my beer and sat facing her. I was curious about what she was doing but didn't want to stand over her and make her nervous. I figured it was important, maybe something that had given her an idea from our meeting with Melina. If so, I didn't want to distract her.

I had a slug of beer. My stomach instantly reminded me in its own loud way how long it had been since I'd last eaten. Once again I thought about fixing something, but Lexi was much too focused on her laptop. I didn't want to make too much noise bustling about, fixing food.

Instead, my thoughts went back to Melina. I still couldn't believe the woman had guided me back to the realm. The more I thought of it, the more I wondered if it had actually happened. I knew it was the skeptic in me, searching for some sort of explanation or logic that would tell me Melina was nothing more than a crackpot, and that she'd simply used her intensity and other strange talents to brainwash me into creating a "realm."

Deep down, I knew there really wasn't such a thing. There couldn't be. A world of dreams? A world of the imagination? It sounded like something right out of a sci-fi novel.

Melina had hypnotized me. Why? I had no idea. For all I knew, she could be some sort of sadist who got off on other people's delusions.

I'd been hallucinating and had fabricated the meadow, the woods, and Alison.

I'm real, Jack...

The memory of her voice was all it took to convince me that my skepticism was nothing more than my fear coming back. Fear of the unknown, of uncertainty. Fear of what would happen if I did return to the realm.

Alison was real--there was no denying that. Nothing would convince me otherwise. I closed my eyes and remembered how she was as she stood there, facing me that one delicious moment before she put her hands on my shoulders and kissed me.

She was just as real as I was.

But the problem remained: How could I find her physical body? It was my only chance--the only way I could bring her back.

Depression set in again, and as the darkness enveloped me, I felt myself slumping in the chair. There had to be a way--just *had* to be...

Lexi stopped punching keys and looked up from the screen. "The lady's name is Alison Grant, right?"

"Yes..."

"And her ex-husband's name is Larry Grant?"

I sat up in the chair. "What are you up to?"

"We need to find her, don't we?"

"Are you telling me you've actually got an idea?"

"The way I see it, if you want to save her, and you can only do it by finding her, then we've got to use whatever sources we have. Melina told us we don't have much time, so we've really got to get on this, right?"

I glanced at her laptop and realized what she was getting at. Lexi was an expert with technology. After all, she'd been using it since she was barely able to walk. But I still had my doubts. Although my memory was still cloudy about certain things, I knew I always had a strong contempt for computers. "What makes you think you can find her this way?"

"Dad, I know this is an emotional issue with you--which is probably why you haven't thought of going this route before."

"What are you talking about?"

"See what I mean? You haven't even considered it, have ya?"

"Maybe I have."

247

"Then why haven't you asked me to look into this already?"

"I'm not exactly the greatest fan of computers. I wish I could remember the number of times I had to make phone calls to find out from people what I'd already tried finding online but couldn't."

"I understand, believe me. I also understand that you're still not at your peak. That's probably why you're so skeptical."

"Lexi, I have my issues, but I'm not going to stand in your way. I don't trust computers, but if there's even the slightest chance of this working in our favor, then yes, please do it."

"Good. Let's start with all the facts first."

"All right…"

"First of all, you were in an accident, which put you in a coma. When you slipped into this coma, it took you to a strange place, that realm of dreams Melina told us about. There, you came across Alison, and then her ex-husband, Larry."

"I think I know what you're getting at."

"'Kay…"

"If I met Alison and her ex in that strange place, then it could mean both she and Larry were also in a coma. Otherwise, how could I have come across them?"

"The problem we have now is that we have to figure out what exactly happened to them."

"When I was with Alison, we were both pretty confused. She couldn't remember Larry picking her up at the airport, her hotel room, or even her plane flight from Flagstaff. But she did

248

remember flying to Orlando for some business-related trip. Larry remembered picking her up at the airport. Other than that, he was just as clueless."

"That's weird…"

"I'm sure it had something to do with our brain injuries. I couldn't remember much, either. I never did, actually--not until after I came out of my coma. All I remembered was driving to work that morning. Eventually a lot of stuff came back, but it took quite a while."

"This could mean Alison and Larry were involved in the same sort of thing that happened to you."

"They weren't involved in my accident. From what I was told, I was the only victim who suffered a coma."

"That doesn't mean Alison and Larry weren't involved in a similar accident, Dad. It only means they weren't involved in yours."

"I guess you could be right. If so, where does this leave us?"

"This could be easier than we think." She went back to her laptop and punched a key. "I'll log into the *Sentinel* website, go back to the main headlines during the last three months, and see if I can find any other serious highway collisions where the names Alison and Larry Grant come up as victims." She punched another key.

This seemed hopeless. "They could have been involved in an accident anywhere, Lexi. What makes you think--"

"Didn't you say Alison came to Orlando for a convention?"

"Yeah…"

"Didn't Larry meet her at the airport so he could take her to her hotel in Disney Village?"

"We also know he worked at Disney as an artist." I suddenly remembered something else and felt my spirits rise. "He said he liked fishing, and he did a lot of it at Lake Monroe. That means, well, it could mean--"

"It means he lives in Central Florida and has contacts--which are like fingerprints, if you want to look at it that way."

"Fingerprints?"

"There's a trail. People know him, work with him. The more people you know and come in contact with, the more fingerprints you leave. In other words, he wasn't just some shadowy figure that stepped off the face of the earth."

I wanted to laugh. "Why aren't you going into Forensics, or CSI work?"

Lexi laughed and had some iced tea. "I'll stick to math, thanks. Besides, I'm a little squeamish about blood spatter." She put her glass down. "Anyway, this is more than enough for me to find out a few things."

"Sounds good to me."

She went back to her screen. "Now all I have to do is get in there and retrieve some data."

"Do you think you can?"

"I know I can. And if I have any trouble, I've got a network of friends who can help me out."

***

250

At ten o'clock, Lexi was still punching keys and picking up her cell phone every few minutes to make a quick call.

While she was preoccupied, I made some turkey and cheese sandwiches, added a bowl of baked potato chips and her favorite mustard-flavored pretzels, and placed them on plates in the center of the table. Lexi snatched half of a sandwich and nibbled on it and some pretzels while working the keyboard.

I picked up a sandwich myself. I was about to sit down with another beer when my cell rang. I put the sandwich back down, fished the cell out of my pocket, left the kitchen and took it down the hall.

It was Claire, and she sounded upset. "Is Lexi there, Jack?"

"She's been with me all afternoon. Why?"

I heard her sigh deeply.

"You okay?"

"*Now* I am, thank God. Quite frankly, I was worried. I haven't heard from her all day, and it's not like her to not keep in touch. She did mention she was going over there to see you, but that was hours ago, and I haven't heard from her since. I've been giving her space the last few months. She's earned my trust in many ways and has demonstrated a common sense I haven't seen in most other kids her age. She's very mature for her age, Jack."

"I know."

"She doesn't have a wild side--unlike most of her friends."

"I know that, too. I believe she once told me everyone thinks she's boring and nerdy."

"I'd rather have her boring and nerdy than wild, popular, and on drugs."

"You're right-on about that…" I hoped she'd get to the point soon.

"Anyway, I figured that since she was with you, things were okay. But it's been hours since I've heard from her. It's now almost ten-thirty, so I decided to get on the phone. Is everything all right?"

"Everything's just fine. She's in the kitchen right now, working on something for me."

A pause. "*Working* on something?"

"She's doing some research on her laptop."

"Is this…something about--"

"It's about something I have to do, and she's helping me with it."

Another pause. "Are *you* all right, Jack?"

"I'm still not a hundred percent, of course, but Lexi's been terrific about all this. I wouldn't have gotten nearly this far without her help and support. I hope you realize what a terrific daughter you've got."

"*We*, Jack. She's *our* daughter. I know you're not her biological father, and that you probably don't consider her your flesh and blood--"

"I consider her the sweetest, most considerate creature on the face of the earth, and I'm proud and very happy that she thinks so much of me, and also that she considers me her friend."

"I'm glad, Jack. I feel really badly that you and I weren't able to stay together, but one thing

I'll always be proud of is that you and Lexi are close, and that you'll always remain close."

I saw no reason to get into an argument with her right now--especially about something that was ancient history and couldn't be undone. It still hurt, but not nearly as much. I didn't know if my coma, my recovery, or my renewed kinship with Lexi had anything to do with that. For all I knew, my strange relationship with Alison could have been instrumental in my recovery. This was something I had to think about when I had the time. Right now, there were more important things to consider.

"I'm happy you feel that way, Claire. I'm also glad that we can still get along."

"Me, too. So…since it's getting so late, I guess she'll be staying there with you tonight."

"Probably."

"I know she's a good driver and all, but when you keep hearing about all the drunks out at this hour…"

"I hear you. Don't worry. I'll make sure she stays in."

"Great. Can you tell me what she's doing?"

"Like I said, she's working on something for me. She's been on her laptop the last hour or so."

"And it's about the accident?"

"Yes."

"Well, make sure she doesn't stay up too long, okay? She may not have a full class load anymore, but she still needs her sleep."

"No problem." I pocketed the phone and went back down the hall and into the kitchen. Lexi was

253

no longer punching keys. She was staring at her screen. Her face was pale. Something was very wrong.

"Lexi?"

It took her a few seconds to notice that I was standing in the doorway. She sighed and closed her eyes. When she opened them again, she said, "I found Larry Grant, Dad."

"What...did you find out?"

Her voice turned into a whisper. "He's dead."

***

The back of my neck buzzed.

"Dad? Are you all right?"

I didn't reply. My limbs had turned cold. The room grew hazy, and for a moment I thought I'd just faded away again.

"Is there...anything I can do?"

"Not for this, baby. This is something I should have already figured out. I should have realized Larry was dead."

"How could you have possibly known?"

I sat down heavily. I suddenly felt a hundred years old. "If I learned anything since my last trip back there, it was that Larry was probably close to death when we saw him lying under that tree."

"Tell me what happened, okay? You might have told me all about it before, but maybe if we go through it again, step by step..."

"Alison and I were walking through the woods, looking for some sign of where we were. We spotted Larry lying there and ran over to see what happened--and, of course, to see if we could help him. We thought he was dead, but he was

254

just unconscious. He woke up about a minute later and we talked for a little while. He seemed all right--well, as all right as Alison and I were. Then he just disappeared. He was there, and then he wasn't. That should have told me something. Anyone with common sense should have figured that out."

"Everything was dreamlike, and everyone knows dreams are freaky, and nothing makes sense in them. If I remember, you were never quite sure if any of this was a dream until we went to see Melina."

"I knew this wasn't a dream, Lexi. So did Alison. It was dreamlike, but too many things about it were much too real. Too detailed."

"Even so, you had no idea what was going on. You couldn't have."

"I should've thought more about his vanishing act. At the time, I thought--just as you did--it was just part of the dream. But now it makes perfect sense that he was probably already dying when Alison and I discovered him."

"We wouldn't have learned any of this without Melina's help, ya know."

"I know, but there are still too many unanswered questions facing us. Even with what we already know, we have no idea where to go, do we?"

"I'm waiting for a friend of mine to call me back. He's going to art school in the fall. His uncle's some sort of engineer and works at Disney. He's been there nearly twenty years. He probably knows a lot of people working there."

"Then he might know someone in Larry's department."

"That's what I'm hoping."

"Lexi, how did you find out Larry was dead?"

"Another friend of mine knows some people at the *Sentinel*. I got with him because I could only find out so much on their site. They have it fixed now so you have to subscribe if you want to really get in there and dig. My friend told me he found out about a two-vehicle accident on the Florida Turnpike eight weeks ago, near one of the Buena Vista exits. It raised a red flag with me because it happened on the same day as your accident on Semoran. There were five people involved, with two fatalities. Both fatalities were males. The names hadn't been made public yet, but one of the descriptions sounded like it could be Larry Grant."

"So…your friend didn't have any trouble finding out?"

"I gave him what I knew, and he gave my stuff to his friends. They went into their archives and found a slew of details that hadn't been in the original news report. I was right. It was Larry, and he was traveling with a female companion."

My pulse hastened. "What else did the report say?"

"Not much. They gave her age and said she was visiting Florida, but nothing else."

I fell back in my chair. Something began nagging at me, something I hadn't remembered until moments ago. "Did he find out when the accident happened? The precise time?"

She glanced at her screen. "The report said between 9:00 and 9:30 in the morning."

9:00. 9:30. My pulse pounded. My God. I'd been right all along.

"Dad?"

It took me several moments to find my voice. "It happened right around 9:07."

"Dad…how do you know--"

"Lexi, when I first started taking inventory in the realm, I checked my watch. It was broken. It had stopped at 9:07."

"In other words, the three of you went into comas at the very same time."

"Apparently."

"Wow…"

"Wow is right."

Lexi's cell buzzed. She picked it up and spoke softly into it. She turned away from me and whispered something, and my heart skipped a beat. "You're sure?" A few moments later, she said, "Thanks, dude. I owe ya one." She lowered the cell and stood there with her back to me. Then she turned around and put the phone back down on the table. She stared at it. It broke my heart that she was avoiding my eyes.

"Lexi?"

She slowly raised her head. Then she said in a soft voice, "It was her, Dad. I'm really sorry."

"It was…Alison?" I could barely feel the chair beneath me.

"My friend said the victim's name is Alison Grant. She's thirty-one and from Flagstaff, Arizona. She was admitted to the local hospital the day of the accident and remained in a coma."

I swallowed a lump in my throat. "Remained?"

"He made a call to someone he knows at Dr. Phillips." She sighed and pushed some hair away from her face. "Alison slipped into a deep coma about an hour ago. She's been placed on life support."

CHAPTER TWENTY-TWO

Alison was now on life support.

I couldn't believe it. Alison had become a vegetable and it was all because of me. I hadn't stayed with her and taken her out of the tunnel, and now she was on life support.

I never hated myself more than I did at that moment.

"Dad?"

The room had grown warm; my temples began pounding. "It's…because of me…"

"No! It's not. You had nothing to do with--"

"If I'd stayed… If I'd at least *tried*…"

"I had to bring you back, Dad…"

"I left her there…and now…now she's--"

"It wasn't your fault. If I hadn't brought you back…"

Her voice trailed off as I zoned out. Everything from that point on turned hazy, indistinct. The kitchen light grew dim, and I had the eerie feeling I was alone in the room. Lexi had disappeared, but for some reason, I no longer cared. I'd abandoned Alison, and because of this, she'd become a vegetable.

I let you down, Alison. I left you alone in the tunnel and I'm so very, very sorry…

My apology sounded so empty, so meaningless. *I'm sorry*. It was nothing more than a sick joke. Something you said when you accidentally bumped into someone or forgot to call them back. *I'm sorry, I forgot your change. I'm sorry, I accidentally dinged your car door.*

Being sorry could never make up for what I'd done.

The damage had been done, and now she was gone forever. I'd left her all alone in the other realm, and she'd become so desperate and terrified, she'd surrendered to the darkness and let it consume her.

Now she was on life support, and it would only be a matter of time before her body shut down. Like Larry, she'd disappear from the realm, and her spirit would enter the afterlife for eternity.

I felt someone touching my arm. I glanced at the hand and saw that it was small, with long fingers and short, jagged nails. The tiny turquoise pinkie ring looked familiar. I'd bought it for Lexi on her fifteenth or sixteenth birthday, which suddenly seemed so long ago, I could scarcely remember the details.

I let my eyes adjust and saw a small, hazy figure standing beside me. The haze gradually thinned, and the figure turned into Lexi. She was trying to coax me out of the chair. I assumed that I'd decided not to resist because I discovered I was suddenly standing. It felt strange; I didn't remember getting up. It didn't matter. I let her guide me out of the kitchen and down the hall, and soon I recognized my bedroom. She whispered something close to my ear, something that sounded like, "just relax and let it go, Dad," but I wasn't sure if I'd heard her right, and decided it didn't matter, either.

I lay down and stared up at the darkness. I soon found that I could almost see the meadow again, as well as the pine forest. I knew I was only wishing it so, but it felt good, being able to see it. Maybe I could see Alison one last time before I closed my eyes and let sleep take me to a softer, warmer place.

Lexi said something else. I felt her moving closer. My vision grew dark, her hair brushed my arm, and her warm lips kissed my forehead. Her shadow moved away, and the room went completely dark.

I closed my eyes and surrendered to the darkness.

I'm so sorry, Alison...so very sorry. If I could somehow return, I'd come for you, I really would...really and truly... I'd come back and find you and find some way of bringing you back here...if only I could find a way back to the realm...

Before I realized it, the shadows had disappeared, and comforting warmth settled around me like a soft blanket.

I'd somehow returned to the meadow, and even though everything looked and felt the same, something was very different. I was alone this time. I was alone because I had no idea where Alison was. I knew only that she wasn't here to walk with me down the grassy path. I'd never be able to see her beautiful face again, her thick black hair, her piercing dark-brown eyes. She was in another place, and because of me, I'd never be able to communicate with her, or touch her, again.

But then it occurred to me that my former thought made no sense. I'd returned, hadn't I? And since I was back, I could find out, once and for all. What if she *hadn't* moved to another place? What if she hadn't moved anywhere at all? What if she was exactly where I'd left her? Now that I'd come back, it would haunt me for the remainder of my life if I didn't try to find her again.

First of all, I had to get my bearings. The place looked no different. It was the same realm-- why wouldn't everything remain the same? I remembered where we'd gone and knew I could take the same path to find the area where Lexi's tunnel had once been.

Alison could still be there. Unless she'd continued farther down the tunnel, she should still be in the same area. Even if her spiritual essence had failed and grown weaker, she'd stay close to the place we were together last, hoping I'd return.

Fired up with fresh enthusiasm, I climbed the grassy rise leading to the woods, and was soon trudging through the tall grass, toward the towering pines. I passed the oak tree where we'd found Larry, and for a moment I expected him to reappear. I stopped for a moment and nervously watched the tree. If he reappeared, it could mean I'd gone back in time and had come back moments before Alison would appear behind me again, gasping as she'd done the first time. I knew this reasoning was merely blind optimism, but I couldn't help myself.

I continued down the path, my ears pricked, my eyes alert. I fully expected a glimpse of a slender black-haired figure moving amongst the trees.

About a hundred yards farther down the path, I reached the clearing.

The glittering doorway was gone. So was the tunnel.

Where the tunnel had once been, a grassy knoll appeared just behind the trees. My heart sank. She was gone forever. Even if she wasn't, my only way of finding her had disappeared.

Alison, I'm so very, very sorry...

I stood there, hating myself worse than ever before. My thoughts went berserk; I let them go. I just didn't care anymore. After several minutes, I could no longer look at the knoll without hating both it and myself. I decided right then that my hatred and contempt were no longer an issue. I'd fucked up, and there was nothing more I could do about it.

I decided to walk away and keep walking as far as my legs would carry me. I didn't even know if I wanted to return to my former life. Everything I knew awaited me there, but I feared I could no longer live as I once did. I didn't even think I could look Lexi in the face without showing her how much I hated myself.

When you've lost your self-respect and your will to survive, what is left?

Just as I turned away, I suddenly heard Alison's voice.

"Jack, *please* come back!"

It sounded like it was coming from inside the grassy knoll.

***

I got up before six the next morning, sweaty and exhausted from a night plagued by dreams, nightmares, and the breathless sounds of Alison calling out to me.

Flustered, angry and confused, I sat on the edge of the bed, struggling to determine if I'd dreamed of the realm or if I'd truly gone there again with the help of my subconscious.

After nearly an hour of agonizing, I decided that it didn't matter. Dream or no dream, I had to take this to the end. Ignoring my aching back, I rushed out of the room to awake Lexi, only to discover that she was already up and sitting in the living room recliner in her shorts and tee shirt, watching the morning news with a cup of hot cocoa and a piece of toast smeared with strawberry jam.

"Lexi, I need to go to the hospital."

She sat up and nearly spilled her coca. "Dad, what's wrong? Are you all right?"

"This isn't for me."

She stared at me for several moments and sighed. I could tell what she was thinking. "Dad, we've already discussed this. Alison's on life support, and nothing you and I can do will help her now…"

"I really need to be there." I tried keeping the panic out of my voice, but it was difficult. I'd never wanted anything so badly before. "It's a matter of life and death."

264

"Dad, we've been through this before. It wasn't your fault..."

"I've got to see her."

She put what was left of her toast back onto the plate and placed the plate on the table next to the recliner. "Even if we can get to the hospital, I don't think they'll let you see her."

"I've got to try. I've got to be there. Maybe she'll know. Maybe she'll sense my presence. Maybe it'll help. What can it hurt?"

"I don't think she's sensing anything, Dad..."

"*Please*, Lexi..."

She started to say something else but stopped. She obviously saw something in my eyes that told her I was desperate. "Give me a few minutes to change." Then she got up and left the room.

***

Lexi handled the morning rush hour traffic well in spite of the fact that she obviously hadn't slept much at all. She kept rubbing her eyes as she drove and yawned frequently.

But her lack of sleep wasn't her main concern. She'd glanced at me several times since we'd gotten into the Challenger. She hadn't said anything but I could tell she was probably worried about my sanity.

About twenty minutes into the drive, she said, "Please tell me why we're doing this, Dad."

"I've already told you." I had a slug of hot coffee from my travel mug, which I'd fixed while I got dressed. "We need to get to the hospital."

"But why? We both know Alison's on life support. She's gone. She's not gonna even know what's going on..."

"She's not *gone*, Lexi." I couldn't let myself accept that notion for even a second. I had to stick to my stubborn and somewhat unrealistic belief that I'd somehow reconnected with Alison's spirit and could bring her back home. "She's still trapped in the realm, calling for me."

"You *dreamed* it, Dad."

"It was just as real as it was when Melina guided me back there."

"Some dreams are pretty vivid."

"I'm not so sure this *was* a dream."

"Dad, I helped you into your bedroom. You'd just freaked and had zoned out. You didn't even know I was there with you. I could've covered you with whipped cream and you wouldn't have noticed."

"I think my subconscious might have somehow reconnected me to the realm."

"It was a recurring *dream*. You want this so badly, you're imagining things. That's why it was so real."

"It doesn't matter."

"It *does* matter."

"Lexi, I don't expect you to understand--"

"Dad, your guilt is eating you up, making you imagine all kinds of things. It's been working on you since you came out of your coma. But it's been much worse since last night, and I'm really starting to worry about you..."

"It's not making me imagine anything, baby. But yes, I feel guilty. In fact, I feel like I killed someone. But this happened. I know it did. I was there last night. I got there, this time without Melina's help. I don't know how I did it. Maybe it was the guilt, I don't know. But I was there. And it was just as clear, as vivid, as--"

"Dad..." She stopped at a red light. In her eyes I saw sadness, disappointment, impatience, and several other unpleasant things I never wanted to see on this lovely girl's face. It was the first time Lexi had ever looked at me this way, and it sent a shiver down my spine. "You've really got to let this go. You can't do anything about it."

"She deserves a chance, Lexi."

She turned back to the wheel and rejoined the flow. She said nothing.

"Lexi?"

She remained silent.

"Doesn't she?"

A deep sigh. "That's the same thing you said about that stray puppy."

"That should tell you something."

"It tells me a lot, but that was different."

"How?"

"I don't know. It just feels different."

"This is about someone who's hurting, who needs help just as much as that puppy did. This lovely lady has a little girl herself. In fact, her daughter is a lot like you--just a few years younger. She lost her daddy and now it looks like she's about to lose her mother. How would *you* feel if you just lost me and knew you were going to lose your mother just days later?"

"That's a seriously low blow, Dad."

"Sorry, baby, but I had to make my point."

After a while, Lexi said, "Yes, Dad. Everyone deserves a chance."

"Then why are you so against this?"

"It's not that I'm against helping her..."

"Then what is it?"

"I just think you've been through enough. You were in a coma, and almost died. The doctors even said you flat-lined for ten seconds when they first brought you in. Your spine will never be the same. You've been plagued by dreams, nightmares, memory loss, and guilt--especially guilt. I just think it's more than enough."

I sighed. Everything she just said was the truth. But somehow none of it mattered.

"Well?" She glanced at me. "Am I right or what?"

"Don't you think Alison's been through much more than I have?"

"She's gone, Dad. Her problems are over."

I refused to believe Alison was gone. "I heard her. I honestly heard her."

"It was a *dream*, Dad..."

"What if it was? What if it was the same dream I had those other times? It was just as real as what I went through in my coma and just as real as when Melina took me back. But what if it *wasn't* a dream? What if I managed to get back there on my own? What if my mind is still connected to her in some way, and I made it back there while I was sleeping? What if she's still trapped there? Shouldn't I find out for sure? Do you honestly expect me to forget about this and spend the rest of my life trying to convince myself that she had no chance? And that it was perfectly okay that I didn't even try to see if I was right about it?"

She didn't reply.

"What if I'm right, Lexi? What if there really *is* a one-in-a-million chance that Alison's spirit is still trapped in that tunnel? Don't you think that after all she's been through, she deserves someone to make a last-ditch effort to find her and try to bring her back?"

CHAPTER TWENTY-THREE

Due to the heavy morning rush hour traffic, it took us more than an hour to reach the western part of town.

It was nearly 8:30 when Lexi turned off Turkey Lake Road, pulled onto Hillenmyer and made a right onto Stonerock Circle, which took us down the short straight stretch that brought us to the front entrance of Dr. P. Phillips Hospital, a large complex of white block buildings, balconies, ramps, and walkways. The lots were nearly filled, and it took us several minutes to find a vacant space.

By this time, I was a physical wreck. My pulse hammered, my back ached from the hour-long trip, and despite the air-conditioning, I'd been sweating. But I forced myself to ignore these minor discomforts and focus on the greater picture. Alison was somewhere in the complex of buildings less than a hundred yards away. If luck favored me and if nothing went wrong, I might be able to see her again.

However, my inner voice, much more skeptical about this whole thing, quickly stepped in. I was reminded of the fruitlessness of this endeavor and realized once again that even if we managed to find out where Alison was, we probably would be shown the door anyway. There would be no reason for them to let us see her, and if we did not comply with their wishes, we could both be arrested.

I refused to listen to this voice. It was grim and depressing and lowered my spirits. I preferred to maintain good thoughts and focused instead on what I could do to help Alison.

After circling the main lots, Lexi found a space on the east side of the complex, about halfway down, in the shade of a couple of palm trees. I opened the door of the Challenger, stepped out and nearly slammed to the pavement when my legs collapsed from under me. Fighting panic, I grabbed the top of the door and braced myself, hoping that the circulation in my lower extremities would quickly return.

Lexi rushed right over. "*Dad*?"

"I'm okay, baby."

"You fell, didn't you?" Her face had turned white with fear.

"My legs went to sleep. I've probably just been sitting too long."

She put an arm around my waist. "Let me help."

"Thanks. Just give me a minute."

"You're sure?"

"Really. I'm good."

She took a deep breath and stayed right where she was.

About a minute later, when tingling warmth trickled down my legs, I began feeling much better. I took a few cautious steps. I felt some tickling in my feet, telling me that normal feeling was returning. Relieved, I closed the door and took her arm, and together we crossed the lot and went up an inclined walkway that led to the administrative area.

The entrance was wide-open and air-conditioned, and smelled faintly of antiseptic, gingery perfume, and fresh vanilla-flavored coffee. At the front desk, a pretty, gray-haired woman in her fifties spoke softly into her headset while scribbling in her appointment book. Her name tag said *Shirley*. She pressed a button on her desk unit, and it went white. She pressed a blinking red button, spoke softly, jotted down something else and smiled up at us.

"May I help you?"

Harsh reality slammed me in the gut. I found that I had no idea what to say to this woman. We weren't Alison's family. Hell, we weren't even friends of the family. To make matters worse, I didn't even know Alison in any normal sense. If I told anyone how I'd met her or what I planned to do, I'd probably be taken straight to their mental facility, strip-searched, and tossed in a padded room.

I knew right then that I should have thought this out in the car on the way over. Lexi had tried to get me to see this logically, but I couldn't accept it. Here I was, Mr. Logic himself, and I couldn't accept something that was right in front of me.

But in this case, I felt justified. I couldn't accept the cold facts because I didn't want depression to set in. It might make me change my mind about this. I also knew that if I procrastinated for any length of time, it might kill any chance I had of helping her.

I *couldn't* think logically or realistically about this. Nothing that had happened to Alison and me could be explained or dealt with in any logical way. As I realized when I'd first awakened in the realm, nothing about our experience was even remotely logical or believable.

I could practically feel my skeptical inner voice laughing at me for not paying attention to it. *What will you do now?* it asked me. *What on earth can you tell this woman that will make her believe you're not a certified fruitcake?*

"Sir?" Shirley was still smiling but clearly getting impatient. She was a busy lady and didn't have time to waste on people who couldn't even tell her why they were here. She glanced at her desk unit. There were now at least six different lines flashing red.

Frustrated and angry with myself, I gave Lexi what was probably the most clueless expression she'd ever see. But instead of laughing at me or taking me back outside, she gave me one of her knowing smiles, turned to Shirley and said, "I'm Lexi Taylor and this is my father, Jack Clarkson. We've come to talk to the relatives of a patient who was brought in here a few weeks ago. She was the victim of a highway accident, and we'd like to--"

"Her name, please?"

"Alison Grant."

She gave the keyboard on her left a few rapid taps and brought up a screen of figures. It only

273

took her a moment to realize our names weren't there. She frowned. "What is this in reference to?"

"Well," Lexi said, "it's kind of complicated, but if we could see someone to explain the situation to them, maybe Alison's next of kin, we'd really appreciate it."

"Is this a legal issue? If so, I'll have one of our attorneys--"

"It's a personal matter," I said, shocked that my brain finally decided to start working again.

"Ms. Grant has been placed under life support, you understand."

Lexi and I both nodded.

"There are now legal issues and all sorts of other health and medical ramifications that have entered into this case, as well. The attorneys representing the relatives of Ms. Grant have been cautioned about communicating with any of the litigants in this case."

"We totally understand," Lexi said.

"Are you friends of the family?"

I started to say something, but my brain had shut down again. I wanted this woman to get with any member of Alison's family who might be in the hospital and ask them to come out and see us, but I was so tense and nervous, I knew that anything I said would come out totally wrong.

"Not exactly," Lexi said, "but if we can just have a moment or two with someone, we'd really--"

"Our policy strictly states that--"

"*Please*," I said, hoping I could appeal to this woman's heart.

Shirley stared at me, then Lexi. She obviously saw the desperation on my face. She finally nodded briefly and gestured to the chairs directly behind us, on the other side of the room. "If you'll have a seat, I'll see if I can get someone to come and talk to you."

"*Thank* you," I said, relieved.

My legs trembled as I followed Lexi across the tile floor, where two chairs awaited us in front of the large, tinted windows facing the lush, well-tended grounds.

***

Ten minutes later, I put the magazine back on the metal table between our chairs and noticed that it was a celebrity fashion magazine.

It struck me as odd; I hadn't paid attention at all as I'd flipped through the pages. My mind was on Alison and what she was going through. I had to somehow make this right and knew I wouldn't be able to get on with my life until I did.

The problem was getting someone to agree to let us visit her. This in itself would take some skill on my part, and this time I had to make sure my mind was clear and didn't freeze up again. If I turned into a zombie again, I'd probably be escorted outside by security long before Lexi had the chance to come to my rescue.

But how could I convince anyone what happened? How could I convince anyone about the existence of another realm?

This situation was ludicrous at best. Alison was hooked up to a machine, for God's sake. Even if someone agreed to let me see her, I

275

couldn't possibly communicate with her. If her brain was still functioning, it would be working at a very minimal capacity. Even if it was operating at a level far above what everyone expected, she probably wouldn't even be able to hear me.

Would this be a total waste of time? Or should I try to find a way to return to the realm one last time?

Even if I did find a way back, could I find Alison?

I was positive I'd somehow returned last night. Despite what Lexi thought, I knew it was the real thing, and not a dream. But even if it *was* real, I had to accept the fact that the tunnel was gone, replaced by a grassy knoll. And this could mean Alison's spirit was trapped inside it.

How could I possibly get to her?

And if I did find her, how could I bring her back?

This all seemed hopeless. But as I'd told Lexi, Alison deserved this, and I owed it to her. Like it or not, I was going to put my life at risk to make sure she was given one last chance.

"You do know what's happening with her condition, don'tcha, Dad?"

"Of course I do."

"I don't mean the life support thing. I mean...what I mean is--"

"Just say it, Lexi..."

"Just be prepared. I hope I'm wrong, but if I'm not, then we could be dealing with massive brain damage."

"I...don't want to think of that."

276

"You have to."

"I know."

"She hasn't been functioning for weeks. Her brain activity has all but shut down."

I felt an unbearable pressure building up in my chest. I had to keep the positive thoughts in there, somehow... "Lexi, I know all this."

"I wasn't sure if it occurred to you."

"It has, believe me."

"But you still want to do it."

"You know I do."

"May I help you?" A tall, slender nurse had crept silently up to us and stopped a couple of feet from our chairs. She was about forty, with thick, curly red hair piled high, large blue eyes, round cheekbones, and a pleasant smile. Her nametag said *ANNE BAILEY, R. N.* She stood with her hands clasped in front of her, her gaze shifting from Lexi to me. Like the receptionist, she seemed to be in a hurry.

Despite my efforts to remain calm and clear-headed, I realized my cursed brain had deserted me once again.

Picking up on my predicament, Lexi jumped right in again. "Hello, Ma'am. I'm Lexi Taylor and this is my dad, Jack Clarkson. If we're permitted to, we'd like to see Alison Grant for a few minutes."

"I was informed that you're not family."

"No, Ma'am. We aren't."

Her apologetic smile told me what would soon follow. "I'm sure you can understand our policy, but only family--"

"We understand, Ma'am. It's just that--"

"You must realize Ms. Grant is on life support, and cannot possibly respond to any sort of--"

"We understand that, too."

"Ms. Grant's family has just come over from Arizona, and--"

"Nurse," I said suddenly, my trembling voice surprisingly strong, "I almost died a couple of months ago."

The woman watched me as one studies something fascinating taking place in a test tube. I could almost hear her brain telling her that she'd just come across someone destined for immediate transferal to the Psych Ward. "Mr. Clarkson, I'm sure you can understand the grave nature of this matter..."

I stood up. "Please let me explain myself. I was involved in a very serious traffic accident on Semoran Boulevard, which put me in a coma for five days. This happened the same day--the very instant, actually--that Alison and her ex-husband were in their accident."

She thought about that for a moment, but it didn't seem to make a difference in her assessment. "Sir, I am very sorry about your accident, but it appears that you have recovered quite well. I just don't see how this concerns Ms. Grant."

"I really need to see her, if only for a few moments."

"I'm sorry." She shook her head and turned to move away.

Panic overtook me. Without thinking, I grabbed her arm. I couldn't let her walk away from me; I had to somehow get her to understand me, why I desperately needed to see Alison. "If you'll just--"

"*Sir!*" She pulled free and glared. "I really wish you wouldn't create a scene. This is a hospital!"

"*Please*, ma'am..." My heart sputtered, and I felt my spirits sinking. The room began fading, and my legs grew weak again. I knew I had to work fast and convince her I was sincere before I collapsed. Otherwise, Alison would die, and I'd end up back in the hospital, this time in the Psych Ward. "*Please* just let me have a minute or so of your--"

"Dad, I think we need to leave..."

"Just five minutes of your time?" I took two steps toward the woman. I lowered my gaze and watched in horror as my hands, with minds of their own, reached out for her again.

She stepped back quickly and jerked her head toward the reception area behind her. "Security, Shirl!"

"*Please...*" The room grew hazier, and the nurse turned into a white blur changing into an indistinct shape in front of me. I caught a flash of gold on my left and figured it was Lexi, and then I watched three or four other blurry shadows scrambling around me. Someone grabbed my arms, and for an instant I thought I heard Lexi's voice, but everything quickly became muffled, as if I was underwater. More than one person began

279

talking at once. I tried to pay attention, but I couldn't understand what was being said. The voices were indistinct and sounded like a group of bore beetles buzzing around. I grew light-headed and realized right then that my legs were about to give out again. I had to say something really clever to convince the nurse to let me see Alison.

"Please," I said, or thought I said, "if you'll just let me…"

My sentence evaporated somewhere in the back of my throat. Cold chills ran down my spine, and my limbs had grown numb. The room turned dark, and I watched in fascination as the shiny tiled floor came up to greet me.

CHAPTER TWENTY-FOUR

The darkness quickly faded, and the shadows moving around me grew more distinct.

I opened my eyes and found myself in a small, dimly lit room. There was some sort of metal table in the center of the room, with several small white boxes stacked on it. A padded chair similar to a barber's chair sat in the far corner, a couple of feet from a small sink and medicine cabinet fixed to the wall directly opposite me. The headrest and seat were covered with square sheets of translucent white paper.

I was sitting in a chair, and the red-headed nurse I'd talked to earlier was bending over me, checking my pulse and forehead. I caught a faint whiff of talcum powder. Two large men in security uniforms flanked her. Lexi knelt beside my chair on my left. She looked frightened; her eyes were wet.

"Mr. Clarkson? Can you hear me?" The nurse's face was less than two feet away.

I tried to sit up, but a sudden heavy pounding in the back of my head made me relax. I let the back of my head rest against the wall. The pounding eased up. I had to clear my throat to get my voice working. "How long...have I been out?"

"Just a few minutes. Are you feeling any better?"

"Yes... I think I'm all right..." I had no intention of telling them about the pounding in my head. It would be a foolish mistake to tell hospital people that you just injured yourself in their hospital and needed to lie down. I came here to see Alison--not spend the next several days in one of their beds, fighting with them. "I'm really sorry if…if I scared you…I didn't mean anything--"

"It's all right."

"Dad?"

I smiled at her and patted her arm. "I'll be okay, baby…"

A woman in her early or mid-fifties was standing behind Lexi. Her salt-and-pepper hair was thick and wavy, reaching well below the level of her shoulders. She wore a long-sleeve red blouse with the collar opened, a black skirt a couple of inches below the knee, and black leather boots. She held a black leather jacket draped over her left forearm, and her large tan leather handbag hung at her side from a thick strap resting on her left shoulder. She wore a large gleaming wedding ring and two other rings on her fingers, several silver bracelets on her wrists, and a small silver crucifix hanging from a slender silver chain around her tanned neck. Her attractive, fine-featured face, long nose and large dark-brown eyes rang of familiarity, but I knew I'd never seen her before.

Or had I? I had to remind myself that my brain still wasn't at a hundred percent. For all I knew, this stunning woman could be someone I once knew. Otherwise, why would I even entertain the notion that I'd seen her before?

But what would she be doing here?

There had to be *some* logical reason why she seemed so familiar... She took a step closer and in a soft voice, said, "Mr. Clarkson?"

"Yes?"

"I understand you've come to see my daughter."

The realization hit me immediately, and the pounding in my head vanished. I sat up sharply and ignored the sudden dizziness. "You're...Alison's mother?"

She nodded.

"From Flagstaff?"

The woman blinked.

Her shocked reaction told me I had to talk quickly. Otherwise, these security guys would pick me up and escort me out of the building. But I quickly found that I was no longer suffering from the same mental paralysis I'd encountered when Lexi and I had first approached the reception desk. My mind was now incredibly sharp, clear, and ready for action. The memories were right there, waiting to be released, and I knew exactly how to use them to get this woman to listen to my story. I couldn't possibly know for sure, but I strongly felt that she'd want to know what I was about to tell her.

"Did Kendra come with you?"

"Yes. As a matter of fact, she--" Then she stiffened. For several moments, she said nothing. Then she straightened and stared at me. I could see confusion, distrust, and caution in her grim expression, all at once. I could tell right then that she was wondering who I was, how I knew

Kendra. Once those two questions entered her brain, a hundred others quickly followed. Her jaw quivered. She opened her mouth and in a soft voice asked, "How...do you know Kendra?"

"I've never actually met her, but Alison told me all about her. Kendra and Alison have been living with you since Alison and Larry divorced. You've been taking care of Kendra since Alison flew to Orlando, haven't you?"

The woman's brows knitted together. The confusion remained, but I could tell that the distrust and caution had been quickly shoved aside to make room for the curiosity that had taken over.

My thoughts remained clear, and my gut urged me to keep going. "From what I remember, Kendra's eight years old, likes the *Wizard of Oz, Narnia,* and other fantasy stories. She's very bright and loves horses. Alison also told me Kendra's world fell apart when her parents separated. Kendra rarely even spoke to her mom or dad for weeks after, which hurt Alison deeply. She said she tried desperately to protect Kendra from her father's indiscretions, but Kendra saw him with another woman out in public one time. Alison carefully smoothed it over, telling her the woman was someone her daddy worked with. Alison wasn't sure if that worked, but Kendra seemed okay with it at the time. But the main issue was the divorce and the split-up. Kendra was really shattered when her dad got the offer from Disney and moved to Orlando. Alison was happy that Kendra seemed to have matured a little since she's been staying with you. Alison knew the horseback riding would be therapeutic…"

"H-how on earth…how could you possibly *know* all this?"

"When Alison first told me her name, I said it was a pretty name. She thanked me, but she really didn't sound sincere. I could tell by her tone and by her expression that something about it was wrong. Guess what she told me."

The woman continued gawking at me.

"She said her father wanted a boy. She told me her dad's name is Alan."

The woman gasped. Her right hand covered her mouth. She trembled and lowered her hand. Her eyes glistened. "H-How do you…how can you possibly *know* all of this?"

I sat back in the chair. The pounding in my head had subsided, but I felt a heavy wave of exhaustion hovering dangerously close. I took a couple of deep breaths and felt some of my strength struggling to come back. I had to see this through. I knew that after what I'd just told her, I might succeed in preventing myself from being thrown out. I just hoped my efforts wouldn't backfire and get me arrested. She could claim stalking or harassment, and I'd find myself sitting at a table in a police interview room for the next seventy-two hours. But if this woman believed me even a little, she might choose to find out what happened, and why I was here, looking for her daughter.

"I honestly don't think you'll believe me." I knew I had to tell her everything--especially my

285

own doubts about all this. "There's really no reason why you should. It's a very fantastic story. If I hadn't been there, I wouldn't believe it myself."

The woman blinked. A tear drifted down one cheek. "Try me."

"If I do tell you, you're probably going to think I'm crazy."

She continued staring at me. I couldn't tell if she was trying to determine if I was lying or if I was actually insane. "Ali was never what you could call an outgoing person. She was popular in school and had a lot of friends, but she's always been very private. She'd tell people--even her best friends--very little about her feelings, hopes, fears, or dreams. Even when she was a child, she held everything in."

"I didn't get that impression when we were together."

"That's what is so baffling about all this. If you know so much about her, then the two of you must have been...well, close."

"What we experienced together brought us closer than anyone can imagine."

She remained silent while watching me. Then she took a deep breath. "Mr. Clarkson, I'm about to lose my beautiful daughter. If I could, I would move heaven and earth to keep her with us. I've been praying constantly since her accident. Ali just turned thirty-one last November. She has a beautiful daughter, people who love her, a promising career, and what should be a wonderful life ahead of her. In other words, she has too much to live for and too many people who don't want to lose her. I have no idea how you know her or how you know so much about her, but if there is anything you can do…anything that can lighten our grief even a little…any effort you make will be very much appreciated."

"I don't know what I can do other than tell you what happened."

"Then tell me. Please. And don't leave anything out. Not a word."

I glanced at the nurse, who'd been staring oddly at me the last few minutes. She frowned and turned to Alison's mom. "Are you sure it's okay, Mrs. Leighton?"

Alison's mom didn't take her eyes off me. "Mr. Clarkson and I have much to talk about. We'd like to be alone, if you don't mind. And we don't wish to be disturbed."

The nurse nodded to the Security guys.

Seconds later, Alison's mom, Lexi and I were alone in the room.

***

"Please tell me what this is all about," Alison's mom said the moment the door closed. "Tell me how you know so much about Ali. And Kendra. And Ali's divorce."

"Like I said, it's gonna sound--"

"I don't care *how* it sounds." She pulled her bag from her shoulder and dropped it on the floor next to the chair on my right. Then she sat in it and leaned close to me. Lexi stayed where she was. "I want to know. I *have* to know."

I started the story from the beginning, when I first opened my eyes and found myself in the lush meadow. I told her about the moment I first saw Alison...and when we began exploring in the woods...and when we stumbled across Larry. I continued up to the point when Lexi pulled me out of the tunnel.

Alison's mother sat in stunned silence, her gaze fixed on me as she took in every word. She didn't said anything, just listened, her expression guarded at first, clearly displaying her skepticism. Then, as my story progressed, her eyes narrowed, her facial muscles relaxed, and her lips parted. By the time I'd finished, her eyes had filled with tears. She sat quite still, her hands clasped in front of her, as if in prayer.

"With Lexi's help and with the help of her geeky friends," I said in conclusion, "we managed to find out about the accident and where Alison was taken. And that's why I've come here to see her. And, of course, to see if there's anything I can do to help."

I sat back in my chair. I was greatly relieved that I was finally able to tell my story. Whether this woman believed me or not was now immaterial. It was the truth. She couldn't possibly think I'd imagined it all. I couldn't have known many of the things I'd told her if I hadn't shared some sort of experience with Alison. I wouldn't have known about Kendra, Larry, or that she lived in Flagstaff. If Alison's mom was thinking along the same lines, she'd figured it out as well.

But whether or not this woman believed me wasn't the main issue. I still had to convince her why I'd come here, and I hoped she'd believe my intentions.

"I'm very fond of Alison," I said. "We shared a closeness few people experience, and even though we weren't together very long, I feel as if we'd shared a lifetime together. I know this is a long shot--and probably senseless and impossible as well--but Alison deserves the same chance Lexi gave me. As long as I'm living and breathing, I intend to do whatever it takes to give her that chance."

She still hadn't said anything. She continued staring at me. I couldn't tell by her blank expression if she believed me or was deciding if she should call Security back in.

"I guess this is where you tell me to get out of here or call for someone to come in and haul me away to the Psych Ward," I said.

She stared at me a while longer, the tears ruining her eye makeup. Then she finally smiled and took my hand. "Please call me Ruth."

I sighed in relief. This was a major triumph. I didn't think someone would have me kicked out of the hospital right after she'd just took my hand and told me her name. "Then I take it you don't think I'm some kind of, well…"

"Fruitcake?"

"That wasn't exactly the term I was shooting for, but yes, that would just about sum it up."

"Mr. Clarkson, you are definitely not a fruitcake."

"I'm glad you think so. And call me Jack."

"You were actually afraid I would consider you...well, mentally challenged?"

"As I already told you, it's a fantastic story. Most people are skeptics."

She let out a deep sigh. "Most people aren't living with their beautiful young daughter hooked up to life support."

I nodded.

"However, you've misjudged me, and you've done it amazingly."

"Pardon?"

"Do you honestly think any mother worth her salt would send away or ignore someone who has obviously shared an extraordinary experience with her daughter? Someone who has chosen to come back--at his own personal risk—to help her? To offer her some relief?"

"Then you actually *believe* my story?"

"Your story doesn't matter, nor does the fact that I believe or disbelieve it. What truly matters is that my daughter is on life support, and everyone in this hospital has given her up for dead. What has really touched me is that you came here of your own free will to tell me this incredible story, and since you obviously know much more about my daughter than most people could ever know, then what you've just described must actually be true. Ali's lying in that room, hooked up with tubes, wires and hoses, and they've given her a less than ten percent chance of ever coming out of it on her own. I could not live with myself for even one moment if I knew there was one chance in a million that someone might be able to help her, even in the smallest way, and I did nothing about it."

"I really couldn't blame you for not trusting me, or for thinking I might be crazy. I could be a con man, for all you know."

She smiled through her tears. "Not with those eyes, you couldn't."

"Pardon?" I had no idea what she was talking about, but something told me she'd obviously seen something in them that I wasn't aware of. For a moment I wondered if she was somehow related to Melina.

"Jack, I can see a person's soul through their eyes. I've always been able to, ever since I was little. My grandparents were both from Southern Italy. In the old days, people relied on one another and knew more about things that really mattered. My grandmother always told me to look into the person's eyes when they spoke. "A person can say anything they wish," she used to tell me in her broken English. "Their words mean nothing. But the eyes...*these* are the tools the Almighty gave us to really see into one another's soul for the important answers. For what really matters. For the truth.""

"What do you see...in my eyes?"

"Truth. Sincerity. Above all, honesty. You care, Jack. I can tell you truly care about my daughter. I don't know exactly what happened between you and Ali in this strange realm you've spoken of. I really don't care, either. All I know is what I see in your eyes. Everything I see feels good and tells me you're a good soul."

"You can see all that?"

Another smile. "And in hers," she replied, shifting her gaze to Lexi. "You're good people, and I trust you both. You've come a long way to help my daughter and you haven't asked for a thing in return. A con man wouldn't do that. Neither would a dishonest man."

"I just hope I can do something to help her."

"I truly believe you can."

Something had been bothering me ever since I started talking to this lady. "I have to ask you something. It's...about Kendra."

"Yes?"

"She hasn't seen her mom, has she?"

Ruth shrugged. "Of course not."

"Did she come with you from Flagstaff?"

"Yes. We didn't want to leave her." She sighed. "She is completely devastated since hearing about the accident--and, of course, of her father's passing two days later. Larry stroked just hours after he went into his coma."

A stroke two days later. This told me a lot about his vanishing act in the realm.

"Larry was only in a coma for two days?"

"Since he was driving, he took the worst part of the impact. It was, after all, a head-on collision. It was horrible."

"And I take it Alison was sitting right beside him?"

"They told me she'd been in the process of climbing into the back seat at the time. She was

292

apparently looking for something in one of her suitcases."

"Lucky for her, I guess."

"Oh, yes. Otherwise…" Ruth shook her head.

"So you haven't told Kendra the details, obviously?"

"We were vague about it and didn't want to tell her anything that would give her nightmares. Like I said, we brought her with us when we were first notified, but she hasn't spoken at all since…since we were told about Larry." She shook her head; her eyes glistened again.

"I understand." I felt like an idiot for not considering what the little girl was going through.

"She knew her father hurt her mother. She's asked us questions during the last few months, and this told us she probably knew what was going on. She is really a very bright child. I've had to be very careful what I say about Larry around her. I never approved of him marrying my daughter. I knew he had a roving eye. But Ali was in love, so Alan and I respected her wishes and didn't stand in her way. As a result, we were forced to stay in the background and watch what we both knew what would happen. I'd hoped Larry would come to his senses and realize what a wonderful girl he'd married, but some things never change with some people. I'm just devastated that Kendra was caught in the middle of their problems."

"Is she far from here?"

"She's in our motel room right now, off Turkey Lake Road. My husband's with her.

Kendra will mend, but it will take time. She has her mother's constitution. She brought along her Kindle, so she has all her favorite books to keep her company."

I knew that if I could somehow get Kendra into the room and have her try and communicate with her mother, it might help Alison. But I realized how traumatic this would be. "Has she asked to see her mom at all?"

She shook her head. "As I said, she hasn't spoken since that phone call. She muttered her father's name a few times in her sleep while we were on the plane, but we didn't let her see him when we got here, of course. She's trying to come to terms with the situation, but I really don't think she'll be able to process it yet. She's in shock."

"I understand. This is horrible for everyone."

"Children should never have to endure something like this."

"No. And as I told you, I'm not sure what I can do. Even if I can find my way back there, it could be a hit or miss, at best."

She gripped both my hands in hers. They were warm and I could feel the strength coursing through her. "Jack, please go in there right now and do whatever you can. If there's a chance anyone can bring my daughter back to us, it's in God's hands, and I have this strong feeling that you could be the one person in the world who might be able to do this for us. At least try. And please don't worry if you're unable to do anything. Please remember--Ali has no other chance."

I returned her smile. I sincerely hoped I wouldn't break this sweet lady's heart. "I'll do my best."

She squeezed my hands even harder. "That's all any of us could ever ask."

CHAPTER TWENTY-FIVE

A sick, pale little girl lay on the bed, smothered in tubes and wires, her pallid face covered with a clear mask, her head heavily bandaged.

Monitors set up near the bed beeped and ticked away, signifying the slow but steady approach to the end of her time left on earth.

My body turned cold when I saw her, a shriveled scrap of a thing totally dependent on the latest medical technology, when only the night before, I'd seen her as a vibrant, fiery beauty desperate and scared, begging me to help her.

I stood frozen in the doorway. My limbs had turned numb. My heart pounded violently. My legs had become concrete pillars, immobile and useless and permanently fixed to the tile floor.

"Dad?" Lexi's voice sounded weak and far away. She was standing next to me, looking up at me in her frightened, little-girl innocence. I knew right then why I was here and what I had to do.

Ruth Leighton stood on my right, holding a handkerchief up to her face. Her gaze focused on the floor halfway to the bed. She obviously could not look at the pathetic figure in the bed. After a few moments, she sighed brokenly and slowly raised her eyes--but only for a moment. She immediately shifted her gaze to me. Her eyes glistened in the semi-dark room. Her voice, muffled by the handkerchief, was surprisingly clear. "Jack...please...do whatever you can... *Please* try and help her..."

I put my hand on her shoulder. Our eyes met, and I finally found the courage to move my legs. I had to do this for her, for Kendra...and, of course, for Alison. I'd come much too far and suffered too much pain, torment, and guilt to back out at this stage.

My legs still felt unusually heavy, but I managed to shuffle into the room. My nerves jerked as I approached the bed and looked down at the motionless body. The shock of seeing her in this state slammed into me, and for a moment I thought I might faint. But I forced myself through it, remembering what she'd looked like in the other place, what sort of person she was. I reminded myself where her spirit was and what she'd been going through. She was alone and terrified, trapped in darkness, and had no idea where she was, why she was alone or why I'd left her.

I'd left her there, all alone...

My anger came thundering back, and with it, all the courage I thought I'd lost. This was no time to be afraid, no time to feel faint. Alison was dying, and I had to save her. I'd left her alone in the tunnel and had to fix that. This time, nothing would stop me.

"It's me, Alison," I said softly. "It's Jack."

No response, of course. All I could hear were the beeps, the humming, the soft slurping sound of the mechanical ventilation hose pumping oxygen into her failing lungs, and the soft ticking

297

of the monitors on the table on the other side of the bed.

"Sit down, Dad."

Lexi had dragged over a chair. I sat and forced myself not to look at Alison's face. I feared that its stillness, its frailty, would bring back my fears. I stared at her hand instead. It was small, much smaller than I remembered in the realm--not much larger, in fact, than the hand of a child. It was white and bloodless, the knuckles covered with bandages, the wrist taped with tubes. This was the same hand that had touched my cheek in the realm. The same hand that had pressed against the back of my neck when she'd kissed me. The same hand that had clutched my own hand so tightly, so desperately, when we'd entered the tunnel.

It had become so small, so frail. So delicate. I wanted to touch it but was afraid I'd hurt her. Then I realized I was being silly. Alison would want me to touch her. If she knew I was here with her, she'd want me to communicate with her in whatever way I could. And if part of her spirit was in this room, watching me, she'd undoubtedly yell at me to find some way to get her out of that tunnel. Melina had mentioned contact, hadn't she? Physical contact. And physical contact meant touch.

My fingers trembled as I brought my hand over, and I felt the fear coming right back. I fought it, reminding myself that this was my fault, that she wouldn't even be here if I hadn't abandoned her. Once again, my returning anger

298

eclipsed my fears, and I brought my hand gently down onto the cold, tiny flesh lying motionless on the mattress in front of me.

I felt only a slow, weak pulse. This wasn't very encouraging, and for a moment I thought all was lost--that Alison was already in the process of dying, and nothing I could do would bring her back. I wanted to pull my hand away. After all, I was no god, no doctor. I couldn't possibly fix this. If she was this close to death, what could I do?

I realized what I'd have to do--what I'd have to face--if I gave up. I'd have to stand up, turn around, face that poor, fractured woman and tell her there was nothing I could do. I'd have to tell her that her daughter was dangerously close to death. I was no doctor, no miracle worker. I was sorry, but she was just going to have to suck it up and accept the fact that she'd just lost her daughter. We all have to face all kinds of disappointments in this world...

At that moment, I heard a voice in my head. It was small and weak, and it sounded like that of a young woman.

Was it Alison's voice? Or was this just my imagination stepping in again? The voice sounded weak and far away. It also sounded muffled, as if trapped inside some sort of barrier, or enclosure.

I gripped her hand more firmly, closed my eyes and focused. "Alison?"

Silence.

"Alison? Can you hear me?"

Moments later, I heard it. It was tiny and distant, but it was there.

"*Jack?*"

My eyes snapped open. The pulse in Alison's tiny lifeless hand had hastened and began beating just a little stronger.

I cringed in the chair. "Alison?"

"*I'm here, Jack...*"

Everything suddenly turned black, and as I felt myself falling. I opened my eyes to see what was going on, but the hospital room had already turned hazy and warm, and the blackness came right back and swallowed me up.

As I fell, I heard other voices. Lexi's voice was among them. She sounded frightened as she kept calling me. I knew right then that I had to let her know I was okay. I started to reply, but then I heard another voice, this one growing farther and farther away. It was the unfamiliar voice of some woman, and she sounded excited as she said, "The EEG. My God, look. It just *jumped*..."

***

I gazed dumbly at the lush grass directly in front of me.

It took only a few moments for reality to set in. I was kneeling on the ground amongst the pine trees. That meant...

I'd returned to the realm. I'd done it. I'd come back.

Now I had to find Alison.

A cold chill swept down my back as I got to my feet. Could I find her again? For that, I'd have to find my way back to the same place. I had to face the fact that we'd only managed to explore a small portion of the woods in the short time we were together. The forest itself was enormous. I had to quickly find my way back to the same area. Otherwise, I could die. If Melina was right, my spirit would eventually convince me to stay here.

The fear quickly dissolved when I went a few yards down the grassy slope and instantly recognized my surroundings. The tree where we'd found Larry Grant stood a few yards off the main path, about thirty yards behind me and to my right, up the weed-choked rise. If I turned left and followed the trail for another hundred yards or so, I'd reach the clearing.

I hurried down the path, my senses alert for any sound or movement coming from among the trees. As I'd expected, I heard nothing and saw nothing. It was just as peaceful this time as the other times I'd been here. But I didn't care about the peace and quiet. I only cared about finding Alison.

I just hoped I could find her before she disappeared. If I believed what I'd seen in my dream the night before, she was still somewhere in this general area. I'd heard her voice just moments ago and refused to believe it was my imagination trying to trick me.

I hurried down the uneven path, stepping over limbs and fallen trees, until I reached the clearing. As I'd suspected, Lexi's glittering doorway was gone. So was the tunnel. Just as I'd seen in my dream, a large grassy knoll blocked the path, rising to a height of nearly twenty feet just beyond the two trees. The grass covering the rise was thick and lush, the weeds rampant. Fresh saplings and wild brush peppered the side of the hill. I was certain this hill hadn't been here very long, but that no longer mattered. It was here now, and it wasn't going anywhere.

I approached it cautiously, listening. When I reached the foot of the rise, I knelt down in the grass, bent and pressed my ear to the cool, soft ground. I knew it was silly, and that I probably wouldn't hear anything, but I had to explore every possibility.

However, my biggest problem was also the most obvious: How could I possibly find Alison when the terrain had changed? Since both the doorway and tunnel were gone, there was no way I knew where she was. This, of course, caused the panic to return. I had no way of knowing how much longer it would be before she disappeared-- or even if she had already done so. I had to force myself to believe she was still here. I'd just heard her voice, hadn't I? That meant she was probably still here.

But even if she was, I was afraid she wouldn't be here much longer. I'd just seen her physical body lying helpless in a hospital bed, hooked up to life support. She was sinking steadily and would soon be gone.

I had to stop this nonsense and concentrate on some sort of plan. There had to be one; otherwise, I wouldn't have been able to return in the first place. But I *had* returned and had to find a way to see this through. I'd already promised Alison I'd come back for her. I intended to fulfill that promise.

I straightened and scanned the area. Nothing but grass, weeds, a hill, and trees. Above me, the flawless clear-blue sky went on forever. There were no clues, no signs. This wouldn't be easy.

My frustration reached new heights. I wanted to scream my lungs out but knew that wouldn't accomplish anything.

Or would it? Screaming my lungs out wouldn't exactly help. However, letting her know I was here would be better than standing here like an idiot, admiring the landscape. Besides, I had no other alternative.

I took a deep breath and yelled at the top of my lungs. "*Alison!*"

Silence.

I took another deep breath and, gathering all my inner strength, let it out again. "*Alison! It's me! Jack! I've come back, and I'm gonna find you!*"

"Jack?" Alison's voice.

I froze. For long, tense moments I didn't move, didn't breathe. I just listened to the silence, desperate to hear her voice again. I waited anxiously, my fists clenched, every muscle in my body tense, for perhaps thirty seconds. Thirty seconds was about all I could handle at the moment. In this case, thirty seconds felt like an eternity. It seemed like hours had passed, and I knew I couldn't wait a second longer.

I tried again. "Alison?"

"Jack?"

It *was* her. It *was* Alison's voice.

"Alison, it's me!"

"You've come back?"

"Yes! I'm back, and I'm gonna take you out of here! Where are you?"

"I'm…in here, Jack… In the tunnel…"

I scanned the area once again, as if I'd missed it the first time around. I hurried down the path a few yards to my right, looked around, turned, and came right back. I saw only the grassy hill. I dropped to my knees and crawled closer to the foot of the hill. "There's no tunnel here anymore!"

"I know." Her voice *was* coming from inside the earth. "It began filling in…after you left… I couldn't get out…in time…"

"Alison, I'm going to get you out of there!"

"You can't, Jack…"

"I'm going to!"

"There's no time… I'm so weak… I'm fading…"

Frantic, I jumped up and began investigating the terrain surrounding the hill. I saw no openings, no holes, ditches or dips in the earth indicating that a tunnel had once been there. Judging by the way it looked, this hill had been here just as long as the rest of the place.

But it didn't make any sense. How would the realm change so drastically? What power would create a hill to conceal the tunnel? It made just as much sense as the time the door disappeared when Alison and I were exploring the woods, and Lexi's voice began getting closer--

Lexi. It had something to do with Lexi. Somehow, there had to be a connection.

304

The glittering doorway had been there before the tunnel, and just as Lexi's voice began growing louder and closer, the doorway disappeared and was replaced by the tunnel.

Had Lexi *created* the doorway? Had she somehow imagined it in an unconscious effort to lure me to it? And had the tunnel materialized as some sort of portal enabling me to return to her?

When Melina told us about the realm, she'd said it was the world of dreams, of the imagination. If this was the case, and Lexi had indeed created the tunnel, this meant someone else had created the hill that now prevented me from reaching Alison.

But who would do it?

Who would create such an impenetrable barrier that would prevent me from rescuing Alison?

I had to stop analyzing this. I was wasting precious time. I had to find a way in there.

Without another moment's hesitation, I crawled up the hill in hopes of seeing something from a different perspective. I moved slowly over the earth, searching for soft spots, holes, and gouges, but saw no sign suggesting any recent disturbance. By the time I reached the top, I'd grown more and more restless, and could feel the panic hovering over me, ready to devour me. My heart raced, and the back of my neck had become soaking wet. But this was the least of my problems. Alison was running out of time. If I didn't find her very soon, she'd disappear. Like

Larry, she'd be gone forever, lost in the realm of wandering souls.

I couldn't go back in defeat. I couldn't face Alison's mother and tell her I'd failed, that Alison was gone forever. If I didn't find Alison, there was no sense returning to the real world. I wouldn't be able to live with myself. Melina had been right; the nightmares would haunt me constantly. In time, this obsession would consume me, and my only relief would be my death.

I took in the beautiful terrain and realized once again that this world was much more beautiful, much more serene, than the world I'd left. The saplings, trees, and bushes--even the grass itself--was much more vibrant, much happier, than anything I'd seen in the real world. This place was like a masterpiece painted with love by someone with a gifted hand. In fact, I discovered that staying here might not really be a bad thing. If I found Alison, we could stay here until both of us vanished, and as spirits, we'd be reunited in the next world...

No. I had to stop thinking like that. I couldn't believe I'd let myself give in to that way of thinking so soon. I needed to focus. Alison couldn't stay here. She had too much to live for. So did I, in fact.

I carefully scanned the top of the hill, examining the earth, the grass and the weeds, while searching for anything that would help me find a way to reach Alison. Once again, I saw nothing, and my heart sunk heavily.

Defeated and frightened, I descended the hill. At the bottom, I sat down in the grass and glared at the earth, hating what I saw and didn't see. I was totally frustrated by my helplessness and began hating myself as well. I had to get to her. I had to somehow find a way of penetrating the earth so I could reach Alison and pull her out. There had to be a legitimate reason why that hill was there--how it had gotten there. There had to be some logical reason why the tunnel was covered up.

It made no sense--no sense at all. How could this be? What power would do such a cruel, senseless thing? Why was it necessary to block up a tunnel?

"Jack? Are you...still there?" Her muffled voice wasn't far away and sounded like it was coming from within the earth.

I lowered my face closer to the ground. "Alison?"

"Jack? Where are you?"

Furiously I snatched clumps of grass and weeds and yanked them out by their roots. They came out easily, and I tossed them wildly in the air. But my impulsive action hadn't accomplished much at all. I'd managed only to create a dozen or so bald patches in the earth. At this rate, Alison would be dead by the time I'd fashioned a decent-sized hole.

Once again, I felt the panic settling in.

"Jack? Is that you...out there? You sound like...you're...so *close...*"

"It's me, Alison. I'm right where the tunnel once was."

"I'm right here, too. The tunnel...it's still here..." Her voice sounded so weak, yet so close. We could be just a few feet from one another, but the ground separating us made any contact impossible.

"I know it's still here. But right now, there seems to be a couple of hundred tons of dirt covering it up."

"Jack? You...really came back?" Her voice was barely a whisper.

"Alison, I've come back for you, and if there's any way I can get to you--"

"N-No, Jack...can't... I'm so...weak... I don't think I...don't...can't make it..."

"Nonsense. You can and you will."

"Can't... No more strength..."

"We're going back, Alison." I scooped out dirt with my fingertips but succeeded only in scraping my knuckles on solid, well-packed soil.

I had to face the fact that I couldn't do it. No matter how much I wanted to, I couldn't use my hands to dig into the earth as deeply as it would take to create a tunnel big enough to crawl through. I closed my eyes, willing myself to disappear, to somehow slither into the earth...but when I opened my eyes, I found myself staring at the same cursed piece of ground. The same weeds. The same bald spots I'd made from yanking out clumps of grass.

I had to accept the cold, miserable fact that I couldn't get to her.

"Jack...Larry came back..."

"Alison, we'll talk about that later--" Then I stopped. The hair on the back on my neck bristled. "*Larry* came back?"

"He was here... I...heard his voice... He told me to come with him..."

Her statement ripped violently through me. Larry had come back. He was dead, but he'd come back. He'd come back to take Alison with him.

He'd come back from the dead to take Alison.

"Dammit." As reality thrashed through me, I grew more and more enraged for not considering it sooner. Fresh saplings. Trees and bushes vibrant and happy. A masterpiece, in other words.

Painted by an artist? Or, more appropriately, someone with artistic talent?

Larry's spirit had come back. He was dead, but his spirit hadn't changed, and the same defects he'd had in life had followed him into the spirit world. He was hot-tempered and possessive, and had barricaded his ex-wife beneath a hill to keep her from being rescued.

In different circumstances, the concept would have been almost humorous.

"*He* did this, dammit. *Larry* did it. I should've known."

"Jack? What did you just say?"

"Alison, Larry was the one who plugged up the tunnel and covered it with this hill."

"Wh-What?"

"He did it to keep you here. Once you die, he'll come back and take you with him."

"*Larry* did this?"

"It's the only thing I can think of that makes any sense. Lexi unconsciously fashioned the doorway to bring me here, and when I reached it, her imagination made the tunnel, enabling me to go back. Larry may be in another world, but his spirit is still wandering around here somewhere. He wants you with him and used his imagination to block the tunnel."

"How come we can't…why can't we open it up, then?"

"I don't know. I guess like with everything else, there are rules about this place. We obviously can't do anything while we're part of the realm. Otherwise, I would have cleared that tunnel long before now."

"Then how…how can I--"

"I'm going to do it, Alison. I'm going to go in there and get you."

"But how *can* you?"

"I don't know. I only know I'm not leaving you here."

"Jack…thank you for coming back, but I don't think I can go back…with you…"

"Alison, you're not going anywhere until I get there. Do you understand?"

Silence.

"Alison? Did you hear me?"

"Jack…I'm so tired…"

"Fight it. You'll have plenty of time to sleep later."

310

"But it's so warm and comfortable here…"

Damn. She was giving in. I couldn't let her do this. "Don't think that way, Alison. You have too much to live for." I had to work faster. I closed my eyes and focused. "Lexi, are you there?"

"I'm here, Dad!" Her voice rang loud and clear, and sounded like it was coming from the other side of the grassy knoll.

"I found her, Lexi, but I can't get to her."

"Whaddya want me to do, Dad?"

"Do what you did the first time, okay?"

A pause. "The *first* time?"

"You brought me back. Think you can do it again?"

"I don't *know* how I did it."

"Think hard, now. You made a doorway, then a tunnel. The doorway was filled with bright lights. It was distinctive and unusual. You must've seen it from something or someone. Something you read, maybe?"

"Well, I just kept thinking about you, and some of the memories we'd shared together. No, wait. I remember now. I'd been reading poetry by Michael E. Riffel. There was an illustration for his poem, "Doorway," that was pretty and very strange. It was done by a lady--I think her name is Claudette McDermott--and I must've been thinking about it when--"

"I don't care *how* you did it, Lexi. Just *do* it, okay? Visualize it!"

"I'll sure give it a try…"

I sat back on the ground and waited. After a few moments, she began calling me, as before, over and over again. Once again, it sounded like she was calling from within the grassy knoll.

"I'm here, Dad…right here…"

Just then, the ground before me trembled. A small opening of darkness appeared, growing larger and larger as the earth separated around it. After about a minute, the darkness grew into a large rectangular opening filled with glittering light. The light gradually dimmed, turning dark and revealing the tunnel just beyond it.

Alison lay on her side three or four feet inside the mouth of the tunnel, her arm outstretched, her hand reaching out. Her face was drawn and pale, her matted hair lying in thick, uneven strands across her cheek. Her eyes were closed.

She didn't move.

CHAPTER TWENTY-SIX

I scrambled into the tunnel, knelt beside her, and gently picked her up.

She was cold and shivering. She weighed practically nothing. It was like picking up a half-empty garment bag. Cold shivers ran down my back as soon as I held her in my arms. The light entering the tunnel opening drifted through parts of her. She was fading quickly; it wouldn't be long before she'd vanished.

I held her close. "Alison? Are you still with me?"

No response.

"Alison?"

Nothing. My pulse raced as I gently shook her. No response. Then, when I could think of nothing else, I pushed her hair away from her face, pulled her closer and kissed her on her cold, damp lips.

She stirred, moaning softly. Her eyes slowly opened partway. "Jack? Is that you?"

"It's me."

"Wh-What happened? What did you...just do?"

Relieved she was coming back, I stroked her damp, matted hair. "I was...trying some CPR. I guess it worked."

She smiled weakly. Trembling a little, she shifted her weight.

"You okay?"

She moaned. "I...I don't know, Jack... I think you need to...maybe try that...again?"

I wanted to laugh and leap with joy. I kissed her again. This time, she kissed me back.

When the kiss ended, she sighed and said, "That was nice...really nice. I feel...much better..."

Relief thundered through me. For the first time, I realized I might be able to get her out of here. "Alison, I can get us back home, but you've got to fight it. You've got to *want* to come back with me."

"I'd like to, Jack, I really would..."

"Then do it. Do it for me. Do it for your mom and your dad, and for Kendra. Please?"

She tensed up and arched her back. Her eyes, now wide-open, searched mine. "Mom? Dad? Kendra?"

"They all want you back, Alison."

"You've...seen them?"

"They're all back there, waiting for you."

She blinked. "Kendra, too?"

"Yes."

She sighed, and I felt her grow colder. "I don't know, Jack... I can barely move... It's been so awful, so cold since you...I've been so...frightened."

The guilt came roaring back, but I ignored it. True, I'd abandoned her, but I hadn't meant to. The important thing was that I'd come back for her, and this time I wouldn't leave without her.

"I'm here, now. And I'm never going to leave you again."

314

"Did you say…Larry closed the tunnel?"

"I think so."

"Then how did you--"

"I asked Lexi to open it back up."

"Lexi?"

"She's back there, waiting for me--for both of us."

"Jack, I don't understand. Why would Larry close the tunnel?"

"He wants you to go with him."

"I don't want to, Jack… I want to go back…with you."

"I want you to come with me, too."

"I just don't think I can make it--"

"Leave her be, Clarkson." The faint voice had come from the darkness of the shaft just a few yards behind me. I practically jumped when I heard it.

I turned but saw no one there. But it was obvious that his spirit had come back.

"Leave her alone, Larry. She doesn't want to go with you."

"Look at her. She's almost dead already. How can you possibly get her out of here?"

"I'll manage."

"Clarkson, she needs to come with me. You know she does. We were married to one another. We were both in the same accident. Doesn't that tell you anything?"

"She wants to go back with me. Otherwise, she would have already gone with you."

"Give her a few more minutes. Then you'll be here all alone."

"Not if I have anything to do with it."

"Larry...I don't...want to go with you..."

"Just let go, Ali. It won't hurt at all. Actually, it's damned peaceful."

"Jack ...I'm so scared... This has been such a nightmare..."

"Hold on, Alison. I'll think of something."

"Let her go in peace, Clarkson. She doesn't have much longer."

"Jack? They're really *back* there? *Waiting* for me?"

"Yes. They're all there. In fact--"

It came to me in a flash, and I knew what had to be done.

I closed my eyes and focused. "Lexi, have Ruth make contact with me."

An instant later, the pressure on my right hand increased as some warm invisible force gripped it. "Jack, I'm right here." It was Ruth, and she sounded very close.

"Ruth, I can't do this alone. Alison needs more help to get her out of here."

"Help?"

"She needs love--as much as she can get. And she needs it ASAP. Do you understand what I'm talking about?"

A moment of silence. Then: "Yes. I think I do."

"The clock's ticking."

"Just give me a moment." The pressure on my hand vanished.

I cradled Alison in my arms and held her tightly. She felt even smaller and lighter than moments before. She was slipping away, and I could do nothing to stop it. I put my face next to hers. "Alison, you've got to fight this. You've got to come back with me."

"I can't, Jack…can't…"

"You have to."

"Can't…"

"Ali, you're coming with me." It was Larry's voice again. His voice sounded as faint as before, but close.

"L-Larry?"

"C'mon, Ali… Just let go and we'll leave this place."

"Stay here, Alison. Fight it." I held her tighter. There was no way I was going to let her give up this easily. *C'mon, Ruth*, I thought furiously.

"Let her go, Clarkson." The voice had edged even closer. "She's my wife. We were destined to be together."

"Your *ex*-wife," I said. "And she doesn't belong with you. She still has much of her life to live."

"Why let her suffer? She's been fading away for quite a while, now."

"Jack, keep holding me…please?"

"I'm right here, Alison." I gripped her tiny lifeless hand with my own.

"Clarkson, you're being selfish. Just let her go."

"You're the one being selfish. If you really cared about her, you'd want her to go on, to be happy."

"She's almost dead, Clarkson."

"Maybe, but she doesn't want to be."

"That's beside the point. Even if she wanted to live, the fact is--"

"Momma?" The tiny voice was right next to my face.

Alison jerked in my arms. Her hand squeezed mine with a surprisingly strong grip. "Jack...that sounded like--"

"Momma, please come back!" We both felt another hand on ours. It was small and cold, and gripped ours very tightly.

"K-Kenny?"

"Momma?"

A moment later, another hand covered mine. This one was larger, stronger. I heard Ruth's voice. "Ali, baby, come back home!"

In the next instant, a much larger hand joined in, applying an even greater pressure to the weight covering my hand. We heard a man's voice. "It's me, baby."

"Daddy?" Alison's face instantly lit up. Her body grew heavier, warmer. Tears filled her eyes. They were happy tears, and glistened like tiny beams of dancing light.

Suddenly the darkness in the tunnel wasn't as dark or overwhelming. Fresh air had drifted in, bringing with it the sweet scents of flowers from the meadow.

"My baby, Jack," she whispered, her voice much stronger. "My baby's come to see me. And Mom. And Daddy."

"I know, Alison. They came all the way from Arizona to see you and bring you back home with them."

"My baby…"

"Momma?"

"Baby, I'm here!" she shouted hoarsely, hurting my ears.

"Ali, honey, please come back to us, okay?"

"Mom?"

"Come back, baby."

"Baby…Mom…"

"Ready to leave this place, Alison?"

She sniffed. "Yes, Jack… I really and truly am!"

"Ali, you've got to come with me!" Larry's voice sounded desperate.

"No, Larry…*please* let me go…"

"You're almost dead, dammit! Be sensible!"

"Jack, please…*hold* me… I don't *want* to die!"

"As long as I'm here, holding you, you're not going to die." I hugged her again, and this time she hugged me back. Her arms were much stronger as she pulled me against her. "Everyone hold on tight, and whatever you do, *don't let go!*"

The pressure on my hand and wrist grew, numbing my arm. I didn't know if Kendra was using both hands to grip me, or if it was the combined efforts of her, Ruth, and Alison's father. Alison's growing strength also added to the pressure. And it was working. I could feel the darkness coming back to envelop us.

Just then, we both heard Larry's voice again. "Come with me, Ali!" he yelled frantically.

"No, Larry… *No!*"

"Just let go and I'll take you to a much better place…"

"*No!*" Alison shifted in my arms. Her face moved closer to mine. Her left arm wrapped around the back of my neck and pulled me closer and her lips, now warm and moist, covered mine. I could feel the passion consuming her and her inner strength increasing as she kissed me. She held my face tightly against hers and pressed her body against me for one hot, delicious moment, and I experienced a sensation of joy, desire and an urgency I'd never known before…

And then it happened.

Long before our kiss had the chance to end, Alison disappeared.

CHAPTER TWENTY-SEVEN

I sat alone in the darkness of the tunnel.

There was no sign of Alison and no sign of Larry. The silence was so heavy, it was suffocating, and I found it difficult to breathe.

I crawled outside and scanned the immediate area. I saw only the trees, grass, fallen limbs, and wild brush. The sky was just as clear and blue, the air just as pure and sweet. Nothing had changed. It was as if my last few minutes with Alison hadn't happened at all.

But those last few minutes *had* happened. Alison had really been with me. I'd held her in my arms, kissed her, held her hand, stroked her hair. She'd come back from near death, regained her strength, and kissed me. Then she disappeared. Aided by the love and devotion of her family, she was finally able to leave the realm.

Now I was alone again. This in itself should have given me some relief. Instead, I found that I was nervous and restless. I was also frightened, and the panic that had repeatedly tried taking over was once again hovering dangerously close. It took only a moment to decide why I felt this way.

I kept wondering if Larry had succeeded--if he'd somehow swooped in at the last moment, snatched Alison's spirit in her most vulnerable moment and took her away with him. I knew it sounded fantastic, but I couldn't help it. I hoped I was worrying for nothing. Kendra, Ruth, and Alan had been at her side. Their love for Alison was strong, true, and lasting; they wouldn't have let her die without a fight.

Because of their efforts, Alison had recovered. She'd immediately grown stronger, her body pulsating with renewed vigor and energy. She'd stirred in my arms, her strength quickly returning.

I could never forget that kiss. But once again, my imagination and fear returned, and I soon found that I was unable to tell if her kiss had been one of passion or of farewell.

Idiot. I had to stop this and look at the situation objectively. And what I deducted was something I could not shake, no matter what my imagination or fear suggested. That was the best kiss I'd ever had in my life. Nothing about it suggested a final good-bye.

Even so, I couldn't shake that nagging feeling of doubt that stubbornly refused to go away. I tried but I just couldn't make it vanish. And until I was totally sure, I knew that I couldn't go back. If Larry had in any way sabotaged Alison's return, I needed to find out.

I forced myself to stay calm as I gathered my thoughts together. I gave the area one last scan and prepared myself mentally for the possibility that I might have to start looking for her again. If she was still somewhere in the realm, I had to find her. If Larry had taken her to the other place, I had to find that out as well.

Gathering up what courage I had left, I took a deep breath and let the sound of my voice ring through the woods straight ahead. "*Alison!*"

Silence.

I waited, but the silence continued. This told me nothing. I took another deep breath and let my next message rip through the silence of the trees and the grass. "*Larry! Are you still here?*"

More silence.

Once again I tried convincing myself I was letting my imagination get the best of me. I had absolutely nothing to worry about and should stop this immediately. Alison's family had joined forces, using all their combined love to help bring her back to the world of the living. There was no way Larry could fight such a powerful force.

I knew I was just giving in to my fears. Larry's appearance in the tunnel had unnerved me. I hadn't expected it. And the desperation in his voice was intimidating. However, it hadn't been intimidating enough to convince Alison to go with him. She didn't want to go because she didn't want to die. She wanted very much to live.

"She deserves a chance at happiness, Larry." I looked around again. I sincerely hoped I wouldn't hear his voice. My gut told me he was gone and would not come back. He'd failed, and there was no further reason for him to stick around.

Just then, I thought I heard something behind me. I spun around.

The grassy knoll was gone. So was the tunnel. What remained were the two giant pine trees that had been standing where I'd first seen Lexi's glittering doorway. The sound of a pinecone dropping to the ground was what I'd just heard.

"That's more like it."

"Dad? Who are you talking to?"

I froze. "L-Lexi?"

"Dad, is someone there with you?"

"No, baby. I'm alone."

"Are you sure you're okay?"

"I'm just fine."

"Good. You've got to come back."

"What about Alison? Is she--"

"You've got to come back now, Dad. It's over."

"But I have to know--"

"C'mon, Dad. You know you shouldn't stay there any longer. Remember what Melina said." The pressure on my right hand had suddenly increased, and I winced and stared at it. I couldn't see hers but knew it was there. It was there because she was in the other realm, holding on tightly to me. She was taking no chances; she wanted to make sure I'd come back. "Don't make me have to hurt you," she added in her impish voice.

"Everything's okay, then?"

"Everything's great, Dad. We did it!"

"But...her coma..." My pulse hammered as I fought for the right words. "Has she...is there any change?"

"There's brain activity, Dad. The monitors...they're hopping all over the place!"

A huge wave of warm relief washed through me. With a deep sigh, I lay on my back in the

324

grass and watched the sky. It was the clearest blue I'd ever seen, and I felt a strange sadness hovering over me.

I'd soon be leaving this quiet, beautiful place. This was peace in its purest form, and I never felt as content or as relaxed anywhere else. The realm of the living would never be as serene or as beautiful--at least, not as long as it was overcome with people. But that was the real world, and I wasn't the one with the power to change it. I wanted only to close my eyes and stay like this until...until--

"Dad?"

Lexi's voice once again crept into my head, and all my previous thoughts vanished. I couldn't stay here--not now, after all this. Lexi would be crushed if I didn't go back. And I had to get back to Alison and see for myself that she survived. I didn't know if anything would develop between us after all this. but I had to see her and find out if there was a chance that something *could* develop.

Once again I thought about that kiss. I'd known a lot of women in my life, but I'd never been kissed like that before. Since I was obviously no expert, I was curious to find out if there really had been more to it than gratitude.

I had to see her again to find out for sure.

Coming back to this beautiful place would have to wait. All things needed to happen a certain way. My return here would take place when it was supposed to--not before. I was pretty certain this wasn't that time.

I took a deep breath and closed my eyes once again.

"Dad? You still there?"

"I'm ready, baby." I felt her hand gripping mine once again. I placed my other hand over it and let her take me out of this strange, beautiful world one last time to bring me back into the realm of the living, where I belonged--at least, for now.

***

Apparently I slept for several hours.

They told me I woke a few minutes after they'd taken me out of Intensive Care. I looked around the room for a moment and went right back to sleep. I didn't move for the rest of the night. I later learned that I'd suffered exhaustion from my efforts, but the doctors didn't seem worried. They'd had my history faxed over from Winter Park and were confident there would be no recurring effects from my coma.

It seemed like only a few minutes had passed since I'd entered the realm, but I could tell my sense of time had been seriously compromised when I first opened my eyes and caught glints of the early morning sunlight peeking through the horizontal blinds on my left. Time obviously passed much differently through the other realms.

When I finally realized what had happened, I discovered that I was lying in a hospital bed in a small private room similar to the one I'd been in following my coma. I also realized that I wasn't alone. Claire had stopped by. Her stylish tan business suit, impeccable makeup and perfect hair told me she'd come over on her way to work. Lexi sat in a chair near my bed, watching me intently. Her hair, recently washed, hung loose, and she wore her favorite red tee shirt and faded jeans. Ruth Leighton and a short, skinny young girl with a long, thick black pigtail and large dark-brown eyes watched me at the foot of the bed, directly in front of the doorway leading to the hall.

"Dad? You awake?"

"I'm back, baby."

She jumped up, covered my hand with both of hers and planted a series of warm kisses on my forehead. "How're ya feeling?"

My limbs were stiff, my neck hurt, and I had the beginnings of a headache. I noticed that my fingers ached.

It took me a few moments to remember that I'd probably stressed them in the realm, when I tried digging into the earth to get to Alison. I didn't think what I'd done as a spirit would show on my physical body. I knew no one would believe me if I told them. I'd tell Lexi about it later on, with no one else around.

But right now, the only thing I cared about was the beautiful young girl smiling at me. It made me warm inside and even dulled the headache and my other aches and pains. It lifted my spirits that Claire was here, too. But nothing felt as good as seeing Lexi at my side.

I smiled. My throat felt raw, but I was able to talk anyway. "I probably can't do a cartwheel right now, but I guess I'll be all right."

"Jack..." Claire shook her head. "You're not the cartwheel type."

"That's only because I don't want any change spilling out of my pockets."

Claire laughed. Lexi bent over and kissed my forehead.

Ruth came closer and stood beside Lexi. The little girl joined her, peering timidly around her. Ruth's eyes were wet, but she was smiling. "Jack, we're *so* glad you're finally coming around."

"How's Alison doing?"

"She's critical, but apparently out of danger. The doctors have no idea what happened. They just can't understand how she came out of such a deep coma so quickly." She smiled. "They're scrambling around, bringing in specialists to look into this "amazing and unusual case," as they keep calling it."

"It'll keep them busy. Hell, it might even give them character. Doctors could use a heavy dose of character from time to time. They could also use a little humility. This case should keep them stumped for a little while."

"This is Kendra, Jack." Ruth stepped back a little.

"I figured as much. You're just as pretty as your mom."

Kendra reached over and placed her tiny hand on Lexi's. "Thank you, Mr. Jack," she said in her soft, high-pitched voice.

"No problem. I was in the neighborhood anyway..." I looked up at Ruth. "By the way, how did you get Alison's dad and Kendra in the life

328

support room so fast? It seemed like only a few minutes--"

"As soon as the monitors began jumping around, I called the motel. It only took them five minutes to get here." She laughed. "I couldn't help it. I got caught up in the moment. When those monitors went crazy, it was a regular madhouse in that room."

"Well, at least everything turned out." I didn't want to tell her how close Alison had come to dying.

"Jack…" Ruth quickly turned serious. "She's very weak and groggy, but they say she's progressing at an astonishing rate."

"Is she really?"

She nodded. "I believe them. I know my daughter. I saw it in her eyes."

"What exactly *did* you see?"

"The most important thing of all, and the only thing I really needed to see: Life. Her strong will to recover. She's always been a fighter, ever since she was a child. When the EEG and the other monitors began showing signs of sudden activity, I looked into her eyes and saw my daughter again. How she once was. How I remembered her. She's come back to us, Jack. Because of you, she's come back."

"It wasn't just because of me. She really wanted to come back. She just needed a little help getting out of there."

"I won't even pretend that I have the slightest idea what happened or where you and Ali actually were. As I told you before, I really don't care. All

329

I do care about is that she's back, and I truly believe that one day, she'll be as she once was. I'll never be able to thank you enough."

I couldn't help thinking Ruth was hiding something. She sounded just a little too optimistic for my taste. "How *is* she? I mean really?"

Ruth sighed, telling me the worst.

"So there *was* brain damage, then?"

"They think so, but after her miraculous recovery, they're not ruling out anything."

"Did she know you when she came out of it? Kendra?"

"She…smiled at us." Ruth shivered. "They said that in itself was miraculous."

I was beginning to wonder if I'd done the right thing by bringing her back. "Did they say anything specific about her recovery?"

"They told me a lot of things that were just a little too complicated for me to comprehend, but I did manage to retain some of the less clinical references. They said the brain is capable of rewiring itself, to some extent, to circumvent dead brain cells. If I'm remembering this correctly, they said there is very little regeneration of neurons in such trauma cases. However, there are cells which remove chemicals and maintain a barrier between blood and the brain. These cells will wrap the neurons in a sort of protective insulation. They also mentioned neurogenesis. They said it's rare, but exercise will help immensely. They have to wait until she gets stronger before subjecting her to other tests, of course, but like I said, they're very hopeful. So are we."

I knew Ruth was struggling to remain optimistic, and I had no desire to cast a cloud over her hopes. Besides, I could be very wrong about this, and probably was. "I hope she'll be just fine."

"I think she will, Jack. I really do."

"She probably didn't say anything yet, did she?"

"From what they told me, that'll take quite a while."

"You didn't say anything for days after you came out of it, Dad," Lexi said.

"I guess we're all in for quite a wait, then."

Ruth nodded. "She's being constantly monitored, and we're going to stick around. My husband runs his own company. He can take off as much time as he wishes. He's got several reliable people directly under him he trusts. For the next few weeks, he can run the company from his cell phone, as he frequently does anyway."

I smiled, but inwardly I was cursing myself for not finding Alison sooner. If my memory had come back quicker...if I'd told Lexi about this a few days earlier--or even one day earlier...if I'd met and talked to Melina weeks before I actually did...

If I'd done any of these things sooner, I might have been able to bring Alison back when her condition wasn't quite as serious--before the brain damage had a chance to really settle in.

"You're blaming yourself," Ruth said. "Please don't."

This woman was reading me again. Between Ruth and Melina, I was beginning to feel like an open book. "How did you know?"

Ruth smiled. "I see the guilt in your eyes."

She was right, but I was pretty sure anyone could read my face at that moment. "If only I'd gotten there a day or two earlier…"

"Stop it, Dad." Lexi patted my hand. "You had your own problems. You'd been through the very same thing and were suffering the same injuries. You were having problems recovering, too. All you knew at the time was that you were hearing voices. You didn't want to go back to the hospital. No one can blame you for that."

Lexi was dead-on. But it didn't make me feel any better.

Ruth touched my arm. "We have to give this time."

"I know."

"She almost died, Jack. Only God knows how close she came. You brought her back to us. That in itself is everything."

I just sighed.

"They're right, Jack," Claire said.

"I know they are."

"But somehow you're not convinced you did everything there was to do."

"I don't think I ever will be." I wanted Alison to return to be the person she was when I'd first met her. For that, she needed to come back.

All the way back.

CHAPTER TWENTY-EIGHT

For the next two weeks, I drove to the hospital between ten and twelve
o'clock each morning.

I spent as much time as I could in the room with Alison, Ruth, Kendra, and Alan. The four of us sat in chairs beside the bed, watching her eagerly for any sort of improvement. We said very little, and as I watched her, I could see only brief shadows of the woman I'd met in that other world. She lay quite still, pale and shrunken, nothing at all like the woman who'd talked with me and laughed with me and shared so much of herself while we both struggled to discover where we were and what had happened to us.

When the nurses finally asked us to leave, we spent another hour or so in the waiting room. Kendra read one of her books on Kindle while the rest of us flipped idly through pages of their dog-eared magazines while waiting for more news. Most of the time, there was none.

We usually left the hospital at around suppertime. Alison's family returned to their hotel on Turkey Lake Road while I drove back to my condo to spend my evenings with Lexi. The evenings Lexi was with her mother or busy with some activity at school, I listened to Journey or Foreigner on the stereo while fondly remembering the times I'd heard Alison's voice calling me from the living room, or kitchen.

There were many times when I thought I heard something. On these occasions I jumped up, turned down the volume on the stereo or TV and stood stock-still in the middle of the living room, my heart pounding as I listened. Usually all I heard was silence, or the humming of the fridge down the hall. Other times I heard the slamming of a car door, or people talking out in front of the complex.

There was one time I was so certain I'd heard her that I jumped up from the couch, turned off the volume of the stereo and stood frozen for the next fifteen minutes, waiting eagerly to hear her again. I was sure it was her voice, and she was calling me from her hospital room. I could envision her lying in her bed, her spirit awakening, leaving her body, and looking for me. I could see her spirit wandering the hospital corridor, searching for the tunnel and wondering why she was in a hospital. I could see the panic taking over, forcing her to decide whether to go back inside herself or venture farther down the corridor to see if she could find me. I could see her standing in the middle of the corridor, shaking, her hands closed into fists, her eyes tightly shut as she focused on me, on where I was and how she could communicate with me.

But after several minutes of the continued heavy silence, I realized I was just imagining things again.

***

The next couple of weeks went by quickly.

I heard from my insurance company, who told me my court case would be coming up in a few weeks and that the settlement would most likely be substantial. A seven-figure amount was mentioned, and they were fairly confident the issue would be settled out of court. They said my presence might not even be required and that all they would need would be my medical records and statements from my doctors. They would keep me updated and send one of their agents to see me in the next couple of weeks to let me know what was going on.

Bill Ziegler from Drayson Industries called Monday morning of the third week and asked when I was coming back to work. I told him it would probably be in the next couple of weeks--as long as he could put me on a restricted four-hour workday for the first month. I still tired easily and had to undergo biweekly sessions with my chiropractor, and there were times when my headaches reoccurred without warning. Ziegler said this arrangement would be perfectly okay with him and that I should take it easy and not stress myself.

I didn't tell him that I had no intention of going back to work until Alison's condition had improved. I couldn't possibly concentrate on anything while she remained in the hospital in critical condition. I didn't mind the long daily drives to and from the hospital. I even began looking forward to seeing Ruth and Alan, as well as getting to know Kendra, who was sweet and just as bright as Alison had told me in the realm.

335

We had long talks about the Narnia and Baum books, and I listened when she told me the things she liked most about the Harry Potter books and the movies they'd made from them. She didn't believe me when I told her I'd never seen any of them, and I had to promise her I'd watch them all with her as soon as her mom got well. Then I promised her we wouldn't see them without her mom.

In the very next moment, Kendra asked me something that practically knocked me on my butt. She asked if I loved her mom. I didn't know what to say. I gazed into those large, dark-brown doe eyes and discovered that it was just like looking into Alison's eyes. I knew I couldn't lie and realized that I really didn't want to. After just a minute or two of soul-searching, I heard myself say, "I think I do. I really think I love your mother."

To my utter astonishment, Kendra smiled.

Lexi came by three times a week and stayed with us until supper, and many times brought along a couple of her sci-fi books and graphic novels for Kendra to read and enjoy. I looked forward to these visits, and on Friday of the fourth week, Lexi and I were asked to join Alison's family for supper at the hotel restaurant.

Things were looking up.

I knew, however, that I could never really be truly happy until Alison's condition began to improve.

***

By the end of the sixth week, Alison began showing clear signs of   progress.

Although she hadn't yet spoken, she could sit up with some help and was even able to stand briefly. The nurse wheeled her out of the room and the five of us followed them out onto the open terrace in back to enjoy the bright afternoon for a pleasant half-hour.

Alison gazed at the lush greenery of the grounds for the longest time. As I watched her, I wondered if she was beginning to remember the meadow in the realm. At least, I hoped she was. I couldn't tell what she was thinking, of course, but something had obviously captured her attention.

After several minutes, she lowered her head and drifted off. A few minutes later, she opened her eyes and raised her head when a man in a suit passed and went down the steps leading to the parking lot. Once he was out of sight, she turned and glanced in my direction. Our eyes met, and my heart leaped. I expected to see some glimmer of recognition. I even thought she might wink at me. I had no idea what I'd do if she *had* winked or even smiled, but I found that I didn't care. I wanted to see her come back and wasn't too concerned about anything else.

There was no glimmer of recognition. She merely lowered her head and went back to staring at her lap. A little while later, she returned her gaze to the greenery and stared at it for the next ten or fifteen minutes. Afterward, she grew tired, and her head lowered again. The nurse decided she'd had enough activity for the day. She gave us her usual brief smile of apology. Then she got behind Alison's wheelchair and pushed her out of the room and back out into the hall.

***

Early on Tuesday morning of the eighth week, Alison spoke for the first
time.

Her voice was extremely weak and rough, her utterances brief, but it was a very good sign that she was getting stronger. After staring at Ruth for the longest time, she whispered, "M-Mom?" which brought them both to tears. Later, as she watched Kendra from her wheelchair, she swallowed and uttered a hoarse, "Ken-ny?"

The rest of the week showed more improvement, much of it occurring daily. After a couple of days of speaking in short, clipped sentences, she was eventually able to ask for water. After she'd sipped nearly half a glass through a straw, she cleared her throat and told her father she loved him.

By the end of the following week, she was able to move about on her own in her wheelchair for brief periods. She made it to the end of the hall and was able to return to her room without help.

After supper on Sunday, much to everyone's astonishment, Alison stared at the napkin in her lap, raised her head, looked at us and smiled. Then she took a deep breath, grabbed the armrests of the wheelchair and, with a loud groan, stood up on her own. The effort destroyed her, and after just a few seconds, her arms gave out and she collapsed back in her seat. For several moments

338

she just sat there, breathing heavily. But when she recovered and looked at us again, she was smiling.

***

The next three weeks came and went without much significant progress.

But on Wednesday during the twelfth week, Alison was able to push herself out of the wheelchair, stand on her own, and take a few steps. She did this two more times that day, and five times the following day. Within the next few days she began walking. Her steps, of course, were tiny; she could only manage ten or twelve feet before exhaustion set in, forcing her back into her chair. But the sight of her walking without assistance was, to me, just as magnificent as if she'd just climbed a mountain.

By this time, she was able to talk in complete sentences and eat on her own. She used the bathroom on her own, ran a comb awkwardly through her hair and even brushed her teeth without making too much of a mess of it. She remembered details of family functions, her job-- even Kendra's first day of school. She was able to recognize their family home in Flagstaff from snapshots Ruth had brought along. Alison even mentioned the name of a former neighbor. She recalled two major world events--9/11 and Hurricane Katrina--and after several minutes of awkward silence, remembered the year she was born. She couldn't remember Kendra's date of birth or Ruth's birthday, but she could recall some special moment she'd shared with her father when she was in grade school.

During the thirteenth week, more snippets of her memory trickled back. She finally remembered Kendra's birthday, which was the day before Halloween, but thought Ruth's birthday was Christmas Day--which was off by three months. She brought up the first names of three high school friends she'd kept in touch with over the years but could not remember their last names or what two of them looked like. She knew the name of her boss at the travel agency. She still couldn't recall her accident, and only remembered the part of her wedding where someone she didn't like very much caught the wedding bouquet. She couldn't remember Larry or why they'd divorced and asked her mother and father to tell her about it only after Kendra had left the room with Lexi.

I was very pleased that her episodic memory loss had been improving and that things were coming back at more or less regular intervals. But I was disappointed that she hadn't shown me any sign of recognition or acknowledged my presence. Most of the time, Alison didn't give any indication that she saw me sitting there. When she did turn my way, she seemed to look through me as if I'd somehow become just another one of the furnishings in the room. I totally understood what she was going through and knew firsthand about the agonizingly slow pace of this sort of recovery, but it still hurt. I'd held this woman in my arms, told her so many things about myself and my life. I'd kissed her and even risked my life to bring her back from the throes of death. We'd shared many moments together--some tender, others frightening. But now, as I watched her taking one baby step after the other to re-enter the world of the living, I had to put my ego aside and remain silent as this same woman ignored me.

As the days progressed, and I sat in the hospital rec room, watching Alison and her family playing cards, watching TV or reminiscing about the past, I found myself growing increasingly uncomfortable. I no longer felt like I belonged with them. I wasn't a family member and was only important to them because of what I'd done to help her out of her coma. I felt more like an intruder than a friend. In fact, I often felt like a voyeur as I listened to their private conversations and tuned out more and more frequently as the days wore on. To avoid embarrassment, I got up quietly and slipped out of the room.

After so many weeks of this, I reached the conclusion that if I left the room and never returned, I probably wouldn't have even been missed.

Although I wanted to stick around and witness Alison's complete recovery firsthand, I knew better. She'd suffered more damage than any of us could realize and possibly might not ever fully recover. I knew I should not take any of this personally because Alison simply could not remember me. I wouldn't have been surprised in the least if she couldn't remember the realm at all.

Although I still blamed myself for not getting back to her sooner, I knew that what I'd done was the best thing I could have done at the time. But now that we were both back among the living, I realized that that adventure and everything about it needed to be forgotten. As with all other memories, it had slipped silently into the past. I couldn't go back and correct it, and I had to force myself to accept the fact that it had to remain the way it had ended. We'd both managed to survive, and that was the end of it.

My next decision was the most difficult one I'd ever made in my life. It was even more difficult than my decision to return to the realm. I chose to come back to see her for one more week. If I saw no sign of recognition in those beautiful dark-brown eyes, I'd have to accept the fact that this was how it would have to end. I would have no choice but walk out of the hospital and never come back.

CHAPTER TWENTY-NINE

On Friday afternoon of the sixteenth week, while Alison sat at the table with her family, reminiscing about more recently remembered events, I decided I'd had enough.

She still hadn't shown me a single sign of recognition, nor had she looked my way during the hour I'd sat next to her mother at the table, just five feet away.

My heart was filled with sadness and tremendous loss as I quietly got up from my chair, left the room and went down the hall. The growing frustration that had been consuming me the last few weeks had finally come to a breaking point. I could feel the tears gathering in my eyes and didn't want anyone to see my torment. I didn't look back. If anyone had turned my way, I couldn't have seen it. I preferred to believe no one did. It would make my decision easier.

The time had come for me to leave this family to themselves. It was the week before Thanksgiving, and time to get back to my life. Besides, my work was done. I'd brought Alison back, and now that she was on the long, steady road to recovery, there could be no room for someone like me to complicate her new life. What we'd been through together was strange, to say the least. But what happened to us had taken place in the past, in another world. This was the real world, the one true place where the here and now mattered. I couldn't possibly expect any of the magic that had happened in the other place to repeat itself here. I now totally understood that what takes place in one world cannot reoccur in another.

Lexi was getting out of the Challenger while I went outside and walked down the ramp to the side lot, where my new Audi was parked. It had been a little chilly the past few days. She wore her maroon windbreaker over her black crop top, jeans and white athletic shoes. Her hair was washed and hung loose, glistening like gold flame in the afternoon sun. She looked very grown up and beautiful, and I knew right then that it wouldn't be long before she'd graduate from college, meet some lucky guy and go her own way. The time to appreciate her, to spend as much time as I could with her, was now. She was a rare gem. Without her love, her caring and her devotion, I wouldn't be standing here today. Unlike Alison and her family, who were strangers I'd met under unusual circumstances, Lexi was a major part of my life. That fact alone should help me forget about everything else and concentrate on what I already had. It would be a waste of time to obsess over what I could never have.

But did I really *want* Alison?

What was *really* bothering me about all this? Was I afraid that I wasn't entitled to have her? Or was it the fact that she didn't remember me that was eating me up inside? Perhaps what I really wanted was some token of thanks from her, some gesture of gratitude, of knowledge, that I'd risked my life and health to bring her back home.

That reasoning sounded foolish, and I considered myself an idiot as soon as I'd thought about it. I had to forget all this nonsense. I was making too much of it. It wasn't thanks that I wanted at all, but some small sign of forgiveness from her for abandoning her in the tunnel. Judging by how she greeted me during my last trip to the realm, she'd already forgiven me. But somehow, that didn't seem quite enough. My ego was apparently so fragile and so flawed that it needed her forgiveness in this realm as well.

Was that all there really was to this? Possibly. Was there anything else that was truly bothering me? Most likely not.

So why couldn't I stop thinking about that kiss? How she'd felt in my arms? How she'd held me when we kissed? How she'd held on to me when she thought Larry was about to take her away?

Lexi watched me curiously as I approached her.

"You okay, Dad?"

"I'm fine."

"You never leave this early. What's up?"

I shrugged. I didn't want to go into it--not here, anyway.

"You'll have to do better than that."

I forced a smile. I knew it looked unnatural, even stupid. So did Lexi, judging by the fact that she shook her head and laughed. "The smile needs work, too."

"They're getting along really well, and it seems like they've returned to where they were before. They're a family again. They don't need me anymore." I knew I sounded bitter, but I couldn't help it. It was how I felt.

"Don't be silly. They want you there with them."

"They didn't even notice when I left."

"You sure about that?"

I nodded. I wasn't sure at all because I hadn't looked back. But Lexi didn't have to know that.

"Let's go back and see."

"I'd rather we went for burgers somewhere."

She didn't move. Her expression told me nothing, but I strongly suspected she wasn't having any of this.

I decided to improvise. "I take it you're not keen on burgers right now. How about pizza?"

"What's really going on, Dad?"

I couldn't lie to this girl. Lexi had a way of looking at you that made you want to tell her everything. She really needed to get into law enforcement. She had a built-in lie detector option that frightened the hell out of me.

"She doesn't remember me, Lexi. She won't even look at me."

Lexi put a hand on my shoulder. "She's still recuperating. You more than most people should know that."

"I started remembering things a lot sooner than--"

"She slipped into a much deeper coma-- remember? She came much closer to death than you did."

346

This time, I was the one who didn't say anything. I couldn't. Lexi was right.

"Well?"

"Well what?"

"Am I right or what?"

"Even if you are, it doesn't change anything. She won't remember things for months. I can't stick around that long, hoping she'll eventually remember me. I have my own life to live. Besides, I've got to go back to work in a few days. Ziegler's been expecting me for the last week. I can't keep putting him off."

"Is this why you're giving up? Because Mr. Ziegler wants you to go back to work?"

"I wouldn't call it giving up…"

"What would you call it, then?"

"I don't know. I just don't think she'll ever remember me."

"Give her time."

"It's been four months."

"Give her more time."

I smiled at her. I couldn't help it.

"C'mon." Lexi took my hand. "Let's go back and see her."

***

"We wondered where you'd gone, Jack." Ruth smiled at us when we came back into the rec room. "Hi, Lexi."

Lexi smiled and waved. "Hi, Mrs. Leighton, Mr. Leighton. Kenny." She nudged me and without looking at me, whispered, "See? They noticed you left."

"Hi, Lexi!" Kendra's face lit up.

"Get over here, Jack." Alison's dad smiled and motioned for us to come over.

Alison glanced my way at the sound of my name. She watched me for a moment and then turned back to Kendra, who'd been talking when Lexi and I had come in.

We pulled out chairs and sat off to the side. About a minute later, Alison glanced at me again. This time, her eyes stayed on me for a full five seconds before she turned back to Kendra.

"That was the same bike you had when you were little, baby," Alan said. "You were being silly when you fell off, too, so don't get on Kenny too much for acting like her mom."

"I wasn't getting on her," she said. "Actually, it was so funny, I wanted to laugh, but she looked so scared, I didn't have the heart to--" She stopped abruptly and glanced at me again.

"Ali?" Ruth placed her hand on Alison's shoulder. "Are you all right?"

Alison didn't reply. She continued staring at me.

"Baby?" Her father looked worried.

Alison's gaze didn't leave me. As I watched her, I could see a flicker of curiosity in her eyes. Her hands rested in her lap. Just then, she raised her left hand and placed it over her right.

"Dad?" Lexi moved closer to me. "It looks like...I think maybe something's coming to her."

My pulse hastened, and the back of my neck grew warm. Lexi could be right. There was something in Alison's eyes that hadn't been there a moment ago. But I didn't want to get my hopes up. "I can't tell for sure."

"Did you see the way she covered her hand?"

"I noticed."

"Any idea why she would do that?"

"I *think* so, but I could be wrong…" If I was right, something had triggered her memory, taking her back to the tunnel, when we were all holding her hand. Or maybe it had something to do with the two of us holding hands when we first entered the tunnel. Ruth and Alan yelling my name just a few minutes earlier could have brought it back, for all I knew. But whatever happened had made her recall *some*thing. And unless I was totally wrong, Alison was now visualizing the tunnel, or perhaps the realm itself.

I knew better than let myself get too optimistic. At this point, anything was possible. I had to accept the fact that this could be just some unrelated subconscious reflex, nothing more.

Lexi nudged me. "Dad, she's still looking at you."

"I see that."

"She hasn't taken her eyes off you."

"I see that, too."

"Dad?" Lexi tapped my arm.

"What, Lexi?"

Lexi was smiling. "Why are you still sitting here?"

"What?" I had no idea what she meant.

"Get up." She elbowed me in the side. "Walk over there. Help her out."

My heart raced as I got up, shuffled unsteadily over to her, and knelt beside her chair. She still hadn't taken her eyes off me. Her expression was a mixture of confusion, fear, and fascination, and for one second I let my hopes run wild. Maybe this was it. Maybe the fog in her mind had finally lifted, revealing things she hadn't been able to see or understand until now. Maybe she'd returned to the realm, at least momentarily. Or maybe the realm had returned to her.

Either way, I had to be sure.

I placed my right hand over her hands. She didn't flinch or pull back, but suddenly her eyes grew, and the beginnings of a smile touched her lips. I closed my eyes and visualized the tunnel, the doorway, the woods, and the meadow, and when I opened them again, she was still watching me, her eyes just as clear as before. I felt her left hand moving, and when I looked down, I saw it pulling out from under mine. She raised it and placed her palm gently against my right cheek. She trembled, but her smile grew.

"Alison?" I whispered uneasily. "Is it...coming back?"

Tears gathered in her eyes. She trembled but didn't pull her hand away from my cheek. Instead, the pressure increased. Her lips parted, and she whispered, "Jack? Is it...really you?"

I felt the tears warming my own eyes and knew right then that she'd finally come back. "It's me, Alison..." I didn't know how I managed to get the words out.

"You came back for me again. You really came back..."

"Yes. I really did."

She was silent, but I could tell something important was weighing on her mind. Her smile suddenly relaxed. "Jack, tell me something."

"Anything."

"What you did before...remember?"

"When?"

"In the tunnel."

"I don't know what you mean..."

"Would you like to give me CPR again?"

The tears kept coming, and I felt myself grinning stupidly. I couldn't help it and made no effort to stop it. Alison's memory had come back, and we were together again. "I've missed you so much, Alison. I know this is all so strange, since we never really knew one another--"

"We know one another very well, Jack. We got to know each other in another place."

"Yes. We sure did."

"I didn't think you'd ever come back."

"I would've come sooner if my brain had cooperated."

She smiled. "I know what you mean."

I stared into those beautiful dark-brown eyes and saw a happiness I'd never seen before. I thought of the moment when I'd first come out of the coma. I hadn't remembered her at all. I hadn't even remembered the realm, for that matter, and I knew right then that this miracle would not have even happened if she hadn't kept calling for me and appearing to me in my dreams.

"I really think this was meant to happen," I finally said.

"I kept calling for you. I never stopped."

"I know. I heard you in my kitchen, my living room--even my bedroom. I didn't know what was happening at the time, but once I found out, I knew what I had to do."

"I did whatever it took. There were times I even thought you heard me. I didn't know if you did, but I kept calling anyway. I even talked to you when I thought I heard your voice. I was probably delirious by that time, but it didn't matter. I was going to keep trying until you heard me. And you did. You heard me and came back. We had a connection, Jack. It kept us together even though we were in different worlds."

"I promised you I wouldn't leave you, Alison. And now that you're finally back, I promise I'll never leave you again."

"Some things will happen, no matter what. They're the good things, Jack. The gifts we've been given."

"I honestly didn't think you'd ever remember me again."

"I'm sorry it took so long."

"At least it's over now."

Her smile returned. "So...how about that CPR thing?"

I glanced at the people watching us--Ruth, Alan, and Kendra--and saw that they were all smiling, with tears in their eyes. Lexi was out of range, but I was sure she was smiling, too. "You mean right here? In front of everyone?"

She nodded, and the tears trickled down her cheeks, making her smile brighter than ever. "Right here. In front of everyone."

I kissed her. It was just as wonderful as our kiss in the tunnel. There was no farewell in it, only love and a passion I hadn't expected at that moment. And when it ended, I kissed her again.

She sighed and rubbed my cheek. Then she looked past me, on my right. "Is that Lexi?"

I nodded.

"She's beautiful, Jack. You do good work."

I stiffened. Apparently some of the fog in her memory hadn't yet lifted. She obviously hadn't remembered what I'd told her. "Alison, Lexi isn't really my--"

"Yes she is. Look at her."

I turned. Lexi stood in front of her chair, watching us. Her hand covered her mouth. Her eyes glistened. I'd never seen her happier.

Alison was still smiling. "She's yours, Jack. Even if it's not a biological thing, I've never seen a stronger bond."

I kissed her again. I knew right at that moment that everything had finally turned out okay. I also knew that whatever this was that had happened between us was meant to happen, and that it didn't matter that all the odds had been against it. Something this pure and this wonderful would beat the odds and endure.

Even in another realm.

THE END

OTHER WORKS BY DAVID BERARDELLI

THE APPRENTICE
THE WAGON DRIVER
DEMON CHASER
DEMON CHASER II
STEPPING OUT OF MY GRAVE
ESCAPE CLAUSE
FATAL INNOCENCE
COLORS
THE FUNNY DETECTIVE
"Taking On the Orlando Mob"
JUST A SIMPLE ERRAND
A Funny Detective Novel
WORKING FOR A MOB BOSS
A Funny Detective Novel
AND DARKNESS FELL
DEMON CHASER III
AFTER DARKNESS FELL

Titles available through:
Fiction4All
Gravestone Press